HUNTED

THE DAWNING OF MUIRWOOD

THE
HUNTED

JEFF
WHEELER

Published by 47North, Seattle

www.apub.com

Amazon, the Amazon logo, and 47North are trademarks of Amazon.com, Inc., or its affiliates.

ISBN-13: 9781542035040 (paperback)
ISBN-10: 154203504X (paperback)
ISBN-13: 9781542035033 (digital)

Cover design by Kirk DouPonce, DogEared Design
Cover Image Credit: © Africa Studio / Shutterstock, © faestock / Shutterstock,
© Michal Balada / Shutterstock, © Viorel Sima / Shutterstock,
© Renata Sedmakova / Shutterstock, © Kirk DouPonce / DogEared Design

Printed in the United States of America

CHAPTER ONE

The Town of Isen

L ady Gwenllian Siar enjoyed her morning walks in the heart of the town of Isen. Only, that was not her true name, nor was she really a lady. She was, in fact, a wretched escaped from Muirwood Abbey. And while she did not know who her parents were or where they had come from, she had knowledge they had likely never possessed. With a word, she could unlock a door. With another, she could summon clouds and rain. With yet another, she could converse in any language in any realm. But speaking those words came with a price. The words of power drained her and left her weak and dizzy if she used them too often. It was a careful balance. And more than once she had pushed herself too far and lost consciousness.

Isen was a beautiful town in the Thuren province of Hautland. The buildings had plaster walls painted dozens of different shades—purple, yellow, orange, pale green, and blue as robins' eggs—and sloped roofs with shake shingles. Businesses were housed on the lower floors, advertised by wooden signs hung from ornate, fanciful iron bars, and upper floors were reserved for living spaces.

At that early hour, there were few carts clacking, and there was a pleasant stillness to the streets. Lady Gwenllian had learned Hautlanders treasured their sleep and didn't start the work of the day until the morning bell was struck from the many bell towers.

As if summoned by her thought, the bells began to toll, and immediately doors opened and people began to bustle about in great urgency, as if they'd been waiting behind the doors with their hands on the knobs.

"Blessed morning, Lady Gwenllian," said a hatmaker from a mint-green building as he carried out a rack with displays to showcase his craft.

"Blessed morning," she answered, fluent in their tongue. After traveling through Hautland for a while, she knew the standard greetings. The spell *xenoglossia* was a tutor of sorts. Each time she used it, she understood more and more about the tones and meanings of the language. There would come a day, if she lingered, when she wouldn't need it at all.

Other than a few pleasant greetings, she kept herself aloof from passersby lest they ask too many questions and force her to use the Medium's power. Passing beneath an arch between two tall stone bell towers, she took a moment to study the side of the nearer building. The ivy climbing the lattice looked faded, and barely any leaves clung to it.

It would be winter soon, and she still hadn't managed to arrange a meeting with Aldermaston Utheros. Time was running out. There was no self-deception on her part. Hoel would find her eventually. And every day, she dreaded that he would do so before she could complete her mission.

She continued to the dwelling that she had rented. It was a narrow building—a delightful ocher color—crammed between two taller ones. The bedroom she shared with "Holly," whom everyone believed to be her maid, was on the top floor. Their home was simple, with a sitting room on the second floor, and beneath it a small kitchen, a fireplace, and very little else. Still, it was more opulent than any personal space they'd had previously, and it provided them with shelter while they continued their attempts to gain admittance to the castle. Better yet, the old woman they rented from left them alone, except when it was time to collect their monthly payment.

Lady Gwenllian approached the house, inserted the key into the lock, and turned it. When she entered, the sizzle and aroma of cooking sausages met her nose. Holly was in the back of the kitchen, preparing the morning meal.

Once the door was closed, the pretense ended. She was Eilean again, and "Holly" was Celyn, her childhood friend and companion. They'd fled Muirwood Abbey to seek out Aldermaston Utheros, who was supposedly guilty of heresy. They believed differently. The maston order had succumbed to pride, and the leaders were acting increasingly despotic. The High Seer's refusal to reveal *why* Utheros was a heretic, despite sentencing him to death, suggested his heresy was anything but. Eilean hoped he would prove an ally capable of making real change in the order. She also hoped he could make use of the tome the druid Mordaunt had entrusted to her and use the knowledge therein to help their world, something Mordaunt, as a prisoner at Muirwood Abbey, could not do directly.

If only they could find a way to reach Utheros.

The Aldermaston had escaped death, temporarily, because he'd been granted a writ of safe conduct to attend his trial. He'd disappeared for a time before it was discovered the prince of this province of Hautland had brought him to the safety of his castle. No one knew why the prince had taken such a risk, but only one explanation made sense: he believed the excommunicated Aldermaston was innocent.

He was certainly taking every precaution to protect him. Entering the castle without an invitation was now a crime.

So Mordaunt's tome sat hidden on the ground floor of the ocher house at the bottom of a barrel of beans they'd purchased after arriving.

"How was your walk, Eilean?" asked her friend.

"It's getting colder each morning. Winter is nearly here, and soon I won't be able to walk outside anymore without freezing." Eilean tugged off her gloves and set them on a small end table by the door. She removed her cloak and hung it from a hook. Her dress, which they'd bought in Bridgestow before crossing to Hautland, gave her a foreign look compared to the costumes of the locals. But that was intentional. She'd hoped to rouse curiosity in her arrival so they'd get an invitation to the castle on the hill.

So far it had not worked.

Celyn took the pan and dumped a sausage each onto two plates on the table, which already held bread and cheese. There was no third plate since Stright spent most nights at a cell among the greyfriars, and he would eat with them. He'd picked up the Hautland tongue very well since they'd arrived, and none of his "brothers" of the order appeared to suspect that he wasn't one of them. His strange ways were attributed to his foreignness, but in truth he was a druid from the Bearden Muir in the kingdom of Moros.

After drinks were poured, Celyn carried the tray up to the sitting room floor. Eilean followed. They ate their meals together by the window so they could observe the foot traffic through the arch at the base of the bell tower. There was less of it than in previous days.

"It is going to start snowing soon," Celyn said after eating some of her sausage and bread. "Then we'll be trapped here all the rest of winter."

Eilean had another bite of the delicious sausage. "I'm wondering if I should just use magic to get into the castle. I think I could do it."

Celyn frowned. "I know you could transform yourself to look like a servant or something, but it would be terribly dangerous. If you had to maintain the illusion too long . . ." She shook her head. "I think we should keep waiting for an invitation."

"But what if one doesn't come? What if Utheros changes locations in the spring? We need to speak with him, Celyn."

"I know, I know. But I'm worried about you. Not even the greyfriars are allowed up there. It's heavily guarded."

Eilean avoided her gaze, looking out the window. A man in gray robes was walking toward their door, and she immediately recognized the stride, his gait. It was their friend.

"Stright is coming," she said.

Celyn's worried eyes brightened upon hearing his name. She was as enamored with him as he was with her. Eilean was a little jealous of their connection, but so far neither of them had confessed their feelings to each other. At night, however, the lady and her maid had many frank discussions about it.

Celyn hurried downstairs to let him in, and the wooden floor was so thin Eilean could feel the vibration through it. A knock sounded, followed by the sound of the door unlatching, and the two exchanging greetings. Soon her friends were both up in the sitting room.

"Blessed morning," Eilean said to Stright in the Hautlander fashion.

"Indeed it is," he replied in their own language. He lifted his eyebrows. "I think I've found a way into the castle."

"Really?" Celyn asked with delight.

There was a third chair by the table, and he sat down, leaning forward eagerly. "I spent the night in the woods near the castle."

"Weren't you cold?" Celyn asked with worry.

Eilean sipped from her drink, suppressing a small smile.

"I'm more comfortable there than in that dank cell at the hostel. It's a punishment, I tell you."

As a druid, Stright preferred dwelling out of doors, in proximity to the spirit creatures that proliferated in the natural parts of the world and shunned towns and cities. The amulet he wore allowed him to commune with them and influence them to use their magic on his behalf. No spirit creatures lived within the town of Isen, so he had been communing with the ones that lived in the woods surrounding the town.

"How close to the castle did you get?" Eilean asked him.

"Very close," he said. "And I know where Utheros is staying within the castle."

"Truly?" Celyn asked with delight. She gripped his wrist with enthusiasm. He looked down at her fingers, his cheeks turning a little pink, and she hurriedly removed her hand.

"Did one of the spirits tell you?" Eilean asked.

"Yes. A púca. They are mischievous sorts. Normally you have to win their trust, but this one was a companion of Mordaunt's."

"Truly?" Eilean said with great interest. "I don't remember seeing it."

"Púcas can alter their form. This one favors the shape of a rather large bat. So it was probably disguised when you were around. It offered me a ride to the castle, but understand that if you accept a ride from a púca, they have power over you until the ride is done."

Eilean's stomach dropped. Fly to the castle? "That is not very reassuring, Stright. What kind of power?"

"It doesn't have to take you there immediately. But you'll be safe. Spirit creatures cannot lie," he said, holding up his hands, "so it would not have claimed to be Mordaunt's companion if it were not true. I know of their kind through the druid lore, but I've never met one before. Since coming here, this púca likes to fly up to the castle at night and torment the soldiers on guard."

"Mischievous indeed," Eilean agreed.

"The púca has seen the man being kept at the castle. It's Utheros. The creature wanted to make contact with you and Celyn, but it came to me when it realized I was a druid. It knew I could pass on its message."

"So it can get us inside the castle?" Eilean asked with interest.

"It'll only come out at night, so we'd have to spend the night outside the city walls."

"Are you sure we can trust it?" Celyn said nervously.

Stright sighed. "As long as you understand these creatures, they will not harm you. I'd be willing to go first, to tell Utheros about Eilean and Mordaunt's tome. That might earn you an invitation at least."

"But what if it doesn't? What if you're captured?"

All druids were considered heretics by the maston order, regardless of whether they worked with the Medium, like Stright, or twisted its power to their demands, like the dark druids. If Stright were taken, the consequences could be severe.

Stright looked at Celyn. "I'm willing to take that risk. It won't be long before Hoel finds us, and if we don't find a way to get into that castle without giving away why we're here and what we have, we'll run out of time. Those guards will never let us in without scrutinizing our story. They're taking serious precautions to keep Utheros safe. We all know his life is in jeopardy."

"What do you think, Eilean?" Celyn asked.

"I should be the one," she answered. "I'm the one who knows Mordaunt. Utheros is more likely to listen to me. Besides, if he calls the guards, at least I could use my magic to get out. Would the púca also bring me back?"

"I'm sure it would try," Stright said with hesitation.

"That doesn't sound comforting," Celyn observed.

"I don't know how brave this particular púca is. They aren't vicious. It might flee if the guards frighten it. Of course, you won't need help if you can convince Utheros you're friendly."

Eilean looked at Celyn.

"If we're patient, an invitation might come anyway," Celyn said. "We've been thinking of nothing else. Surely the Medium will find a way for us to get in there."

"Maybe the Medium has," Stright said. Even though he was a druid, he had been open to learning about the Medium from them.

It was a good point. The Medium *did* deliver the results of thoughts mixed with emotions. Eilean had been desperately trying to figure out a way to get to the castle. Earlier attempts had yielded no gains. But perhaps the Medium had finally provided them with a solution.

"I'll do it," she said. "Where should I meet you?"

"I'm coming too," Celyn said, her chin jutting out.

Eilean took her friend's hand. "I doubt it can take us both."

"She's right," Stright agreed. "It can only carry one person at a time."

"It will be fine," Eilean reassured, squeezing Celyn's hand and then releasing it. To Stright, she added, "I will slip out of the court, invisibly, so that our neighbors won't know I'm gone. Then I'll walk to the edge of town and leave before dark. Where do I meet you?"

"The road that leads to the castle hill," he said. "I'll be in the woods watching for you. Come at dusk."

Eilean felt good about the plan, although Celyn clearly disagreed.

Frowning, her friend said, "I'll be worried all night."

Eilean patted her arm. "It'll work out. This is the Medium's will. I'm sure of it."

His eyes intent, Stright leaned forward as if to make a weighty pronouncement. Then he motioned to Eilean's plate. "Are you going to eat the rest of that?"

***

Eilean's nerves prickled like a hedgehog for the rest of the day, which she spent roaming the streets of Isen—sometimes alone, sometimes with Celyn. As the sun began to sink, they returned to the ocher house for a quick meal, and then at last it was time to leave.

Celyn helped Eilean fasten her cloak and then lifted the cowl to cover her hair. "Be safe," she whispered.

"They will try," said the prince with a solemn look. Then he patted the table. "Let us see the tome. I myself was a learner at Dochte Abbey in Dahomey." He regarded Eilean with a kindly smile. "That is where all the rulers train in the Medium. I would have preferred my native Severus Abbey, of course, but tradition binds us."

Eilean listened for a warning from the Medium. It was her charge to keep the tome safe, and hers alone. When no whispers came, she nodded to Stright.

Utheros leaned closer, his eyes eager, as the druid lifted the tome out and handed it to Eilean. It was heavy, but she'd handled it enough to be familiar with its weight. She set it down in front of the prince. His eyes were interested. He lifted one page and then the next, his brow furrowing.

"Can you read this, my friend?" he asked of the Aldermaston.

Utheros craned his neck and leaned in even closer. He looked at the engraved words. Then turned the page. Again and again. The look on his face made Eilean's stomach sink. She had hoped bringing the tome to the Aldermaston would end her quest.

"I don't know this language," said Utheros. "It is all written in it?" He turned all the pages methodically until he reached the middle portion, where the tome was empty.

The prince frowned with disappointment. He tapped the page next to the blank one with a thick finger and looked at Eilean. "The markings are fresh on this page. You can tell they haven't been smoothed with time. But the tongue it is written in . . ."

"I don't think it is a cipher," said Utheros. "It is an ancient tongue. Which would make sense since the druid was one of the original Twelve. I know the tongue of the old empire but not this one."

"So do I," said the prince. "I thought it would be written in Calvrian. But this . . . this is older still. Why not use the Gift of Xenoglossia to understand it?"

Utheros shook his head. "That Gifting only works on spoken languages. If I *heard* this being read, I could understand it. But it would take a seering stone to read a lost language. And those departed with Safehome. Hmmm . . . it looks vaguely familiar. I might have seen it once before in an old tome."

"I desire to know what this tome says," said the prince. "I would pay a hefty fortune to learn from it."

The Aldermaston sat back in his chair. "Perhaps another Aldermaston could help us decipher it, but the Aldermaston of the closest abbey is loyal to the High Seer. We are running out of time. After winter, when the snow begins to melt, Hautland will be invaded by the emperor's men."

"It will take months before they reach Isen," said the prince. "And they will fail to conquer this castle. I assure you, we are safe enough."

Eilean was equally disappointed. Then a memory came to her. Just the snatch of one of the many conversations she'd had with Mordaunt. "There is another abbey, known for its various languages, is there not? Mordaunt told me of it."

He'd said it was the source of the word "*pethet*," an insult he was fond of using. The memory nagged at her, although she couldn't access it fully. *In the Peliyey Mountains, there are several abbeys that are especially secluded.*

"Sumeela Abbey?" Utheros said. "They have many tongues there."

Eilean shook her head. "Another one, in the mountains."

"Sumeela *is* in the mountains," the Aldermaston said.

"It was another one," she said, frustrated with herself. "On the border between two other realms."

"Dochte Abbey has many languages, but it is on an island, not in the mountains," said the prince. "I would not take the tome there. It is loyal to the Dagenais family."

"What about Cruix Abbey?" Utheros said.

Eilean recognized the name instantly, relief radiating through her. "Yes! That is the place."

Had Mordaunt mentioned it on purpose because he knew she would need to go there? Had he been planting the seed in her mind?

"Cruix is in the Peliyey Mountains," said the prince, frowning. "You will not get there during winter."

"What of the Apse Veil?" suggested the Aldermaston.

The prince rubbed his mouth. "All the abbeys in Hautland are under watch by the High Seer and her Apocrisarius."

Eilean looked from the prince to the Aldermaston. "I am not a maston," she confessed.

The prince's eyebrows lifted. "You did not pass the test? That is nothing to be ashamed of, my dear. Many don't."

The Medium pressed on her heart. She needed to be truthful. In talking to both men, she felt their sincerity. They were good people. The Medium was with them both.

"I didn't even take the maston test," she said. "Because I'm not who you think I am."

She heard Celyn's sharp intake of breath. She glanced back, and her friend nodded in approval.

Looking back at the prince and the Aldermaston, she confessed, "I'm a wretched. I was assigned to serve Mordaunt at Muirwood."

Both men looked dumbstruck.

While they both stared at her in surprise, the door opened, and a knight entered with snow still clinging to his cloak. He marched up to the prince and dropped to one knee.

"Prince Derik."

The prince turned, frowning, to the kneeling man. "Speak."

The knight lifted his head. "The guards at the south gate were attacked. And defeated. Someone escaped."

The prince's eyes went livid with rage. "How many men conquered my guards at the gate?" he demanded.

The knight swallowed, his eyes fearful. "Only one."

It is almost the celebration of wintertide, and the snow lies heavy on the abbey grounds. But I am in no mood for the reveling. The entire castle has been searched—and searched again—for the fugitive. Every room, every closet, every crate large enough to hold a man.

I've delayed sending word to the High Seer. I must find Mordaunt. He cannot have escaped the bounds of the castle. I've had the Leering in his chamber inspected by several trustworthy mastons, all of whom say it has not been tampered with. My instincts tell me that he is here but invisible, avoiding contact and moving freely when others are asleep. A slippery fish, though still trapped within a pond.

So there is hope, even if very little of it. As Ovidius said: "Endure and persist; this pain will turn to good by and by."

—Sivart Gilifil, Aldermaston of Muirwood Abbey

CHAPTER FIVE

Wintertide

The tradition of wintertide preexisted the maston order, but the mastons had adopted it and turned it into a celebration of the Medium's benevolence. First begun in Hautland, it was now practiced as far away as the savage lands of the Naestors. It was a three-day celebration ushering in the darkest days of the year, filled with lights, feasts, holly boughs, group songs, and the traditional burning of a massive yule log cut from the densest part of the wood.

Eilean and the others had stayed at the prince's castle since their arrival, for the roads were bogged with snow. The hush of the ice brought a feeling of rest and calm; however, Captain Hoel had escaped Isen. She thought about him on occasion, wondering where he was and when he would come next. That uneasy feeling of being hunted made her study the faces of the servants she passed in the corridors of the castle.

An interesting friendship had been formed between Stright and Aldermaston Utheros when it was finally revealed that her friend was a druid, not one of the greyfriars. Stright had explained much of the druid lore, describing the different kinds of spirit creatures, from the terrifying Fear Liath to the mischievous púca, who showed up at the tower window haphazardly.

At first Utheros remained frightened of the creature, but when he began to realize the púca didn't mean him harm, he dared to let it sniff at his collar and only flinched a little. Amazed that there really was another manner of beings not acknowledged by the maston order, he soaked up as much knowledge as he could from Stright.

Celyn, known as Holly to everyone, aided in the castle kitchen and delighted everyone with her creations, which were unfamiliar to the folk in Hautland.

Eilean spent part of each day reading Utheros's tome, a record that was being copied by his followers, young mastons who admired him for his intelligence and conviction and shared his belief that the maston order had become corrupted by pride. Utheros was both passionate and articulate in his defense of the poor, arguing that they should not be turned away from studying as learners for lack of funds. The costly building projects underway throughout the realms, especially those in Moros, had meant that there were less means to assist local communities. His arguments were supported with meticulously cited passages from the Twelve.

No wonder the High Seer had attacked him so swiftly and brutally, while being vague about his supposed crimes. No one in the maston order wished for him to be looked upon as anything but a quack.

Reading his tome, Eilean felt like a learner at last, and within a few weeks she no longer needed the word of power to communicate freely in his language.

A month after their arrival, she and some of the other learners were gathered around a trestle table in the hall, drinking vassail, a kind of spiced cider, while they shared things they'd learned from the different tomes. The yule log had been nestled in the hearth and lit, beginning its three-day ordeal of being slowly consumed by flame, and the halls were festooned with holly. Still, they'd gotten no further with their efforts to translate Mordaunt's tome. No one in the castle could understand the ancient language it was written in, although everyone was equally enthusiastic to discover its native tongue.

Tombert, one of the more outspoken learners, gave Eilean a pointed look and said, "I think Cruix is the place you'll find the answer."

"I'd go with you if the Aldermaston permits it," said Johanns bravely. "But I imagine your friend, the greyfriar, will be accompanying you after the snows stop."

The others didn't know about Stright's true identity. It was a secret only the Aldermaston and the prince knew.

Tombert held up his empty cup and waved it toward a servant, who refilled it from a pitcher and was promptly thanked. Eilean remembered being a wretched and serving others at Tintern. Now, here she was, being treated as though she belonged among these young mastons who'd risked their lives to follow Utheros. Based on her observations, the servants were all treated respectfully in the prince's castle, never derided or ignored. If a tray fell or mess was made, Utheros and his learners were among the first to help clean it. She respected all of them and felt she belonged with them, even though she hadn't been born to their station.

"It won't be possible to travel until the roads are clear of snow," Eilean said. "The Peliyey Mountains run through Paeiz, where the holy emperor reigns. The abbey is on their southern border, shared between Dahomey and Mon. It won't be easy to get there."

"Oh, there's the Aldermaston!" said another learner, his face brightening.

Eilean turned to look as the Aldermaston and Stright entered the great hall. Utheros was gesticulating with animation, and the two were given cups of vassail.

Tombert waved until the Aldermaston noticed, and then the men headed toward their trestle table.

"There are tomes to be read and work to be done, and I find all my learners sitting at a table?" said Utheros with an exaggerated look of impatience.

"It's wintertide, master," said Johanns, lifting his cup for a toast.

"So it is. But when that huge log burns to ash, I expect you to be back at work again, scriving diligently."

"Yes, Aldermaston," they replied in unison.

Stright stopped at Eilean's shoulder. He lowered himself to whisper in her ear. "Have you seen Holly?"

"I think she's in the kitchen still," Eilean answered.

"She works harder than all of us," he said, then let out a sigh. "I'll go find her."

She watched as he wandered across the hall, moving around the flaming yule log. The blue flames dancing at its base reminded her of the fire he could summon in his hands. Some sprigs of mistletoe had been suspended above the exit to the hall. It was a Hautlander tradition that a man and woman would kiss should they pass beneath one. According to Stright, the tradition had started with the druids, in remembrance of the great love between the first of their kind, Phae and Isic, but the mastons had squelched that lore. It was just a tradition now, one that kept everyone on their toes, for the young of both sexes were keenly aware of where the sprigs were hung, and they vied to either seek out or avoid each other at such openings.

So perhaps it was more than luck that Celyn stepped forward at that exact moment to meet Stright. Had her friend been waiting in the shadows for just such a chance?

Stright seemed a little embarrassed, but he pressed a kiss to Celyn's cheek in acknowledgment of the tradition. It made Eilean smile. Her friends had still not openly shared their feelings, although their attachment seemed to grow stronger every day.

Her mind took an unexpected turn, and she found herself thinking of Hoel. Would she have been pleased or pained if they met beneath mistletoe? The unbidden thought made her cheeks burn, and she cast it away. She was still dreaming of him, of that awful day by the cave, and she told herself that was the only reason her mind had summoned him.

Still, she couldn't help wondering what had become of him. Was he somewhere in Isen, plotting to abduct her again?

Would he still think Utheros a heretic if he met him? If he listened to him speak? Despite Hoel's iron-clad dependence on the rules, she saw him as a man of sense. A man of empathy. She liked to think that he could be persuaded, that his mind was open enough and sharp enough to grasp the truth.

As her mind wandered, someone jostled her elbow.

"The Aldermaston asked you a question," said Ruhe, another learner.

Eilean turned. "I'm sorry, Aldermaston."

"You were watching your friends kissing, no doubt," said the Aldermaston with a sly smile, and the other learners all exchanged knowing looks.

Actually, she had imagined herself doing it . . . with the very man who hunted her. She tilted her head. "What did you ask?"

"I asked if there was vassail at Tintern Abbey."

She shook her head. "None. There was cider at Muirwood, which was very popular, but it had none of these spices."

"It's the spices that make it vassail," said Utheros. "The winters are even worse in Naess, so I've heard. Such traditions help its people survive the bleakness of the season. We have snow, as you've seen, but it's not as deep as it is farther north."

"The snow is the only thing keeping us safe from the emperor," said one of the other learners in a worried voice. "When spring comes, they will come for us. They think us heretics."

"So we are to most of them," said Utheros. "Traditions can be more confining to the mind than chains. Those who break them are always treated with suspicion and fear."

As Stright and Celyn reached the table, the Aldermaston raised his cup to them. *"Vassail!"* he said.

The other learners joined in the salute. Eilean felt she'd been with the others long enough and rose from the bench. "What did you teach the cook today?" she asked her friend.

"Gooseberry fool," replied Celyn proudly. "She loved it."

A servant approached the table and bowed stiffly to Eilean. "The prince requests your company."

She offered her cup to Celyn before following the servant. As she left, she sensed disappointment from the young men who'd gathered around her. More than one of them had hoped to catch her at the nearest doorway when she left. It was strange how the Medium revealed things to her, especially glimpses of what others were thinking.

Although none of the servants were bound by the tradition, she let the man who'd summoned her precede her out of the room, her gaze drawn to the clump of mistletoe. It put her in mind of the Dryad trees in the Bearden Muir, distinguishable from other oaks because of the mistletoe found in their gnarled branches. Knowing a Dryad's name unlocked a secret part of their magic, but the Dryad who had assisted them had revoked Eilean's knowledge of her name. She wished she could remember it. It seemed . . . significant somehow. All she could recall was something about a fountain.

The servant escorted her down a long corridor bedecked with holly and up some stairs to the top floor. Another servant stood waiting there, holding a thick velvet cloak with a fur trim, which he helped drape over Eilean's shoulders. They opened the door to the snowy battlement walk, and she saw the prince ahead of her, his footprints in the snow.

The air outside was brisk and cold, especially after leaving the warmth of the hall, but the cloak was sufficient to keep her warm. Her clothes and sturdy leather boots had been provided by the prince since her wardrobe was so limited.

As she made her way toward him, she could see her own breath and feel a tickle in her nose caused by the cold. The sound of crunching snow filled her ears. Prince Derik waited for her to reach him and bowed slightly as she did.

From the battlement walls, she could see the town of Isen nestled beneath the snow-shrouded trees. Lazy plumes of chimney smoke curled up from the sloped rooftops.

Now that she'd seen Isen in winter, she understood why the roofs were so steep—the snow had a more difficult time clinging to them at that angle.

"You wanted to see me, my lord?" she said.

"I didn't want to walk alone," he answered. He wore comfortable gloves to protect his hands, but his full cheeks were ruddy from the cold. A velvet, feathered hat covered his ears and hair, and the gold chain around his neck glimmered.

She walked next to him as they continued along the battlement wall.

"You know so much about my people, about our ways," said the prince. "But did you know that my rank is that of prince-*elector*?"

"Yes," Eilean said. "Mordaunt taught me about the electors, the noblemen in each realm who are entitled to vote for the next holy emperor." It was one of the many fascinating facts he'd taught her about the intrigues of their world.

He sniffed. "Of course he did. I was a fool to think otherwise. I tell you that it is hard, for many of us, to know that our authority is *below* that of other men. That we exist to bring honor to others, which we ourselves do not receive."

"Isn't it prideful to seek honors?" Eilean asked him.

"It is," he agreed. He was a very plainspoken man, not easily offended or angered. He was logical and studious. Even though he didn't agree with all of Utheros's arguments against the High Seer—who *did* have the right to divert funds as she deemed prudent—he was determined that the rule of law would prevail. An Aldermaston should not be deposed or condemned to death for speaking according to conscience. The judgment against Utheros, he believed, had been unrighteous.

He came to stand against the balustrade overlooking the town below. Waving his arm before him, he said, "The people do not know the holy emperor, a man from the neighboring kingdom of Paeiz. I am the only nobleman they know. But who am I? But for an accident of birth, I could have been a blacksmith or a wheel maker." He turned and looked down his pointed nose at her. "But for an accident of birth, *you* could have been born a lady."

Eilean wasn't sure what he meant by that. Nor did the Medium help her follow his thoughts.

"Whether or not it was an accident," Eilean said, "the Medium does not condemn me for it."

"I spoke rashly, I fear. I only meant you know not who your parents were. I tell you, I'm grateful to speak to you in my own tongue. You've learned our language quickly."

"Any skill I have is a Gift of the Medium," she answered. "But no, I don't know who my parents were, let alone if they are still living."

"One of them could have been a noble," suggested the prince. "You are strong with the Medium."

"Isn't it also likely that I'm strong in the Medium because I grew up at an abbey instead of in a hovel?"

His eyes crinkled. "Too true. You act like a lady. Isn't that a more important indication of nobility than blood?" He looked back down at the town. "When the winter ends, I must sue for peace with the holy emperor. This castle has stood against our rivals for ages past. I should not like to be the caretaker of it should it fall."

Eilean felt uneasiness in her belly. "Would you turn over the Aldermaston if the emperor demanded it?"

"No," said the prince. "I must hope that reason prevails." He turned and looked at her. "Nor will I turn you over, should the High Seer herself demand it. It may be time to choose another emperor. A new High Seer."

Her mind thought back to Captain Hoel again. She knew of his Gift, the one he'd kept secret. While the High Seer pretended to have special Gifts from the Medium, the captain had the rarest of all—the Gift of Seering. He could see glimpses of the future. She hadn't told anyone what she'd learned about him. For some reason, she wanted to keep that secret to herself.

"Just as the electors choose the emperor, so must a convocation of Aldermastons agree to choose a new High Seer. Lady Dagenais is still quite young."

"Death is usually the cause of transition, to be sure," said the prince. "But it is not the only way. She could voluntarily step down. Or she could be deposed because of an illness or transgression."

"Are there grounds for such a dismissal?" Eilean asked. She felt the queasy feeling again.

"As to illness, I know not of any. Whether she's transgressed— it would take an investigation to conclude that. It would be difficult because her advisor is very cunning."

"You mean the head of the Apocrisarius?"

"Yes, Lord Nostradamus. A Dahomeyjan." His lips curled. "I believe him to be an unscrupulous man. She would be accountable for any crime he commits." He sighed. "It's not much to hope for, but it is something. The snow you see, the thick walls, they give us the illusion of protection."

A spasm of pain struck her insides. She grimaced and held her stomach.

"You are unwell," said the prince with concern. He gripped her arm to steady her.

She felt a warning throb from the Medium. Turning her head, she saw a man half-hidden in the shadows of a tower across from them. He was raising a bow and drawing back the arrow.

"Gheb-ool," she whispered, feeling the rush of the Medium come to her.

Was it Captain Hoel come to kill her? To kill the prince?

The arrow streaked at them and struck the invisible barrier she'd summoned with the word. Another draw, another pull, another arrow. It, too, struck the barrier and glanced to the side. Her vision began to blur as the pain in her insides turned more violent.

"Guards! Guards!" the prince bellowed.

One answered in a shout and started to run toward them. The next arrow caught him instead.

First appearance deceives many. The castle was searched and searched again. Captain Cimber then suggested the fugitive might have discovered the entrance to the tunnels beneath the castle. Not knowing if this was the case, they mixed some chalk dust with the earth in the tunnel and forbade any man from traveling within those places. The workers were extending the tunnel to the Pilgrim Inn at the village, but that work was halted.

What did we behold? Chalk prints in the shape of shoes. He is a clever man, clever indeed. Of course he would be. Now we know where he is. We just need to lure him out. How true the saying is from the tome of St. Petrus, another of the Twelve. He was a fisherman, which makes his words all the more fitting: "Let your hook be always cast. In the pool where you least expect it will be fish."

—Sivart Gilifil, Aldermaston of Muirwood Abbey

CHAPTER SIX

Kishion

The man with the bow strode forward, loosing another arrow to kill another rushing guard. The chunks of snow sticking to his cloak revealed he'd been outside for a while, and his gait reminded Eilean immediately of Captain Hoel.

"We're doomed," said Prince Derik worriedly. He only had a dagger at his belt, but he drew it and put himself in front of her.

Although her bowels were thrashing with pain now, and she felt dizzy from invoking the word of power, she refused to back down.

"He will not reach us," she said and then stepped in front of him. "Behind me."

"I will not—"

"My lord, I can defend us both."

The archer drew another deadly shaft, aimed it directly at them as he continued his advance, and let it fly. The magic of her barrier deflected it again. She felt the strain against her will.

An arrow shot by another hand ricocheted off the battlement wall, missing the advancing attacker by the span of a hand. Eilean saw one of the castle defenders draw another one. The intruder turned, nocked another arrow, and aimed at the man who had shot at him. Eilean watched with sickened fascination as the arrow pierced the fellow and dropped him from the tower.

When the attacker turned back, she saw his eyes were glowing silver. A blast from the Medium struck fear in her heart, making her insides shrivel, and she wanted to flee. The invisible shield she'd created wavered and collapsed.

Slay him.

The whisper from the Medium came to her mind, piercing the terror that still held a stranglehold on her heart. She stared at the silver eyes, half-hidden by the shadow of his cowl. Was it Captain Hoel? It seemed like him, and she knew the captain's skill with a bow to be astonishing. She'd seen it herself.

She couldn't look away from the mesmerizing eyes, radiating a power that was unnatural and compelling. That baleful stare commanded her to run.

The prince sucked in a breath as the man drew another arrow.

Slay him.

Again came the command from the Medium, urgent and unmistakable. Her mind recoiled from it. Could she kill Hoel? She had never killed anyone before. The idea of it was abhorrent, especially if it were *him.* The guilt would surely haunt her. But this man—Hoel or not—had clearly been sent to murder Prince Derik, and if she didn't stop him, he would do just that. He certainly had the skill.

The doors they'd used to walk onto the battlements were flung open, and more soldiers emerged brandishing weapons. But they were too far away. She saw the tip of the arrow as it was leveled above her head, a clear shot at the prince.

Surely Hoel wouldn't slay someone like this. It wasn't him. It couldn't be.

You can't let it matter.

Before the Medium could command her a third time, she raised her hands and uttered the words of power she had only heard once, although she'd practiced them with the null gesture. These were the words Mordaunt had used to slay the dark druid attacking them in the tower in Muirwood.

"Ke-ev had," she said forcefully, opening her palm to the man.

The hooded man loosed his arrow.

A hail of invisible blades rushed from her body, and the arrow was shattered midflight. The attacker grunted as he was struck in dozens of places in an instant. She heard the sounds of the invisible blades clipping against the stone of the battlements, sending up sprays of dust and shards of stone.

As she stood there, palm still raised, she watched the man sag to his knees, the bow still clenched in his left hand. Her heart lurched as he bent forward, clutching his chest with his other arm and struggling to breathe. Blood dripped into the pale snow beneath him. He looked up at her, his glowing eyes fading to dark, and then collapsed.

Eilean gulped, feeling dizzy, but didn't sway or faint. She stared at the fallen body, shocked by the evidence of the invisible blades that had pierced him through. This man had been slain by her words. She'd killed him and, in doing so, saved the prince's life.

Let it be someone other than Hoel. Please. Please.

"By Idumea's hand," the prince whispered in shock. His big hands gripped her shoulders from behind, and he pulled her to the side. The advancing guards reached them, their eyes wide as they looked from her to the prince to the dead man in the snow.

One of the soldiers crouched by the body and touched his neck.

"He's dead, my lord," said the man.

"Turn him over," said the prince, releasing Eilean's shoulder and using his hand to mimic the action he wanted.

Eilean's stomach clenched with nerves as the soldier turned the body over and lowered the cowl. An almost dizzying relief came over her the moment she saw the stranger's face, his close-cropped beard similar to that of Hoel's. She whispered a silent prayer of thanks to the Medium that she hadn't killed a man she esteemed.

"Search him," ordered the prince. "Bring anything indicative of his identity to my solar at once. Come, Gwenllian. Away from this awful scene." To one of the soldiers, he added, "Send for the Aldermaston immediately."

She felt his hands on her shoulders, pushing her away from the dead man, but she couldn't take her eyes off the fallen man's face, not understanding why she felt so relieved it wasn't Hoel. She only knew that she would have regretted killing him if he had been the one to come.

***

When they reached the solar, the prince brought her to a chair to sit down.

Eilean felt dizzy, but she was not on the verge of fainting. Her bowels still twisted and ached.

The prince was pacing, his expression haunted. "In my own castle," he kept repeating, then he stopped in his tracks and stared at her. "You saved my life."

She didn't know how to respond to that, or to the look of gratitude in his eyes. "It was the Medium," she said, being honest.

"Praise the Medium," he replied. "I've never seen it used in such a way. It was terrifying but effective."

"I've seen it done once before. When dark druids attacked the grounds at Muirwood before the abbey was finished."

The door opened, and Utheros strode in worriedly. "My lord, many in the castle are sick, especially your guards. The mastons at the table with Gwenllian have also fallen ill. I think the vassail was poisoned." He looked at Eilean worriedly. "You don't look well, my dear. Neither did our mutual friends, but they are better now."

"I do feel terrible," she said, still clutching her stomach.

The Aldermaston strode up to her and immediately laid his hand atop her head. He lifted his other arm. "By the Medium, I command you to be hale and whole. I Gift you with healing that you may conquer this terrible affliction. By Idumea's hand, make it so."

The power of the Medium rushed inside her at his words, and the tight clenching of her bowels released. She gasped as power suffused her, giving her strength.

Gazing up at the Aldermaston, she felt a swelling of gratitude in her breast. This was a true Aldermaston, one who was honest and upright, one who knew the Medium should not be commanded or controlled but allowed to flow through him.

"I must attend to the others who are sick," he said with intense eyes. "With your permission, Prince Derik."

"Of course. Heal who you can. Then come back. I want to know how many fell victim to this barbarous attack."

Utheros nodded in agreement and rushed from the room.

"You are feeling better." The prince scrutinized her. "I can see it already in your countenance."

Smiling, she rose from the chair. "I should see if my friends are—"

"Stay," he entreated, holding up his palm to make her wait.

"I'm concerned for my friends," she said to him, not understanding the look in his eyes.

"The Aldermaston will help them," he said. "There is something I have been meaning to tell you, and this experience has only heightened the urgency. Please . . . stay with me a little longer."

Uneasiness began to creep inside her. Was this why he'd summoned her to the battlements? What could he possibly want?

In her mind, she heard Mordaunt telling her, *You can be more than what you are, Eilean. You are not like the laundry girls, whose thoughts are as fleeting as flax in the wind. You have potential they do not.*

"I am no longer a young man," the prince said softly. "I know that. I have given my heart and mind to ruling justly in this province of Hautland."

Nervousness began to tremble inside her. The prince was going to ask her to marry him, wasn't he? Even though he knew she was a wretched. A nobody. The castle, the very castle she stood in, could be hers if she accepted.

She wouldn't be a lady's maid—something she used to aspire to— she would be the lady in her own right.

He was still talking, and she forced herself to concentrate through the bubbling panic inside her.

". . . free from excess taxation, from border squabbles with the other prince-electors. But since you came, I have come to understand what I was missing before."

Her hands squeezed the top of the chair she'd vacated. She did *not* want to marry the prince. The idea of marrying someone of his age and . . . honestly . . . girth filled her with dread, as did the thought of having to reject a man who probably assumed his station would entice someone of her low birth.

"My lord," she said uneasily. "I . . . I do not think you should speak so familiarly with someone like me."

"I care not for propriety," he said, plowing straight on. "You must believe that I have given this tremendous thought. I am not known for being impulsive. There is no law that forbids what I envision, and it would add to your honor immeasurably."

She dreaded what was coming next. She would have to refuse him, but how to do so without injuring his feelings? Until now, it had never crossed her mind that his kindness toward her had been anything more than brotherly.

"Hear my proposal if you would. Please. Do not be impulsive either. Consider the merits of what I offer."

A knock sounded on the door. Eilean watched in desperation as a servant opened it and addressed the visitor in a low voice. The prince looked annoyed by the interruption.

"Captain Garn is here," said the servant.

"I'll be but a moment," said the prince civilly, motioning for the door to be shut again.

Eilean pressed her nails into her palms, anguished that the sudden reprieve had been thwarted.

"This is my offer," said the prince with a coaxing smile. "I would have you be my chief advisor. Your wisdom and prudence come from one of the Twelve, as we all suppose Mordaunt to be. He has trained you well. I know you will get other offers, but I implore you to consider mine."

His words were so shocking, she struggled to control her expression. Still, the prince must have noticed her surprise.

"Ah, my dear. I see you had mistaken my intentions." He shrugged, and she felt her ears start to burn with embarrassment. "I am much older than you, and too wise to imagine any maiden as beautiful as yourself could ever be truly contented with me. I've long reconciled that I'm married to my realm, and I've no resentment on that score." He gave her a short bow. "But it would be a great honor to me and to Hautland if, when your duty to the Medium is fulfilled, you chose to align yourself with us. I'm prepared to offer very generous terms for your service."

"I'm flattered, my lord," she answered truthfully. "I'm sorry if I've offended you."

He shook his head, again with a pleasant smile. "We will speak no more of this now. I just wanted you to know my intentions." Turning, he gestured to his servant, who was still at the door, and motioned for him to let the new arrival in.

The door opened, and in walked Captain Garn. Eilean did not know the man personally but recognized him from her sojourn at the castle. He had a grizzled goatee with a scar on his left cheek. He carried a bow and a gladius, and a quiver of arrows was slung around his shoulder.

"What have you discovered, Captain?" asked the prince.

The captain brought the gear and settled it on the table. The weapons were the same sort carried by Hoel and his hunters.

"Those are the arms of the Apocrisarius," said Eilean to the prince.

"Indeed," said the captain. "I've had the pleasure, although in my case it was not very pleasurable, of training with one of them years back. The man who attacked us today killed six of my men and wounded four more, one of whom was stabbed in the groin." His eyebrows narrowed with controlled fury. "My lord, your life was endangered. If that young lass hadn't been there, you'd be dead. It's unforgiveable. I've disgraced you."

The prince made a waving gesture with his hand. "Speak no more of it, Captain. We assumed the hunter had fled, but it was clearly a deception. He was waiting for the festival, thinking our celebration would lessen our vigilance."

"My lord, the man who attacked us was *not* Captain Hoel," Eilean said, shaking her head. "I'd never seen him before. And his eyes glowed silver; did you notice that?"

The prince frowned. "I was so frightened, I don't remember well . . . but yes, now I recall it."

"Was he wearing a medallion?" Eilean asked the captain.

The man gave her an appraising look. One of his hands had been closed in a fist, but he opened it and showed them the medallion and coiled chain in his gloved palm.

Its whorl-shaped pattern did not resemble the druid talisman Stright wore, nor the kind of amulet favored by the dark druids. She could sense, even in his palm, the power of the Medium within it.

The prince looked closely at it, disturbed. "What is that?"

"I'd hoped you'd know," said the captain. "He had coins in a purse from Paeiz and Dahomey."

"I know the Aldermaston is busy healing those weakened by the poison, but send for one of his scholars," said the prince.

The servant stationed at the door left in a hurry.

The captain pushed the bow to one side and then adjusted the blade. "No evidence of poison in his things. No vials or anything of that sort."

"He probably used it all before he attacked me," said the prince. "How did he get in the castle, do you think?"

The captain rubbed the bridge of his nose. "A wagon from town came with barrels of vassail. The driver was new, said the usual man was sick and couldn't make the journey. He started feeling ill soon after he arrived, so they took him to a healer. The man snuck off soon afterward. I asked the healer to look at the body, and she confirmed it was him. I've sent riders down to the town, but I believe the man we purchased the drinks from will be found dead or injured."

The prince grunted. "I don't like the taste of vassail myself. I didn't drink any of it."

"Nor I, my lord," said the captain.

Shortly afterward, one of the other learners arrived. Ruhe. "The Aldermaston already healed me," he announced. "I was sick as a dog not long ago."

"Thank you," said the prince. "Can you look at this medallion? Tell me if you recognize it."

The learner approached and looked down at the charm. As soon as he saw it, his eyes widened with fear. "That's a kystrel."

"Isn't that a kind of bird?" asked the prince.

"Yes, but it also refers to these amulets. I've only seen a single drawing of them. Back in the original empire, the empress was served by courtesans who wore these as necklaces. They were called the hetaera. The kystrels left marks on the chest of the wearer."

Eilean felt a jolt of memory. Utheros had asked if she was a hetaera.

"Did the man who wore this have marks on his chest?" the prince asked.

"He did," said the captain, rubbing his brow. "I thought only women could use them?"

"No," said Ruhe. He looked from the prince to Eilean. "The hetaera created the kishion with these amulets."

That was a name Eilean recognized. They all did. The kishion were dangerous and deadly, murderers of the vilest sort. Leaders of old had used them as assassins to kill their enemies and each other.

The prince looked at the captain. "Who hired a kishion to try and kill *me?*"

Eilean wondered the same thing. Was the man part of the Apocrisarius? Or not?

The fish has proven to be adept at eluding the fishermen. Winter is ending, the snow has turned to slush, and still we cannot catch Mordaunt. We know he wanders the tunnels and has even entered the abbey itself. But by the time we send hunters to catch him, he is always gone, back to the labyrinth. One tunnel, the one that goes to the quarry, has been sealed off. By Mordaunt himself. A stone slab blocks the way, protected by a Leering. How he did this in the course of one night is impossible to understand. But none at the abbey, and I doubt the High Seer herself, could force this Leering to obey.

Of course, we've tried to demolish the wall. But it is embedded with a word of power that takes the force of any tool used against it to recoil with double force back against the wielder. Obviously, there is a word of release that would open the stone door. We know not what it is, though we have tried every tongue, every language, every word. The other side of the door leads to the quarry at the hillside, so there are walls of solid rock preventing us from getting in that way. The ground has been too frozen for us to dig from above. But that is changing now that the thaw has begun.

I must make my report to the High Seer soon. She is not a patient woman. I know she has more compelling imperatives than this. The invasion of Hautland begins shortly.

—Sivart Gilifil, Aldermaston of Muirwood Abbey

CHAPTER SEVEN

Allies and Enemies

Surely you could pass the maston test right now," said the Aldermaston from near the window. He shook his head and grimaced. "If I dared bring you to the closest abbey, I could grant you that status this very day. The roads are now passable by horse. But all of the abbeys in Hautland are bound to the High Seer. Though I am safe here in the castle, her power holds at the abbeys."

Eilean appreciated his confidence in her. She had spent the winter months studying with him and the learners devoted to him and knew more about the maston rites than she'd ever learned at Tintern or Muirwood. But with no abbey available, there was no way to pass the test. She would just have to wait until it was safe enough to travel to Cruix.

"Why does she even need the test?" Stright asked. "She can command Leerings well enough on her own."

The three of them were meeting in Utheros's tower, a place of privacy and learning. It had become special to Eilean since their arrival. Stright was pacing. Eilean sat at the table.

The Aldermaston arched an eyebrow. "Would a spirit creature listen to your thoughts even if you did not wear your druid talisman?"

"Yes, my thoughts would be transparent to them regardless."

"Then why do you wear one?" prodded the Aldermaston.

"It signifies that I have learned sufficient lore, that I respect the ways of the spirit realm." Comprehension dawned, and Stright pursed his lips and nodded. "I see your point. It is the same with the Medium."

"Exactly," said the Aldermaston. "You wear a medallion as a symbol of the agreement you made. A maston wears the chaen—an article of clothing—to represent a similar symbol. And, as we saw last month, the kishion also wear tokens of belief that grant them powers."

"Which is another reason for me to go to Cruix Abbey," Eilean said. "I will hopefully learn what language Mordaunt's tome is written in so I can translate it. He seemed convinced the information would help us restore the maston order. I'm also hoping to persuade the Aldermaston to let me take the maston test."

"Yes!" said the Aldermaston eagerly. "Once you pass it, you can travel through the Apse Veil to a closer abbey, disguise yourself with a word of power, and return here much faster than you could by foot. I recommend you go as soon as possible. Tomorrow, even."

Stright looked from her to the Aldermaston. "I will go with her."

The Aldermaston cringed. "I need you here, my friend. Prince Derik has already willingly offered warriors to protect her on her journey. Warriors he can ill afford to spare."

Considering the coming conflict with Emperor Carolus of Paeiz, Eilean knew the Aldermaston was right, but she could see the resistance in Stright's eyes. The Aldermaston and the druid had indeed formed a bond during the winter months. In the past, the Aldermaston would have been unwilling to see the druid's beliefs as anything but heresy, but being condemned of heresy had rendered him more open-minded and interested in learning. Besides which, he could see the spirit animals with his own eyes and knew them to be real and connected to the Medium. A common belief seemed to intertwine the two traditions. They hadn't reconciled everything yet, but their respect for each other was sincere.

"I made a promise to help Eilean," Stright said. While that was true, Eilean also knew that he didn't wish to leave Celyn. If she went to Cruix Abbey too, then Stright would insist on going as well.

"I cannot force you to stay," the Aldermaston said. "But truly, you are needed here. Your powers might be limited down in the town. But you could do us much good in the forests surrounding Isen. The spirit creatures could spy on our enemies. They could even torment them before they reach us."

Stright looked to Eilean, the conflict showing in his strained expression.

"He looks to you, so I must persuade you," the Aldermaston said, coming closer to Eilean. "The journey to Cruix Abbey will be dangerous."

"All the more reason for me to go," Stright interjected.

"But it will be even more dangerous here," said the Aldermaston, tapping the tabletop. "Emperor Carolus will come at us with all his might. He will try and crush what he was told is heresy. If we had a hundred druids who wielded the fireblood, we might be able to stop him." He shook his head. "But the druids were driven from Hautland ages ago. All we have is a greyfriar in masquerade."

Put that way, the odds were daunting. Utheros might be able to last a year, maybe two. But in the end, Hautland alone could not withstand the force of the maston order and all the kingdoms unified against it. It was the same situation that had convinced King Aengus of Moros to bend the knee before he was compelled to. But what if there were someone else who could help them?

"If only we had an emperor less bound to maintaining the order in its current form," Eilean said, the idea just starting to flutter in her mind.

"You mean if Carolus died?" asked the Aldermaston. "I do not condone murder."

Stright was staring intently at her, his eyes searching. "I don't think she meant that," he finally said.

She rose from the chair and began to pace while the two men gazed at her. "We must endure what we have. I just recalled that Mordaunt taught me of another man he served, a high king in another world. There's a sordid history, but I'll summarize it thus. A young man became king and then unified the other kingdoms under his dominion. The kingdom was based on an order of righteousness, and justice and mercy were served by its knights. It was a kingdom where people lived their ideals."

"It would seem he had more success in that world than in this one," the Aldermaston said. "Our people seem determined to tear one another down." Looking to Stright, he added, "I wish we had more druids to help us. Now that I know more about your order, I fully support it. If I had the authority, I would allow the druids free worship in this world."

Stright brightened. "Thank you, but there aren't many of us here anymore, and we've no way of communicating with our home world."

The Aldermaston rubbed his chin thoughtfully. "But Mordaunt could travel between the worlds. Somehow. Perhaps he told you that story for a reason, Eilean, perhaps . . ." He sighed. "I think our first priority should be translating the tome. That is why Mordaunt sent you away from Muirwood, Eilean. As for the rest, I will think on it. I must use the garderobe, so if you both would talk it over amongst yourselves, we can discuss our approach again later this evening. Do you agree?"

They did, and Stright and Eilean left the chamber, the Aldermaston bolting the door behind them.

"He uses it quite often," Stright said with a rakish smile. She had, of course, told him all about her first meeting with the Aldermaston, including what the púca had done.

As they walked together along the battlements, she could see the green in the valley below. The snow still prevailed on the mountaintop, but the vibrant evergreens below were no longer weighed down. Smoke from the chimneys of Isen could be seen rising into the crisp, cool air above the town. The sun hadn't fully breached the snow-packed roads, but as the Aldermaston had said, they were passable by horse.

"I can tell you don't want to be left behind," Eilean said to him.

He shook his head. "I didn't come here to fight a maston's war."

"It's not a war we could win, anyway. But your skills would be valuable in buying us time. With the spirits you could enlist to help, you'd see the enemy coming from afar. You could learn their plans . . . even cause some trouble as Utheros said."

"True, but I'll not leave you and Celyn."

Eilean paused and touched his arm. "What if she stayed too?"

He stopped and turned to look at her. "I can't believe you'd go on without her."

"The thought frightens me," Eilean admitted. "Remember when we went to the Dryad tree and I set loose the Fear Liath?"

He grunted. "Who could forget that?"

She looked him in the eye. "Captain Hoel used both of you to try and stop me. If I'd been alone, I could have turned invisible, I could have done other things to defend myself."

He shook his head. "You faint when you use the words too often. Hoel and his men are stronger than you."

She nodded and sighed. "Maybe that's because I'm *not* a maston yet. I haven't made the promises that allow me to use the magic with authority. And what would you and Celyn do while I'm at Cruix? You'd be sitting targets. I know you care for her, Stright."

Working his jaw, he clenched his hands into fists. "I made a promise to you."

"And you've fulfilled it. You promised to come with me to Hautland." She peered into his eyes. "And you've not been persecuted here. But if you go south, if someone in Paeiz or Dahomey discovers you, then you'll be killed on the spot." She thought again of Hoel, who'd spared Stright's life despite knowing the possible consequences. It occurred to her that she and Hoel were much the same—she'd spared *him* under similar circumstances. Shaking off the thought, she added, "Aldermaston Utheros will help protect you. I think that's why you're supposed to be *here*."

His shoulders slumped. "I do care about her," he confessed. "I never thought you'd part from her."

"I don't want to," Eilean said. "For the time being, however, it's safer here than where I'm going. And if this castle were to fall later on, you'd be able to get her out and to safety. I need to talk to Celyn, of course. She would want to go with me."

"She's expecting to," Stright said with a chuckle. "She will go wherever you go. Her loyalty is one of the things I admire about her."

"And yours is one of the reasons that I admire you," Eilean said. "I'll talk to her. We have to make this decision together. All three of us."

"Do you . . ." He scratched the back of his head. "Do you think she cares for me?"

Eilean couldn't believe he'd even asked the question. "Are all druids such fools about love?" she answered.

He gave her a sheepish smile. "Wasn't it Maston Ovidius who said, 'Many women long for what eludes them, and like not what is offered them?'"

"Have you been reading the tomes, Stright?"

"It's been a long winter."

Eilean smiled. "If you can't tell the way she brightens up the moment you walk into the kitchen, then you're blind as well as foolish.

Tell her how you feel. You don't need to wait for another clump of mistletoe to get permission to kiss her again."

"I've been a fool, haven't I?" he said, his cheeks turning the slightest bit pink.

"Maybe a little."

Together, they entered the castle doors to seek out someone they both knew was in the kitchen.

Either do not attempt at all, or go through with it. That is the lesson of the Medium. Setbacks plague all mankind. I will prove to this fugitive that my will is stronger than his. Defy me, bait me, torment me—it matters not. You will not prevail. I will have him back in custody. A way is always provided to the diligent. It is true what the tomes say: "Time is the devourer of all things."

—Sivart Gilifil, Aldermaston of Muirwood Abbey

CHAPTER EIGHT

Consequences

Eilean left Stright and Celyn to their discussion. Back in her room, she began to pace, thinking about the upcoming journey to Cruix Abbey. Having studied the prince's maps, she knew the way to the abbey. The mountain ranges would be her guide. Once they crossed the mountains outside the castle, they would travel to the town of Fenton. From there, a ship would take them to the coast of the neighboring kingdom, Mon, where they'd be dropped off before reaching a port. If they followed the mountains westward from there, they'd reach Cruix.

It would take a fortnight to reach Cruix if all went well. As she paced, she went to the window and gazed at the snowy crags of the Watzholt, which could be seen from her room. It would be a cold journey, but there was little chance of running into enemy soldiers. The mountains provided a natural barricade.

The thought of going without her friends made her heart hurt. Although she'd never known her parents, she'd always had Celyn, except for those awful days after her friend's death from the sweating sickness. It was Mordaunt who'd saved her, using a word of power to bring her back to life. The experience had changed her friend, making her more sensitive to the Medium's whispers, and it had changed Eilean as well.

A knock sounded on the door, startling her from her reverie. When she answered it, she saw one of the prince's men standing there.

"His Highness is in the solar and wishes to consult with you."

Eilean had told Celyn she'd wait in her chamber, but she could hardly refuse the summons, so she nodded and followed the man to the solar.

Prince Derik had spread maps on the tabletop, and he stood there with a bluff-faced man who wore a hauberk beneath a plain-looking tunic splotched with damp spots. A brace of knives were belted at his waist, and a broad velvet hat covered his light brown hair.

"Ah, Lady Gwenllian," said the prince when she arrived. "Come closer. This is Gropf, my best hunter. He just returned from the mountains. I sent him out days ago to see which passes were clear. Gropf is not a man of many words, but he is a rugged fellow and knows the Watzholt better than any man in Hautland, I daresay. He will be your guide."

The hunter was true to the prince's description. He nodded to Eilean and said nothing.

"I'm sending six soldiers with you," said the prince. Studying her, he added, "I must ask. Have you ever ridden a horse?"

Eilean shook her head no. Most ladies rode in carriages. The more adventurous had learned the art of riding, but not all. As a wretched, she hadn't been afforded the opportunity to learn.

The prince tapped his lip. "The mountains are rugged, and you'll make better time on horseback. It would be best if you had your own horse instead of burdening one with two people." He turned to Gropf. "Is there a gentle one you can recommend?"

The hunter made a grunt and nodded curtly.

"See to it, Gropf. You choose the men to escort the lady to Cruix, but I commission you to see that it is done properly. Do not leave her side unless you are convinced it is safe. Once you have crossed into Mon, there are roads that will take you to Cruix."

"Thank you, Master Gropf," Eilean said.

The hunter turned to her without emotion or expression. He shrugged, nodded to the prince, and left the solar.

The prince chuckled. "You won't find him to be a conversationalist, but he truly is the best I have. The Apocrisarius tried to recruit him years ago. He refused. But he's worked with them over the years and knows their ways."

"Thank you for letting him come." She was relieved and put her hand to her chest. "I feel better. I've never ridden a horse, but only because I never had the opportunity."

"Understandable, considering your circumstances," said the prince drily. "It will take several days to cross the Watzholt. There are no inns within the mountains. It will be cold."

"We'll dress accordingly," Eilean said. "And the days are getting warmer."

"True. Can you start a fire with your hands . . . like your friend?"

"Not in the same way, but the effect is the same."

"It will serve you well."

The door opened, and the messenger appeared again. "My lord, the Aldermaston is coming. News from Erfar."

"Send him in," said the prince, his brow crinkling with worry.

The Aldermaston soon arrived, out of breath. "My friend," he huffed out, "it begins."

"What happened?" asked the prince, his posture stiffening.

"I have several acolytes still at the abbey at Erfar. Knight-mastons began crossing the Apse Veil. First a dozen, then hundreds. They have taken over the city by order of Emperor Carolus and by the authority of the High Seer of Avinion. Thankfully, one of the acolytes was able to escape before they closed the city gates and barred anyone from leaving. He's just arrived."

Eilean's stomach tightened. Erfar was a two-day journey from Isen.

The prince sighed. "It was only a matter of time, I suppose. The snow in the mountains gave me a false sense that we had more time."

The Aldermaston looked at Eilean. "The druid will be even more necessary now, I'm afraid. The road to Isen goes through the woods. His help is urgently needed."

"He's talking to Celyn right now," she answered, gesturing to the door. "I will go get him."

She paused at the Aldermaston's intense look of worry as he turned toward the prince. "I have brought much trouble to you, my prince."

"Not all the prince-electors will side with the emperor," the prince said firmly. "We need allies. And soon. I must send messengers to beseech for it."

Eilean felt the urgency of her mission. "I'll do what I can to learn what is in the tome. I'm convinced it will aid our cause."

"It may not come soon enough," the prince said, doffing his hat. "No doubt the emperor's emissaries will send a summons for me to go to Erfar. If I refuse, I will be excommunicated."

The Aldermaston lifted his hands, giving him a slight smile. "It's not so bad."

The prince chuckled. "I wish I had your courage."

"You have plenty of your own."

But courage wouldn't get him far. If he were excommunicated, everything he owned could be stripped from him. There had to be a way to avoid it, or at least put it off . . .

A thought came to Eilean as she was on her way to the door. She turned and said, "You could send a reply that you were nearly killed by an Apocrisarius this winter. You could even send the sword as evidence of the attempted murder and confirm that the man wore a kystrel. That gives you a fair reason not to come in person."

The prince looked at the Aldermaston and then back at her. "I knew I was right in choosing you. I only wait to hear whether you will choose *me*. Your counsel is excellent, my lady. It will buy some time and force them to offer assurances or explain who sent the kishion."

Her chest throbbed at his approval. "And I'll go find Stright and Celyn."

She quickly walked down to the kitchen on the lower level, surprised to see that her friends weren't there. Then she returned to her room and found Celyn inside, the travel bag already stuffed and strapped. When Eilean entered, her friend rushed to her, tears in her eyes, and hugged her fiercely.

"Thank the Medium you haven't already left," she said, sobbing.

Tears stung Eilean's eyes as she gave herself over to the embrace. "I have to go." She forced the words through her thickening throat. "The emperor has sent knight-mastons to Erfar, only two days from here."

"I'm going with you," Celyn said, swiping tears from her eyes.

Eilean shook her head. "They need Stright *here* to help them defend the castle."

"I know. That's what he said. Eilean, I'm going with you."

"But I'll feel guilty if he comes too when he's so needed here. The Aldermaston is begging for his help. After all they've done for us, it seems like we should reciprocate."

Celyn released her and turned away, her shoulders trembling. "I told him to stay."

"What?"

Celyn nodded, choking down tears. When she turned back, they were streaming down her cheeks. "He loves me, Eilean. He finally told me, the *dolt*." That was the Hautlander word for a fool. "Now, you must listen to me. When the Medium brought me back to life, I made a promise to do its will, no matter what. I knew I was supposed to go to Hautland. And I know just as *strongly* that I'm supposed to go with you to Cruix Abbey."

Eilean stared at her friend, speechless. Her own heart quivered with relief and pain.

Celyn sniffled. "I told Stright that I loved him too. But sometimes love means parting for a season. It doesn't feel right, sending you off alone. I'm your companion and your friend. If Stright's love is real, then he'll wait for me to come back."

Eilean tried to stifle a sob, failed, and the two embraced again. She could only imagine how devastated Stright must feel. He'd finally confessed his love, only to be forbidden to go with them.

"That must have been so painful for you both," Eilean finally managed to say.

"It was the hardest thing I've ever done. He didn't understand. But I told him that I was following the Medium. I wouldn't even be *alive* today if not for the Medium. He said that he was confused because both sides of this conflict are claiming the Medium's power. Remember the word Aldermaston Utheros taught us? 'Schism'?"

Eilean remembered that lesson well. Aldermaston Utheros had told them he didn't want to be the cause of a schism in the order. When the Medium was made to fight against itself, a Blight always came of it—a punishment from the Medium. And yet Utheros had seen the truth and been unable to stay silent. The power of the High Seer and the emperor had grown tyrannical, and the unity they had brought to the world was forced.

"A Blight is coming, Eilean," said Celyn. "I don't know what kind or how it will happen, but I can feel it, like the wind."

Her insides felt like churning butter, but Eilean nodded. "It does feel wrong, doesn't it? Something is coming. A danger we cannot see. We cannot lose hope, though."

Celyn gripped Eilean's arms. "Mordaunt gave you his tome for a reason. He wanted you to learn how to translate it. Your task isn't finished. And neither is mine."

Eilean's heart constricted with pain. She wanted Celyn to join her, but she was conscious of causing her friends pain.

"How did Stright take it?"

Celyn sighed. "I've never seen him cry before. It hurt. We're both hurting. We have to trust that we'll see each other again. And that is hard. If I find out the emperor is attacking this castle, it'll be a torment. But it would be an even greater one knowing I was betraying my promise." She swallowed and then took Eilean's hand and squeezed it firmly. "When are we going?"

✳✳✳

There were two ways in and out of the castle—the prominent western gate, which linked to the road going down the mountain to Isen, and a carefully concealed postern door, which Eilean had not known about until that afternoon. The prince explained that it was kept secret because it allowed people to exit and enter the castle inconspicuously. It also gave his soldiers a way to launch an attack without risking opening the main gate, and because it was smaller, it was easier to defend.

The postern door was wide enough for a horse to go through, but not for a horse and rider, so they would have to lead their mounts out one at a time. A small yard abutted the wall, and by the time Eilean and Celyn joined the group, their mounts had already been brought out. Gropf had a smaller pony, or maybe it was a mule, which he'd ride at the head of the party. He was busily checking all the saddles himself.

Eilean and Celyn were both dressed for the weather, with leggings beneath their dresses, jackets over them, and heavy cloaks over that. Their thick boots were lined with muskrat fur, making them very plush and comfortable. Eilean had personally packed Mordaunt's tome in the bag she would wear around her shoulder, not trusting even the saddlebag to carry it. The sword she'd found with the tome was wrapped up and strapped to the pack, but the hilt had been left exposed, the raven symbol on the pommel a curiosity.

Could it be from the realm of the king Mordaunt had told her about? Would it even be possible to find and access that realm? The uncertainty made her excited and nervous at the same time.

The six soldiers who would accompany them were also bundled for warmth and armed with swords. Two of them had bows and arrows as well, both for hunting meat and for defense.

"His Majesty would address you before you leave."

The voice called to them from above, and they all turned and looked up to the edge of the battlement wall higher up the cliffside. Prince Derik approached the edge and gripped the stones as he looked down at their gathering in the small bailey yard.

"As I feared, the summons to meet the emperor's battle commander has just arrived. Hasten on your journey. Be loyal and true. Protect Lady Gwenllian and her maid with your lives."

Gropf ran his gloved hands across his nose, hocked, and spat. Then he nodded submissively.

"Farewell," said the prince, his gaze shifting to Eilean. He gave her an encouraging nod, a reminder of his request to serve him, and then he was gone.

Gropf pulled on his line and led his mount to the postern door. The porter unlocked it and then yanked the heavy door open, although it made no sound. The gruff hunter trudged through first.

Eilean heard another door open, closer, and then Stright came rushing out in his gray robes. For an instant, Eilean thought he had changed his mind and chosen to go with them. But then he came up to Celyn and kissed her firmly on the mouth. Some of the soldiers exchanged looks, and a few chuckled. Neither of them seemed to notice.

Stright ended the kiss and held Celyn tightly. Then he dipped his forehead until it touched hers.

"I will wait," he said. "However long it takes."

"Thank you," Celyn whispered huskily. "I will wait for you here or until Idumea."

The druid's face was mottled with emotion, but he firmed his features and kissed her again on the cheek. Then he approached Eilean.

"I've told the púca to follow you to Cruix," he told her in a low voice. "If there is danger you cannot see, it will try to warn you. And it can get you away faster if needed. It still wants to help us."

"You might need it to help you," Eilean said, but she was grateful.

"I have other spirits willing to help me here. I think the púca took a fancy to you after you flattered it. It wanted to go."

Eilean hugged him, grateful for all he'd done for them.

Stright looked abashed, and then he stood by to watch them leave. Two soldiers followed the hunter out of the opening, and then it was Eilean's turn. She watched as Celyn and Stright clasped hands, his thumb gently caressing her gloved hand.

They both had tears in their eyes as they parted.

Eilean felt some guilt at causing their parting. What worried her even more was the uncertainty of when—or whether—the two would see each other again.

We had the dubious honor of a visit from Mícheál Nostradamus, the head of the High Seer's Apocrisarius. He traveled by means of the Apse Veil to Dochte Abbey, and then by ship to Moros, and lastly by horse to Muirwood Abbey. He came himself because he did not trust any underling to determine the cause of our disobedience to the High Seer's order to send Mordaunt to Avinion.

I'm relieved that he didn't revoke my office on the spot. I explained, as best I could, the cause of the delay and even showed him the tunnels where our quarry has hidden himself. Stone masons hammer night and day now, trying to breach the lair of stone where he has sealed himself since we cannot damage the Leering.

Master Nostradamus implied I was neglectful in not having the man in irons, but I explained to him that such irons are useless against a man who can remove them by uttering a single word. He revealed that the Emperor Carolus Magnim has begun to besiege Hautland to pursue the heretic Utheros. But he also let slip that the Naestors have been launching raids against abbeys, especially any situated near the coast. They use longboats, no sails, and brave the open seas before launching up rivers where our ships cannot follow. He suggested I contact the sheriff of Mendenhall and warn him to be vigilant. There is a small town created upriver a short distance from the abbey, which would be a prime place to set a watch.

He will be staying for several days to monitor the progress and consult with Captain Cimber. As Ovidius says, "Like fragile ice, anger passes away in time." That is my hope.

—Sivart Gilifil, Aldermaston of Muirwood Abbey

CHAPTER NINE

The Watzholt

None of the evergreens had snow on them farther down the mountain, but there was still an abundance of ice to cross. Eilean admired the scenery, which was surprisingly colorful in spite of the snow, from the sharp blue sky to the deep green trees and the dark gray water of the river that wove its way down the mountain.

When Eilean asked Gropf the name of the river, the taciturn hunter said simply, "The Gray's River." And that was the end of his communication.

The layers of clothing combined with the brightness of the sun meant that there was no discomfort from the cold, no frigid hands or freezing toes. Before nightfall, they reached a broad plateau in the mountains and found a small cabin awaiting them. Gropf led the horses to it and then dismounted and opened the door, which had no lock on it.

"What is this place?" Eilean asked one of the soldiers.

"It's a warming hut," said the soldier. "The prince has several of them throughout the Watzholt for hunting. Sometimes a blizzard can come suddenly. These provide shelter, a stove, and they're all stocked with wood."

Two soldiers helped her and Celyn dismount and began to tend their horses. Both of the women rubbed their thighs and backsides. After spending a day in the saddle, Eilean was used to the sway of the horse's back and the gentle nature of the beast, but it was still painful to hold the same position for so long. The mare's name was Fügsam, the Hautlander word for "docile."

"Looks like we're spending the night in the warming hut," Celyn said. She stretched from side to side and tilted her head back and forth. "*Shaw*, look at the mountains," she gasped with awe.

Eilean had already noticed them. Mountains surrounded them. The white snowy field exposed no gorse, just snow and a few scraggly stands of quaking aspens. A wall of fir trees rose beyond the aspens, but the trees became sparser as the ground climbed higher. Everywhere she looked, there were rugged, vast peaks of stone rising around them. It seemed like a large crinkle against the fleecy blue sky.

Snapping and crackling sounds issued from the hut, and then Gropf emerged, brushing his hands. He hocked and spat, hands on his hips, and gazed out at the vast scene as if unimpressed.

"That stand of trees is your privy," he said to Eilean and Celyn, nodding to the nearest group of evergreen across a short field of untrampled snow. "There's naught inside."

Celyn hooked arms with Eilean, and they both trudged through the snow to the privacy offered by the trees.

After they were done, they walked slowly back to the hut, noticing the sky getting darker and darker after the setting of the sun. The cold began to increase, and puffs of mist came from their mouths.

"Are you missing him?" Eilean asked softly.

"It hasn't even been a day yet. We left this afternoon. He *kissed* me in front of everyone." Celyn paused, then added, "Yes . . . I'm missing him very much, but I don't regret my decision. If the love is true, it'll last. If not . . . better to know that too."

"You're very patient."

"Well, he's a different sort of man than Aisic."

Eilean shuddered. "Don't even say his name." The memories of her first love were bitter now, although the pain had dimmed with time. She didn't understand what she'd seen in that selfish man. Or why his days as a soldier had turned him into someone who'd take advantage of a woman.

"He wasn't always a *pethet*," Celyn said, using Mordaunt's favorite term of scorn.

"Maybe not," Eilean conceded. "But there were seeds of it in him at Tintern. I just chose not to see them."

"I'm sorry you had your heart broken," Celyn said, then she heaved a weighty sigh. "I hope it doesn't happen to me."

"Stright is a good man."

A snickering noise came from the direction of the trees. A thump hit the snow behind them, and they whirled around in unison.

The púca couldn't be seen in the shadows, but Eilean heard its claws scraping against the wood of a branch.

"Hello," Eilean said in greeting, nodding to the shadows. She heard the flapping of wings and another snicker.

"Are we in danger?" Celyn asked in an undertone.

"Púca," Eilean said, her heart racing. "If we're in danger, show yourself."

But the magical creature did not reveal itself. All was silent.

"Thank you for watching over us," Eilean said. "You're so good at that." When there was no reply to that comment either, she and Celyn started back to the warming hut, which now had a stream of lazy smoke coming from the chimney.

When they entered it, an oil lamp was glowing to provide light. There were benches along the walls, a potbelly stove in the corner with a mound of wood stacked nearby. The fire in the belly of the stove crackled with warmth. Some of the soldiers had spread out blankets on the floor for them.

The lead soldier, Sergeant Nimrue, explained that two men would guard the hut and the horses in shifts throughout the night. Rations were handed out, and Gropf melted snow in a pot on the stove and gave them all warm water to drink.

"Will we cross the mountain pass tomorrow?" Eilean asked him.

He nodded curtly and said nothing.

The soldiers spoke in hushed voices among themselves. It grew darker and darker, and the wind began to rustle through the trees. A thump struck the roof, and a snickering noise could be heard through the windows.

Eilean and Celyn exchanged a look.

"What was that?" said one of the startled soldiers.

Nimrue pursed his lips. "An owl, probably."

"Sounded too heavy for an owl, sir."

One of the soldiers went out and then came back in. "It must have flown off," he said. "I didn't see anything."

"You're lucky," Gropf said gruffly.

Eilean remembered that the púca were pranksters. It would try to lure one of the soldiers into touching its fur so it could fly off with him for a while. The surly hunter had probably had some experience with that.

Eilean snuggled down in her blanket, resting her head against the pack holding Mordaunt's tome as a pillow. More antics followed as the púca continued to fly to and from the cottage, but she didn't feel any threat. The creature was following its natural instincts. It was drawn to people and enjoyed the game it was playing.

"Good night," Celyn whispered.

That was the last thing Eilean remembered before she fell asleep.

***

The next day was even more tiring as their horses climbed up the mountainside to the pass. Once they reached a certain height, the trees disappeared, and there was just rock and snow lining the way. The air was colder up there, and Eilean felt the sting of it on the tip of her nose. The cowl of her cloak was thick, thankfully, and Fügsam was steady and patient. Some of the soldiers grumbled about the conditions, but nothing out of the ordinary happened.

Eilean noticed that Gropf, who took the lead on his mule, was following a set of tracks—likely his own from having investigated the pass earlier. The snow was deep but not enough to exhaust the horses. When they reached the top, she turned around in the saddle and looked down, soaking in the thrilling view. She glanced at Celyn, who nodded in appreciation at the beautiful scene.

Then the horses began their downward trek. It seemed that there was no end to the Watzholt, that nothing lay ahead other than more mountains, but on the journey down, the snow began to reveal pockets of scrub. Later in the afternoon, they came across another river that wound its way down from the heights. Gropf pointed to the left, and they saw a few elk standing at the bank. One by one, the tawny creatures bounded over the river and disappeared into a stand of trees.

Halting, Gropf waved Nimrue to him. They huddled together for a moment, and then Nimrue announced that the group should follow him because Gropf was going to bring down one of the elk for their dinner.

They went on ahead, leaving the hunter to his task. Eilean felt uneasy without him, but Nimrue displayed confidence, and the rest followed him. When they reached the bottom of the mountain, there was a small stone bridge spanning the river. The snow was much shallower there, and large swaths of scrub could be seen, as well as fallen trees with silver-barked trunks.

"He said to wait for him here," said Nimrue. They dismounted and rested the horses, and Eilean and Celyn crossed to the middle of the bridge and stared down at the frigid waters passing beneath them.

Nimrue ordered the men to gather some brush, which they did, but they struggled to start a fire with a piece of flint and steel. They kept at it, getting increasingly frustrated.

Eilean left the bridge and went to them.

"May I try?" she asked, holding out her hand.

"The wood's too cold, my lady," said one of the soldiers. "Needs a bit of oil to get it going, and only the hunter has any."

"Let her try," said Nimrue.

The soldier handed her the flint and steel. Eilean knelt by the mass of sticks and branches, her back to the men.

"Pyricanthas, sericanthas, thas," she whispered as she struck the flint with the edge of the steel blade.

The magic of the Medium responded to her command, and suddenly tongues of flames were licking at the branches. Heat followed.

"Of all the garmed," said one of the soldiers, impressed.

Nimrue nodded to her, and the soldiers kept feeding the flames until a nice bonfire was burning. Not long afterward, Gropf came walking down the trail they'd come from, an elk slumped over the back of his mule. When he arrived, he gazed at the crackling fire, shrugged, and then took the kill and began to dress it.

Celyn helped him slice the bits of meat and then made skewers for each of the soldiers to roast over the flames. They added some crushed salt and ground herbs, and it was really very delicious.

The horses were fed provender, and they drank from the cold river water. It was as good a place as any to camp for the night, and with enough deadwood to feed the flames, they set up their blankets around the fire. It was much colder without a warming hut, and Eilean found herself shivering when the night came. Gropf filled two leather flasks with warm water from the kettle and handed one each to Celyn and Eilean.

"Keep these under the blankets. They'll help you stay warm."

They each thanked him, and Eilean tried to fall asleep, but it was strange being out of doors in the middle of strange mountains at night. Watching Gropf move about, calm and capable, reminded her of Captain Hoel. She found herself wishing that they weren't enemies, that *he* were their escort to Cruix Abbey. As she lay beneath her blanket, feeling the warmth from the flask against her stomach, she wondered where he was at that moment. Was he with the force in Erfar coming to attack the castle? Was he hoping to find her there?

"Look at the stars," Celyn whispered nearby.

Eilean rolled onto her back, gazed up, and was entranced by the tiny lights scattered across the sky. The smoke from the fire wasn't thick enough to blur them out. Taking in the sight, she couldn't help but consider how small she was in the vast world.

You are not insignificant.

It was a whisper of the Medium. Once again, she felt an overwhelming surge of love and care, like the time she had ventured past the protections of Muirwood to see if the Medium would speak to her.

There was something about being in nature that made it so much easier to feel. To *hear*. And it struck her that the druids experienced the same thing. Few spirit creatures resided inside the towns.

All of this was made for you.

She felt her throat tighten with tears, and gratitude surged in her heart. The snow, the trees, the seasons, the mountains. They were gifts from the Medium, meant to be enjoyed.

Thank you, Eilean thought as another shiver, a different kind, came over her body.

Sergeant Nimrue approached her blankets and squatted down. "The hunter says we should reach Fenton tomorrow night if we ride hard. You do the best you can, my lady. Both of you. We've had an easy pace so far. Tomorrow will be different."

"Thank you," Eilean said, leaning up on her arm.

As the soldier gazed at her in the firelight, she saw a little flush come to his cheeks.

"Get some rest," he said.

"We'll do our best," she said.

"I know. But if we can get there by tomorrow night, you'll be able to stay in an inn. That would be much more comfortable than sleeping out in the woods like this. I'll try to get us a ship that leaves with the tide the next day. But I don't know what we'll find when we get there. The High Seer may already control the town because of the abbey there."

"We'll be careful," Eilean said.

"I'll see you safe, my lady. I promise."

He rose and walked away to give orders for the night watch.

Eilean turned around, her back to the fire now. As she closed her eyes and tried to fall asleep, she found herself thinking again of Captain Hoel, lying bleeding near the Dryad tree, quivering in pain. Telling her to hide. Trying to help her. The way he'd looked at her then, without any disgust or judgment, had stayed with her. Because, in that moment, he had seemed to care for her as a person. Not as an enemy to be tracked or destroyed. Not as a problem to be solved. But as Eilean, a wretched who was becoming something else.

At times it is folly to hasten, at other times, to delay. I have had both work crews hammering furiously at the stones that make up Mordaunt's strange tomb for three solid days, in the dark and in the light, and we have finally broken in. He's inside a little cell of sorts, a natural fissure in the quarry. He's crafted a Leering for light, and the crew from the tunnel has seen him. There is a stone bench of sorts, and he's fashioning a Leering out of another stone. The gap is small, but the workers continue to crack the rocks. By the end of this third day, I think we'll have broken a large enough space to get at him. He's taken no interest in speaking to us and works with the methodical precision of a man bent on finishing his craft. I've spoken to him, but he will not answer me. He acts as if we are not even there.

—Sivart Gilifil, Aldermaston of Muirwood Abbey

CHAPTER TEN

Disguised

They reached Fenton well after dark, but they had no trouble finding the abbey. The facade was engraved with so many Leerings the building glowed like a beacon from far away. Although the design was similar to the other abbeys Eilean had seen, it was notable for the twin towers that rose on its eastern end, which were about as tall as the abbey was long. The entire abbey was surrounded by large stone buttresses, each with a decorative spire that added to the grandeur of the construction.

Nimrue said it was the oldest abbey in Hautland, built on a site originally founded by an ancient empire. It was late, but lights still glimmered in the town surrounding the abbey.

"Will the gates be closed?" Eilean asked Nimrue.

"Yes, but I bear orders from the prince. They'll let us in."

"I'll go ahead and make sure the town hasn't been taken," Gropf suggested, and they all agreed and hung back as he rode ahead.

Fenton was surrounded by a fortified wall, and the road they traveled led to the front gate. There were no wagons or camps outside the port town. All had made it in before the curfew, presumably.

Eilean was weary from the long ride, her thighs and back sore, but she was grateful to have reached their destination. As they drew nearer, the abbey loomed above them. It was the highest point of the town, clearly visible above the walls as they approached.

Celyn stifled a yawn and shook her head. They were all weary from the journey.

Finally, Gropf returned. "No imperial soldiers here."

"Thank Idumea," Nimrue said with relief. They went to the gate, and the sergeant lingered a moment, talking to the guards. When he finished, he rejoined their group on the inner part of the gate.

"They've heard nothing of the invasion of Erfar. An Apocrisarius ship came to the dock about a fortnight ago and stopped for supplies, but it left again. The abbey is still ours."

Eilean bit her lip. "You knew the guards?"

"Aye, my lady. Two of them. They're loyal to Prince Derik. There's an inn called the Schonburg that the prince likes to stay at when he visits. They'll open the doors to us, even at this late hour."

"That would be lovely," Eilean sighed.

The streets were all paved in tightly packed cobbles, and the buildings reminded her of those in Isen, only they weren't as colorful, and the rooftops were not as sharply sloped. There probably wasn't as much snow in the plains as there was in higher elevations. Even though it was late in the evening, the streets were still crowded with people, making merry and dancing to street players performing with flutes.

Some street vendors sold pies and sausages to the crowds, and a few offered their wares to the riders passing through, but Nimrue waved them off. Gropf kept a wary eye on everyone, one hand on the reins and the other on the hilt of a long dagger.

They followed the twisting roads southward, away from the abbey, but those gleaming spires kept drawing Eilean's eye.

At last, before midnight, they arrived at the Schonburg, and Nimrue dismounted and ordered two of the soldiers to care for the horses. The door of the inn was locked, but he rapped on it anyway, and the hostess answered it quickly. The smell of strong ale wafted from the doorway, along with the clinking of pewter mugs.

The hostess looked first at the soldiers, then at the two women farther back. Her head tilted slightly. "What is this?" she asked in a thick Hautlander accent, jutting her chin.

"We traveled from the prince's castle in Isen," said Nimrue. "We require shelter."

"Prince Derik?"

"The same. You have rooms?"

"Of course! There are few travelers these days. Who are they?" she asked, looking at Eilean and Celyn.

"The prince's guests," said Nimrue. "You have room in the stables? My men will see to the horses."

"Of course." She smiled and opened the door wide. "Everyone looks hungry. I'll have food brought to you while the rooms are prepared."

"One room for the ladies. We'll share one next to them, and I'll have guards watching them all night."

"As you wish," said the woman with a shrug. "Welcome."

When Eilean dismounted, her knees felt wobbly. She gazed up at the brick siding of the wall. The upper rooms had windows made of smoky glass.

"It's shaped a little like the Pilgrim Inn near Muirwood," Celyn said.

Eilean paused and acknowledged the similarity. "It does remind me of it. I'm glad you came with me." She squeezed Celyn's hand.

"I never imagined we'd come this far."

As they entered, Eilean was surprised to find the common room so crowded. There was a roaring fire in the hearth and about a dozen other patrons, mostly men, laughing and joking with each other.

The hostess brought them to a table, and the other guests cheered at their arrival. Eilean searched the faces but didn't recognize any of them. The dialect they spoke was more guttural than that of Isen, with other words slurred in that didn't seem Hautlander at all.

After sitting at the table with some of the soldiers, Eilean noticed that Gropf went to a small table in the corner and sat by himself, away from the rest of the group. His back was to the corner, giving him a view of everyone there. A serving girl brought him a tankard, which he accepted.

The hostess's husband came out to greet them, rubbing sleep from his eyes, and Nimrue asked him about any boats heading out in the morning. He wasn't aware of any but promised to send a boy at first light to the docks to inquire for them.

Nimrue declined the offer, saying he would send one of his own men to do the task.

Food arrived shortly thereafter, and the smell of the breaded schnitzel made Eilean realize how hungry she'd been. They ate quickly, the warm food reviving them. The soldiers looked to be enjoying themselves with the ale after the long journey, but by the time the hostess came back and offered to show Eilean and Celyn to their room, they were more than ready.

Nimrue sent two soldiers to escort them and stand guard. The room was spacious, and the crackling fire in the brazier reminded Eilean of Mordaunt's chambers at the castle at Muirwood. One of the beds was large and swathed with velvet curtains, while the other was smaller and simpler, for a servant.

Eilean pulled off the strap of her leather bag and massaged her shoulder to ease the knots from the burden she'd been carrying. Her friend went to the window, but the mottled glass must have made it impossible to see out of. She unlatched it and pushed it open, leaning out a little and breathing out a sigh. There was a garderobe in the corner, a desk, and several dressers for clothes. The decorations were lavish, suggesting the inn was used to serving royalty.

"I could fall asleep in an instant," Celyn said, yawning again as she lowered onto the smaller bed. "It was a long day."

"Beautiful, though," Eilean answered. "And tomorrow, we'll be in another kingdom yet. More traditions to learn."

"I like Hautland," Celyn said. "But sometimes I still miss Pry-Ree."

A soft knock sounded on the door. Celyn rose to answer it, but Eilean was closer and opened the door.

The hostess had come with a silver tray arrayed with fruit, cheese, and a bottle of wine. "In case you get hungry later on."

"Thank you," Eilean said. She moved aside, and the hostess came in and set the tray on the short round table in the middle of the room.

That done, the hostess turned to Eilean. "Sergeant Nimrue is speaking with my husband and someone who knows about a ship. If you are not too tired, would you come downstairs and join them?"

"Yes, I will," Eilean said. She turned to Celyn and pointed to the leather satchel.

Her friend nodded, taking her meaning to hide it in the room, and Eilean followed the hostess out. The two guards nodded to her, although they looked a little disgruntled at having been chosen to stand watch while the others celebrated below.

After going downstairs, they passed through the common room. Gropf was still at the table, arms folded, watching the ruckus with obvious disaffection. He probably would have preferred guarding their room. The hostess led Eilean down a short hall and motioned to the door at the end.

"That one," she said and then turned back toward the common room.

Eilean rapped her knuckles on the door. She heard the sound of boots coming toward it from the other side. And suddenly, she felt a warning from the Medium.

Disguise yourself.

She whispered the word of power that altered one's appearance—"*mareh.*" Having only a moment to decide, she made herself look like Celyn.

The door opened, and she saw Captain Hoel standing before her.

He seized her arm and yanked her into the room. In a few fluid motions, he pushed the door shut with the toe of his boot before pressing her against it and clamping a hand over her mouth. His body weight pressed against her, trapping her to the door. The smell of him, the scent of leather and something uniquely him, struck her strongly.

His eyes narrowed with disappointment. He'd been expecting *her*, Eilean.

Blinking rapidly, she noticed Nimrue on the floor in the corner to her right, unconscious and gagged, his wrists bound in shackles behind him. No one else was there. It was a bedroom, the only light coming from the brazier and a lamp burning atop a dresser. A small bed was pushed up against the wall.

Eilean felt panic bubble up inside her, but she tried to remain calm.

Captain Hoel's closeness was unnerving. She thought about biting his hand so that he'd release her and she could blast him with her magic, but that thought felt wrong. The Medium had warned her to disguise herself. There had to be a reason for that.

"I'm going to pull my hand away, Celyn," he said. "Don't scream, or you'll end up like him. Your friends wouldn't hear you anyway. It's noisy out there on purpose. Will you stay quiet? I have questions."

Eilean swallowed, wanting that smothering hand away from her face. She nodded slowly.

Hoel lifted his hand away from her lips but kept it close in case she double-crossed him. Her mind was a wild mix of emotion and worry as she peered into his eyes. Strangely, the first thought that surfaced was that she couldn't remember ever being this close to him. It made her feel very aware of him and notice details she hadn't before. His eyes weren't green or brown but a mix of the two.

"Is Eilean in the room still? She's the one I asked for."

"She's . . . she's tired," Eilean answered, her throat dry.

"How many guards at her door?"

Eilean stared at him and didn't answer.

Though he still had a firm grip on her arm, he backed off, allowing her to move, only to immediately pull her toward the table. He grabbed a set of irons from its surface and expertly locked them around her wrists, behind her back.

"Sit down," he said, pointing to the bed.

"How did you know we'd be here?" she asked him, lowering herself down. With a word, she could make the chains fall off her wrists. With a word, she could kill him. But that thought made her feel horrible. The image of him lying bleeding by the Dryad tree rose in her mind.

He rubbed his mouth, his eyes darting to the door and back again. He waited a moment. Had he heard something? Dare she hope Gropf had followed her down the hall?

"I'll be the one asking questions," he said. "It was dangerous crossing the Watzholt. Those mountains are known for avalanches."

"We had a guide," she answered. Her mouth was so dry. She felt the strain of maintaining her disguise, but she'd used her power infrequently of late. It would last a while yet.

"So there were no avalanches when you crossed the mountains?"

She looked at him in confusion. "No."

He pursed his lips and nodded curtly. "I'm glad you're both safe. How is she?"

"She" meaning her, Eilean. It was the strangest thing, talking to Captain Hoel about herself, and he'd asked the question in a manner that indicated he was worried about her. For some reason she found that pleasing. "Well enough now."

He inclined his head. "What do you mean?"

"A kishion attacked her and Prince Derik during yuletide." She watched his face closely for a reaction.

He was gracious enough to supply a look of shock and concern. "A kishion?"

The news had definitely surprised him, and the relief she felt surprised *her*. Although she'd struggled to believe Hoel would kill someone in cold blood, she'd feared he knew about the plan. That he'd maybe agreed with it.

"Yes. He had a kystrel around his neck. But he was dressed like *you*."

"What do you mean like *me*?"

"Like you and your hunters," she answered. "*Shaw*, you don't think I know what you look like?" Under Mordaunt's tutelage, she'd stopped using the sayings she'd grown up with, but Celyn had not. She couldn't help thinking the word was a nice touch to her deception.

"I know nothing about it," he answered. But the brooding look in his eyes suggested he knew more than he was letting on.

"She almost *died*, Captain Hoel," she said urgently. "If not for what she'd learned from the druid, she would have. Who sent the kishion?"

His lips firmed. "I don't know . . . for certain. Where is the kystrel now?"

"It's still with the prince at the castle. And now he's facing the emperor by himself. It's not right."

"It's a consequence of his choices. And hers." His tone turned impatient. "She's upstairs, then. How many guards?"

Eilean pressed her lips closed.

"You do your friend credit," he said coaxingly, "but consider what Eilean would want. Half of your men are drunk already, and I'd rather not kill them if possible. The only one who would give me any concern at all is that stone-faced hunter. Even then, I would win."

A muffled groan came from Nimrue. Eilean saw him slowly turn his head, his eyelids fluttering.

Hoel gazed down at the man with contempt and then shot a warning look her way. He drew his gladius, the blade gleaming. "How many? Two? Three?"

She felt an urge to tell him. It would be all right. "Two."

He nodded. "You're not lying. Thank you."

"Nnnghhmrrfff," moaned Nimrue from behind the gag. He struggled against the iron cuffs at his wrists.

Captain Hoel turned the pommel, looking as if he intended to club the soldier on the head.

"Leave him be," she entreated. "He can't go anywhere. Neither can I. Eilean is probably asleep upstairs right now."

The soldier's eyes were wide with fear as he continued to struggle against the bonds.

"Two guards," Captain Hoel mused. "I can handle two with no problem. I'll be back with Eilean."

He slid the gladius back into its scabbard, withdrew a rag from his pocket, and came toward her.

"I won't scream, Captain," she said. "You've won. Just don't hurt them too badly."

He twisted the rag in his hands. "Does she have the tome with her?"

Eilean nodded.

The captain gave a low chuckle. Then he stuffed the rag into his pocket and went to the door, his boots making no sound at all this time. He paused there, listening.

"It's getting quieter," he whispered. Then he opened the door and slipped out into the hall.

The prostrate soldier looked up at her pleadingly, nodding at her to come to help him.

Eilean rose from the bed and walked over to him. *"Ephatha,"* she said. The chains slumped from her wrists, but she caught them before they rattled to the floor. The sergeant's chains had fallen away with the same command. With eyes full of excitement, he yanked the gag out of his mouth.

The magic was making her head swim, so she let the illusion of Celyn melt away.

"It's . . . it's you!" he gasped.

"Hurry. Let's get Gropf and trap the captain between us."

The hunter was now the prey.

In an easy matter, anyone can be eloquent. But this is no easy matter. I can scarce lift my stylus and write these words. Let it suffice to say that we who thought we were the gaolers have become imprisoned in our own abbey. The breach we made in the stone was nearing completion. The tunnel entrance was the closest to success, but I did not cease excavating from the quarry side either. Even with all the hammering and noise of cracking stone, the druid sat at his table, working on his Leering, ignoring the tumult. Again I tried to reason with the man. He would say nothing.

At last, the breach was done. The workers stepped aside, and Captain Cimber and four of his hunters entered the stone chamber to apprehend the fugitive. Lord Nostradamus remained with me in the shaft. Mordaunt uttered a word, and everyone was shoved violently away. Then he said another, and the wall opposite him exploded in a plume of pulverized stone.

By the time we'd rallied our senses and given chase, what did we behold? The hillside had collapsed in rubble, yet there were stones suspended in the air, forming a strange stairway down to the bottom of the quarry. As men screamed and gave chase, the heretic hastened down the boulder steps into the quarry at a breakneck pace, his staff in hand.

Lord Nostradamus ordered the hunters to shoot arrows at him, but despite their skill with their bows, all the arrows veered to the side. When Mordaunt reached the ground, he turned, lifted the staff, and a boulder in the quarry flew up toward us. We scrambled in terror and barely avoided being crushed by stone.

By the time we had abandoned the tunnel and arrived on the scene from aboveground, the workers had scattered in fear, and there was no sign of the man. Lord Nostradamus was furious, as you can imagine, but he also was witness to the terrible power of the heretic.

After all these weeks of digging and attempting to prevail against the stone, I discovered we were doing nothing more than excavating a path for the fugitive. He can return to his dwelling at any time. I don't fear that he has left. I fear that he is wandering the abbey grounds now unchecked.

—Sivart Gilifil, Aldermaston of Muirwood Abbey

CHAPTER ELEVEN

A Broken Window

Intent on stopping Captain Hoel, Eilean hurried with Nimrue to the common room.

"One of the Apocrisarius is here, right now!" the sergeant shouted to his men. Gropf came out of his chair and drew his dagger, his face suddenly tight with anger, a dangerous scowl twisting his mouth.

The rest of the men slammed down their drinks and pushed back in their chairs, which squealed on the wood floor. The other patrons went silent at the shouted words. Some began to head for the exit and found the door still locked.

A cry of pain came from the corridor above, followed by a thump on the floor. As Gropf rushed toward the stairs, a body came tumbling down and nearly bowled him over. But the canny hunter leaped over the sprawled body of Eilean's guard, now sprawled at the foot of the stairs, and continued up the steps, Eilean rushing after him.

"My lady, wait!" Nimrue warned.

"Open the door! Let us out!" shouted one of the patrons, his fist banging against the door. Several other men took up the call.

Eilean reached the stairs before any of the other soldiers and stepped over the fallen man, who was blinking distractedly from his tumble. Grabbing the railing, she pulled herself up, taking the steps two at a time. Her heart seemed to be pounding in her ears, so loudly she barely heard the noise of boots coming behind her as the other soldiers were spurred to action.

When she reached the top of the stairs, Gropf and Hoel were exchanging blows, a gladius against a dagger. Her throat caught with fear. What word of power could she use that wouldn't injure the older hunter as well?

Hoel kneed the older man in the stomach, making Gropf grimace, but the hunter brought his dagger down toward his opponent's neck. Only Hoel's quick reflexes saved him. He deflected the blow by catching the hunter's wrist, then shoved his forearm into Gropf's throat and pressed him back against the door of one of the guest rooms.

"Don't kill him!" Eilean yelled.

Gropf dropped his dagger and grabbed Hoel around the waist, hoisting him up off his feet. Both men smashed into the wall on the other side of the corridor, whereupon Hoel promptly slammed the pommel of his gladius against Gropf's skull. All the fight went out of him, and he collapsed in a heap on the floor.

Hoel's gaze turned to Eilean. She sensed in a glimpse, through the Medium's power, his thoughts as he realized he'd been tricked, that he'd had her in his possession and walked away. Chagrin was one emotion he felt, but there was another, one that flickered through him like an errant flame and was gone in an instant.

"So that was you after all," Hoel said.

She shrugged and smiled.

Nimrue and two other men had come up behind her. "Stand aside, my lady!" the sergeant shouted.

Hoel looked past her, the hint of a mocking smile curling his lips. He didn't doubt for a moment he'd win.

She didn't stand aside. Instead, she took three bold strides forward and said, *"Kozkah gheb-ool."*

The words of power flung Hoel away from her. She watched his eyes widen with shock as he was thrust violently away, so fast and so hard that he crashed through the window at the end of the corridor. His boots disappeared as he plummeted down amidst the sound of shattering glass.

"By Idumea!" gasped Nimrue from behind her.

Worried she'd killed him, Eilean rushed to the end of the hall. Some chunks of plaster had fallen with the captain, and part of the window-sill had cracked. Poking her head outside into the cold night air, she saw Hoel sprawled on the cobblestone courtyard near the stables. For a moment, the vision of him dying from the Fear Liath slammed into her, and her heart twisted with a rush of pain and regret.

But he wasn't dead. He sat up, holding his ribs, and gazed up at the window he'd been shoved out of. The wind blew her hair in front of her face, and she idly brushed it back.

"What's happening?" Celyn asked from behind her. She'd obviously heard the commotion and come out.

Eilean stared down at Hoel as he limped toward the gate leading out.

Her first feeling, oddly, was relief, and then—

She turned and shouted to Nimrue, "He's getting away! In the back, by the stables!"

Nimrue turned, and the soldiers rushed down the steps with a great rush of noise. There was no moon in the sky, so when she turned back, Hoel couldn't be seen, but she heard the gate unlatching and then saw it swing open on one side.

"Hurry!" Eilean shouted back down the corridor. She saw Celyn kneeling by Gropf's still body. Of course her friend would be helping the injured man.

When she turned back to the shattered window, she still couldn't see Hoel through the darkness, but in a few moments, Nimrue and two soldiers came charging out through the rear door of the inn, their boots crunching in the broken glass. She wondered if Hoel was cut and bleeding. Despite everything, the thought of him in pain troubled her. When they brought him back, she would tend to him herself. But he would be her prisoner this time.

"Which way did he go?" Nimrue shouted.

"Through the gate! It's still open!" she called, pointing. Again the wind blew her hair, and she angrily swiped it away. The chill of the night air tasted of sea salt.

Nimrue and the other soldiers hurried out through the gate, and she waited, listening for the sound of conflict.

"Help me bring him to our room," Celyn said to her.

There wasn't much else she could do to assist in the chase, so she hastened to help her friend. While Celyn hoisted from beneath Gropf's arms, Eilean grabbed his ankles, and the two hefted the heavy man into the bedroom and managed to lift him onto the short bed. Gropf's eyes were closed, but they danced beneath the lids.

Suddenly, he gasped, and his eyes flew open. "What?" He glanced at the two of them gazing down at him. "Is it dinner?" he grunted.

Eilean and Celyn exchanged a confused look.

"We've already been fed," Celyn said.

"You took a blow to the head," Eilean added.

Gropf squinted and massaged his scalp. He nodded and then sat up groggily. A few moments later, he glanced back at them. "Oh, is it time for dinner?"

This time the look they exchanged was worried. "I think he needs a healer," Celyn suggested.

"I'll be fine after I've eaten," Gropf said. He tried to stand, wobbled, and sat back down.

"Do you remember getting attacked?" Eilean asked.

"Who? Who attacked me?" he said angrily.

"The Apocrisarius was here."

Gropf looked confused. He shook his head. He looked around at the room. "Where are we?" he asked. "Is it time for dinner?"

And he asked, over and over, about dinner until the healer finally arrived.

***

"My lady."

A hand nudged her shoulder, waking her. Eilean had fallen asleep at the small table. Celyn was sprawled on the couch with a blanket on her, and Gropf lay on the small bed, snoring robustly. The healer was gone.

Nimrue stood at her elbow, his eyes bleary from lack of sleep.

Rubbing her eyes, Eilean noticed the faint glow of dawn coming from the window. Her neck was stiff and pained her. "What news?" she asked.

"We couldn't find him, my lady. I'm sorry, but we searched every alley. Knocked on doors. When the night watch finally came, I enlisted their help as well. We've searched for hours to no avail. It was like chasing a shadow."

Eilean closed her eyes, wrestling with disappointment. She still worried that Hoel had been injured by the fall through the window, but the news that he'd escaped was even more concerning.

"I'm sure you did everything you could," she said with a sigh.

"I apologize, my lady. Truly, after what he did to my men, I'd see justice on the man. But there's no denying those Apocrisarius are skilled at evasion. I've not given up all hope yet. He's still in Fenton. And we have men standing guard at the gates of the abbey in case he tries to go there."

"Thank you," she said. "How did you end up getting captured?"

Nimrue chuckled. "That's a story. So the hostess, well . . . she feels terrible this has happened. Captain Hoel came in disguised as a merchant. He's been here for weeks on business. Paid handsomely too. She said . . . she said he asked about you when he first came, thinking we might already be here. Strange, is it not?"

Eilean frowned. She knew Hoel had the Gift of Seering. Was that how he'd known they'd come to Fenton? But why was the Medium helping Hoel intercept them? Was it merely because his thoughts were so strong, his determination so committed? Because, if not for the Medium's warning, she would have been captured by him again.

Nimrue was still talking, and she'd missed part of what he'd said. ". . . fault. The hostess knew we were looking for a ship, so she suggested rousing our friend. She informed him of our arrival and brought me to him. I, of course, didn't recognize him, since I've never met him and he wasn't dressed as an Apocrisarius. He said he was already bound for Mon when his ship arrived, but he wanted to see you, my lady, to be assured of the truth. The hostess, believing she'd earn a bonus for arranging the deal, went to get you. As soon as she left, he clubbed me on the head and tied me up." He held up his hands. "Again, I'm very sorry."

Gropf's voice interjected. "You're lucky he didn't kill you."

Eilean hadn't noticed him sitting up. His eyes weren't darting like they had been the night before. A pained expression was on his face as he rubbed his scalp again.

"Are you remembering now?" Eilean asked.

Gropf winced and nodded, then lowered his hand.

"So the hostess was ignorant of the plot; I'm convinced of that," Nimrue said. "She offered us the rooms for free and then boarded up the broken window until the glass can be replaced." He sighed. "Our friend had a long fall from that window. I'm surprised he walked away."

"He was hurt, I'm pretty sure of that," Eilean said.

Nimrue scratched his head. "I'm exhausted. I'll keep a guard on you, but we're all needing to sleep. We won't be leaving today anyway, not until we have a ship. But I've got a man trying to arrange one for us. Get some more rest, and I'll be back in a few hours."

"Thank you, Sergeant Nimrue," Eilean said.

He was about to leave and paused. "To be honest, my lady, we're not much help. You're the one who saved *us* last night. Just as you saved Prince Derik. I'm in your debt."

Gropf scooted off the bed and rose, this time with no wobble in his balance. Once Nimrue was gone, he came over to the table. He put his hands on the surface and gazed down at her seriously.

"I'm bringing you to Cruix," he growled. She could see the determination in his eyes, and the Medium revealed a glimpse of his thoughts to her as well. He was embarrassed that he'd lost the fight. And he was ready to go another round with Captain Hoel.

In fact, he was hoping to.

He came again. Well after dark, he opened the door to my study, where Lord Nostradamus and I were consulting with each other. His sudden arrival startled us both. Before Nostradamus could call for his guards, Mordaunt revoked his power of speech through Idumea's hand and then gave us a warning.

The Naestors have witnessed our prosperity and are greedy to partake in it. They will afflict our several kingdoms in raids that will cost us in blood and treasure, and the Medium will not aid us unless we return to it with the humility it requires. It is a punishment for the pride existing within the maston order, starting at its head, the High Seer.

Then he looked at me with those unnerving dark eyes and said that everyone at Muirwood would be slaughtered unless I made a sacrifice acceptable to the Medium. The defensive Leerings of the abbey would not protect us, for the marauders travel by river—the flooding would only help them.

Then he looked at Nostradamus with contempt and said that his voice would return as soon as his faith did. He urged us both to notify the High Seer of this prophecy.

—Sivart Gilifil, Aldermaston of Muirwood Abbey

CHAPTER TWELVE

Naked Shields

Eilean had never sailed on a holk before. On the crossing to Hautland with Celyn and Stright, they'd traveled on a merchant's cog, a wide and flat type of ship with cargo strapped on deck and below. A holk was a fighting ship, with a square sail in the middle and a slanted sail near the front, both of which were sluggish in the lackluster breeze.

It had taken two more days to secure the vessel, which had been ordered to deviate course from its usual patrol to bring them as far as the coast of Mon. They'd left at the morning tide and were making good progress. Celyn hadn't favored the voyage so far and was pale with seasickness.

All attempts to find Captain Hoel had been thwarted by his cleverness. It concerned her that they'd left Fenton without knowing where he was, but it did fulfill the Dryad's prophecy that he would continue to hunt her.

Gropf wandered back and forth from one end of the ship to the other. He continued to cast longing glances at the shoreline. Their hope was to reach the coast of Mon by nightfall, use the small boat kept aboard to ferry to shore, and have no one be the wiser about their passage.

As she stared back the way they'd come, she thought again of Captain Hoel. If his Seering Gift had sent him to Fenton, then perhaps he could beat her to Cruix Abbey as well. That realization only increased the ache of uneasiness in her stomach. She folded her arms as she leaned against the railing.

Nimrue approached from behind, and she turned to look at him. He bowed his head respectfully. "The lack of wind is slowing our progress, my lady. It may be closer to midnight before we reach shore. The captain suggests you get some rest now."

"I'm not tired," she answered, "but thank you for the information."

"Do you see the mountains yonder?" He pointed. "Those are the Peliyey. There isn't so vast a range anywhere, and Cruix is in the center of it."

"The abbey may still have some snow, then, judging by what we've seen."

"Aye, my lady."

Not for the first time, she wondered about the Aldermaston of Cruix. Did he know Mordaunt was one of the Twelve? Would he try to seize the tome from her? Before leaving the prince's castle, she had copied a few lines from one of the aurichalcum pages of the tome so she could share the nature of the language she wished to translate without revealing what she possessed. For herself, the reassuring bulk of the tome against her lower back reminded her that she was a fugitive of the High Seer.

The captain came up to them, his swarthy face showing his many years at sea. His long black hair, striped with gray, was tied back in a queue.

"Sergeant Nimrue, come," said the captain, motioning to him.

Nimrue nodded to Eilean and then spanned the short distance to the captain. The older man spoke in short, urgent tones and pointed to the other side of the ship, where Gropf and some of the sailors had gathered. Nimrue's countenance fell.

He returned to her, agitated.

"Something tells me this isn't good news," she said.

He gripped the hilt of his sword. "A boat is coming this way. It's very long, with naked shields hanging from its sides. Gropf says it's a Naestor warcraft. It has but a single sail, but they're rowing hard. If we had some wind, we'd be outrunning it." He looked at her with fear in his eyes. "It's gaining on us."

Eilean walked across the deck to the other side, where the captain, his men, and Gropf had gathered. Once she was there, she quickly caught sight of the longboat. The oars bristled from the sides of what looked like a giant set of ribs as the crew pulled in unison. She'd never seen that kind of ship before. In addition to being long, it was lower in the water but for the two peaked ends. The warriors inside could be seen over the edges, through the striped and colored shields that hung against the siding like a turtle's hide. It was sleek and fast and heading at an angle that would catch them.

"We're outnumbered," said the captain with a look of dread. "I think those *faerings* can hold upward of fifty men. Aye, maybe more. And they're all warriors, by the looks of it."

"How many sailors do you have?" she asked.

"Twenty-five. Plus your men, my lady." He rubbed his beard worriedly. "We'd best turn to shore now and risk the rocks."

"What are they doing out here, so far from Naess?" wondered Nimrue.

Grunting, Gropf gazed at the longboat through narrowed eyes. "We can't win against that thing," he said. He looked at the captain. "Get the skiff ready. If they can row, so can we."

Eilean's stomach clenched again. She gazed across the open water, wishing the sun had gone farther down. In the dark, they could have hidden.

She knew how to summon a storm. That would increase the winds, but it might do more damage than good if it drove them into the rocks. Her magic could help with the defense of the ship, but the thought of sending invisible blades against the enemy craft sickened her. Besides, they had those shields as a protection, and she wondered at how much damage such an attack could do.

"Give the order," Gropf said sternly to the captain. "Whatever happens to this ship, *she* must be taken hence."

The captain gave Gropf a black look. "It's my ship."

"That's why you need to give the order. You know what those Naestors will do if we don't act swiftly. We'll all be killed. They'll be taken back as slaves."

The captain put his hands on his hips. "You know the Naestors?"

"Aye. I fought them when a raiding party struck the hamlet where I was stationed." The look of horror in his eyes said enough. "I killed seven of them, then fled. They hunted me for three days, sun up and down, out of revenge. The Naestors have no pity. Blood is honor to them. We must get her out."

It was the most she'd heard Gropf say.

The captain was appeased. "We'll get the skiff ready." He whistled and gave the order. "And we'll fight like Hautlanders too. Every man, take your arms!"

Word had traveled quickly. Eilean saw Celyn coming to her, blanched with worry and seasickness. "What's happening?" her friend asked.

Eilean pointed to the longboat. "They're attacking us."

More color leached from Celyn's face. "Can't we do something?"

"The captain is getting the skiff ready. We're going to try and make it to shore while the sailors get ready to fight."

"This can't be happening," Celyn muttered in a shaking voice as she stared at the oncoming ship.

Eilean embraced her for comfort. She had hoped finding Mordaunt's tome would be the most challenging part of her journey. But it had only been the beginning. Looking to the sky, she searched for signs of the púca, but they'd lost track of the spirit creature after coming to Fenton.

"If Stright were here, he'd burn their boat to ash," Celyn said.

The suggestion summoned an image in Eilean's mind. Smoke, swathing everything around it. Her mind itched, an idea surfacing, and—

"Not fire," she said. "Fog!"

It had been a long time since she'd practiced that command. She needed to practice it, to make sure she had it right.

"Give me a moment," she said to Celyn and started pacing. She crossed the adjoining fingers of her left hand, making the null sigil.

"Vey-ed . . . min . . ." Oh, what was the rest?

She'd used the command to create a fog near the Dryad tree. What was it? Had the Dryad made her forget this too, or was worry making her forgetful?

"Vey-ed . . . min . . ." she whispered again, her mind blank.

Panic choked her. The captain and his sailors were all going to perish because of her forgetfulness. She had to remember the words of power. What *were* they?

"Stop," Celyn said, grabbing her by the shoulders. "You're panicking. That will only make it worse. You can do this. I know you can. Quiet yourself. Breathe slowly. It will come to you."

Eilean looked at her friend, grateful for her calming presence, and felt the panic ease its hold on her. Closing her eyes, trying to drown out the commotion on the deck, Eilean sensed the fear of the men but tried to divorce herself from the tumult of emotion.

She could remember. The Medium would help her.

Vey-ed min ha-ay-retz.

She opened her eyes, a smile brightening her face.

"You remembered!" Celyn exclaimed and hugged her fiercely.

No, it was the Medium that had whispered it to her, but she'd needed to be calm enough to hear it. She relaxed her hand and gazed back at the Naestor longboat and its hide of shields. The warriors were coming on strong. But soon they'd be blind.

"Vey-ed min ha-ay-retz."

The prickle of the Medium went down her arms, making the gooseflesh return. A tingle went down her back.

A ripple of wind began to flutter the sails, and the air turned cold.

"Captain! Captain!" one of the crew shouted. "Sea fog! Look!"

"Praise the Medium," said the captain with relief. "Sail toward it!"

"It's coming to us!" shouted the sailor.

***

Everything was deathly quiet. Dark had come, and the fog had made it even more impenetrable. A throbbing headache thudded in Eilean's skull, but she held on to the magic, keeping their vessel enshrouded in fog. They could no longer hear the splashing of the oars from the longboat. Slowly and cautiously, the skiff had been lowered into the water, and Gropf and Nimrue hunkered down inside. Occasionally the skiff would butt against the hull of the holk, so the two other soldiers who'd already been lowered could use their oars to keep it distant until the next person was ready to be brought down by rope.

It was Eilean's turn. With the headache, she'd wondered if she would black out, but the knowledge that their safety and the lives of every man on that ship depended on her had kept her conscious up until now.

The captain helped secure the rope around her. She had to clamp her arms against her sides and hold on tightly as they used the pulley to hoist her up. With help, she got her legs over the side and then swung and swayed as the sailors clenched their teeth and slowly loosed the rope, lowering her. Gropf waited for her, hand outstretched. He caught her boot first, then her leg, and the sailors let her the rest of the way down to be caught. The skiff was crowded now, rocking back and forth. The smell of the sea surrounded them, and she shivered in the cold brought by the fog.

Gropf helped remove the rope, and then it was brought back up for Celyn. She was the last to board. Slowly, carefully, she came down, and then they were all aboard.

They were close enough to shore to hear the sound of the surf to their right. Two sailors would help navigate the skiff to the beach and then row it back to the ship again, assuming they could find it in the dark. Without the stars, there was no way to discern the hour, but they'd managed to escape capture so far.

Celyn was lowered next to Eilean on the bench, and the sailors began to wrestle the oars and propel them toward the noise of the beach.

"Rock," Gropf whispered. He had taken position at the prow and hunched forward, peering through the mist. In response to his utterance, they adjusted course.

That happened several more times before Gropf fell silent, leaving no sounds other than the churn of the surf striking the sand. Eilean patted her leather pack and hoped they wouldn't all get dunked into the sea.

The weariness of sustaining the magic continued to drain her, but she kept it going, not wanting to disperse the fog until she absolutely couldn't endure it anymore.

Celyn gripped her arm, rubbed her back, and they waited for an interminable amount of time until the current carried them without the need to row. The oars came back in, and the boat began to buck.

"Almost," whispered Gropf.

They came over a swell, and then the boat lurched forward sharply. The roar of the wave filled her ears, and suddenly the boat was in the shallows, scraping against sand.

Gropf was the first to jump ashore, followed quickly by one of the sailors, who yanked and shoved at the prow to keep it free in the water. Some of the soldiers spilled out, splashing into the shallows, and Eilean began to stand. Another wave struck just then, but Nimrue caught her and kept her from falling overboard. Celyn, who'd also risen, clutched the sidewall with both hands.

When the boat settled, Gropf grabbed Eilean beneath her arms and hoisted her off the skiff. She landed in the shallow waters and immediately it felt like her boots were getting sucked into the sand as the waters receded. Trudging through the sand, she went to firmer ground and turned in time to see Nimrue disembark. Gropf lifted Celyn out next, leaving just the two sailors behind. He helped shove the boat back, and soon the skiff was on its way again, paddling against the rushing waves.

Gropf waited there, knee-deep in the waters, until they were over the first breakers and the mist began to swallow them again.

Eilean felt a surge of relief. They were ashore. At last, she released the magic she had summoned. The dizziness was almost unbearable, but she endured it and didn't collapse. Her head continued to throb, and salt from the spray made her thirsty. But none of that mattered. She'd done it; she'd held the magic longer than ever before and hadn't passed out.

Celyn reached her, and they locked arms, climbing away from the beach and stealing glances over their shoulders as the mist began to dissolve. As they moved, the scenery changed. Scrubby plants began to appear along the shore, along with rocks of different sizes. The soldiers and Nimrue marched solidly around them.

Dawn was coming now, bringing colors all around.

"We'd best hide in those sea caves," Gropf said suddenly to Nimrue, catching up.

He was right. With dawn came danger.

They were in the kingdom of Mon, a kingdom loyal to the holy emperor and the High Seer.

Ovidius said that tears can have the weight of speech. Lord Nostradamus fled Muirwood after his voice was stripped away through the power of the Medium. He wrote a message to me, asking for a Gifting. But I could not do it. My shame has been made bare at last. When he returns to Avinion, I will be stripped of my rank.

For many years, I have striven to conceal the truth. I have relied on others to mask my inability, my impotence. No more. I only hope that a new Aldermaston can be brought to serve before Mordaunt's prophecy is fulfilled, and the inhabitants of Muirwood perish. I've warned the sheriff of Mendenhall, but he already knew. A village in the north was recently attacked by raiders. Everyone was slaughtered.

Once more, I weep.

—Sivart Gilifil, Aldermaston of Muirwood Abbey

CHAPTER THIRTEEN

Seeking the Stars

The fire roared with tongues of yellow and orange as it devoured the deadwood Gropf fed it. The shadows of those huddled around it were outlined starkly against the rough walls of the cave they'd found for shelter. Eilean was weary from the long walk that day but grateful for the protection and warmth. The hunter had placed a ring of stones around the fire, and there was enough wood to last the night. Celyn had already fallen asleep on her bedroll, her arm stretched out, her face smudged with dirt.

Gropf sniffed and held a log in his hands, then tossed it into the fiery mass before rising from his haunches and brushing his hands.

"It's a good fire," Eilean complimented.

The hunter shrugged and walked back to the opening of the cave, where the stars could be seen in the sliver of sky beyond. The sound of boots scuffing on stone preceded Sergeant Nimrue's reappearance. He and some of his men had lit torches to explore the depths of the cavern. The rest of the men stood guard just outside the mouth of the cave.

"He was right," Nimrue said, coming closer to the fire but remaining at a distance because of the intensity of the heat and flames. He tossed his torch into the fire. "The tunnel goes on and on. We didn't see an end to it."

"No animal scat?" Eilean asked.

"Nothing," said the soldier. "It's black as pitch farther in. No one could walk far in the dark. I think our only threat is from the entrance."

"How far away is Cruix Abbey?" she asked.

Nimrue held up his hands. "That I can't say for certain, my lady. We didn't land where we expected, and there's no sign of any nearby towns where we could seek directions and provisions. It's possible we could go off course, and if it takes us weeks to get there, we'll need Gropf to hunt for meat. I'm sorry I can't be more hopeful right now. None of us know this land well."

Gropf returned and knelt by his pack. He pulled out some strips of dried beef and a small bread roll, supplies the sailors had no doubt offered. Tearing the roll in half, he tossed a piece to Eilean. He offered her some of the beef too, but she shook her head. It would be too tiring to chew it, and she didn't want to waste any of their dwindling provisions.

The hunter pointed at Celyn and gestured with the other half of bread, but Eilean shook her head no. If Celyn was that tired, she wouldn't want to be awakened.

Nimrue assigned the guard rotation and then bedded down for the night, his back to the fire. Some of the others took food themselves and drank from flasks they'd filled at a stream along the way. Eilean was tired in body, but her mind was racing with thoughts of Mordaunt's tome, the secrets it contained, and the man himself. She missed his untidy room, the things he deliberately left for her to fix. The memory made her smile.

Gropf sat down by his pack and began sharpening his knife on a whetstone. The sound of it, mingled with the crackling of the fire, finally made her drowsy. She lay on the blanket, gazing at the sizzling coals, and felt her eyelids begin to close.

One of the guards came up to Gropf and whispered to him. The hunter went instantly alert, and Eilean sat up again, rubbing her eyes. The hunter took his bow and followed the soldier back to the mouth of the cave.

After several moments of waiting, Eilean rose from her bedroll and walked to the mouth to join them. As she got closer, she heard the familiar snickering sound. It was the púca.

Gropf stood at the opening, his bow at the ready, including an arrow already nocked. He was searching the trees, but the darkness concealed the creature.

"It won't harm us," Eilean said, touching the hunter's arm and pushing him to lower the bow.

Once he did, she walked past him, feeling the coolness of the night.

"It followed us?" Gropf asked.

"Yes," she answered. "It may be here to warn us. Don't threaten it."

She walked farther away from the cave and heard the snickering sound again to her left. One of the soldiers whispered something to a comrade. When she looked back, Gropf was scowling, but he'd kept his bow down.

Eilean heard the fluttering of wings, and then the púca floated down from one of the trees and landed in front of her. Her body blocked it from the others watching. It chuckled again as it folded its wings and snuffled at her boots. The fur looked so soft and inviting. Did it want her to touch it?

"What is it, púca?" she asked coaxingly, lowering herself down. "Is there danger?"

The creature snuffled more and then looked up at her, baring its teeth as if it were grinning. A low purring noise came from its throat.

Touch it.

She obeyed the whisper of the Medium.

As soon as her hand lowered to the warm fur, she felt the magic of the creature seize her. It leaped into the air, flapping its leathery wings and hoisting her off her feet as its body expanded to accommodate a rider.

Gropf let out a cry of outrage and rushed after her, but she already was on its back, rushing into the chilling night air. She remembered her last flight and knew the púca would torment her a while before taking her where it wanted her to go. An involuntary cry burst from her lips as the púca suddenly swooped down and banked so hard she feared she would fall. The rush of cold wind half blinded her, but the púca's pelt was soft and warm, and she buried her cheek against it, gasping as the beast whipped her one way and then another. Terror wriggled in her throat, but she'd had this experience before, and it wasn't as daunting the second time.

The spirit creature soared up and down, careening over the treetops one moment before sinking amidst them the next, dodging the trees at a perverse speed that made Eilean squeeze her eyes shut for fear they'd collide with one. Then it yanked her upward again, higher and higher, until they were level with the jagged peaks of the Peliyey, and it felt as if she were breathing ice. The mountains were still packed with snow, and her muscles ached from quivering.

"Down, púca, down!" she gasped.

The creature twirled several times before leveling off and racing downward. Her fingers were numb, and her lips hurt from the harsh wind, but the majesty of the mountains had been so inspiring.

And then she saw Cruix Abbey gleaming against the side of a cliff.

She gasped once more, not from the chill or excitement, but from the sheer beauty of the place. It had been built into the side of the mountain, multiple levels tall and narrow. There were outer buildings, smaller dwellings clustered against the thick, high walls of the abbey. It was more humble in design than the abbey in Fenton, more like Tintern Abbey, although much higher. Still, the upper portion of the abbey, with twin domes on each end and a slanted roofline between them, was still unequal to the heights of the mountains that loomed above it. The walls of the abbey glowed with Leerings, making the structure stand out against the snow and stone of the mountainside.

There was no way they would have missed seeing it. And it was much, much closer than Nimrue had feared it would be. They would reach it in a day or two, not a week.

The púca carried her toward it, closer and closer, until she could see the windows in the gray walls, the smoke still coming from chimneys. It was so glorious that she felt tears sting her eyes. There had to be a trail leading to the abbey from the plains, but in the dark she couldn't see it. Then the púca took her closer still, toward the upper heights of the abbey. She saw, lower down, a bridge connecting two of the outbuildings.

There was a wide balcony of sorts near the top, and the púca brought her down, fluttering and snickering, and then it shrunk to its normal size again and left her on the floor. A small garden decorated the space, along with some statuary and a Leering carved into the doorway at the far end of the platform. She shivered uncontrollably as she took in her surroundings and felt, unmistakably, the presence of the Medium.

She heard a latch click, and the door opened.

Be invisible. Listen.

"Sahn-veh-reem," she whispered, invoking the word of power. Then another. *"Xenoglossia."*

The strain from the words of power was immediate, for she hadn't fully recuperated after summoning the mist to protect them from the Naestor longboat.

A man emerged from the doorway, clad in the gray cassock of an Aldermaston. He had thick dark hair shorn down at the nape of his neck, an angular face with deeply intelligent eyes, and a pronounced limp. The tightness of his mouth indicated he was in great pain.

He reached the edge of the wall, giving him a view of the lower portion of the abbey. There was a desperate look in his eyes, a gnawing concern, and when he lifted a hand to the stone, she noticed a ring on his finger.

He stood there, breathing softly, then stared into the sky, looking up at the stars.

"It hurts," he whispered, his knuckles tightening as he gripped the stone hard. "Help me conceal it a little longer."

He was speaking to the Medium. Her heart throbbed with compassion and surprise, emotions not fully her own. With sudden clarity, she knew this was an upright man inflicted with an illness that was killing him.

"Kal?"

It was a woman's voice. Eilean turned to see a woman appear in the doorway, also dressed in the gray cassock of the order. She was petite and appeared to be of an age with the man, whom she approached from behind.

Eilean felt she was violating their privacy, but she'd been brought there by the Medium. Nor could she easily leave.

The man, Kal, lowered his head after hearing the woman's voice. He gripped the stone harder. "Help me," he whispered again, his voice throbbing. Then he feigned a smile and turned his head. "Yes?" he asked with a cheerful manner.

"It's cold tonight. Come back inside."

"I wanted to see the stars," he said. "Only in the spring can we see some of the constellations. That one is Ardore." He pointed to the sky. "Next to it, the great hunter Nimrod."

"They're beautiful. But come inside. It's still very cold."

Eilean could feel the woman's worry as she hesitantly touched his sleeve.

The man turned and took her hands. "I haven't told you recently how much I love you." He kissed her knuckles. "You mean everything to me."

Eilean felt her throat catch. She could feel the sincerity in his thoughts, his carefully concealed grief that he was dying and would be leaving her.

"You tell me every day, many times," she said, smiling. Then, freeing one of her hands, she stroked his smooth cheek. "I haven't forgotten, Husband."

"Nor do I ever want you to," he said. "I would not be an Aldermaston today without you. But the title means nothing to me next to my other one—Kal, the husband of Anya."

"You gave up a kingdom to be an Aldermaston."

"And I would do it again, for the Medium . . . for you." He kissed her hands again.

"Come inside. I worry about you."

"I'll be there shortly. I just want to see the stars for a little while. I'm still seeking one."

"The star of Idumea?"

He turned back to the balcony and gazed up at the sky. "It has to be one of them."

She wrapped her arms around his thin waist and pressed her head to his chest.

Eilean felt the strain from the Medium wearing her down, and she could neither see nor hear the púca. She wondered if she should reveal herself to the Aldermaston and his wife, but that felt wrong.

"I'll wait up for you," said the woman, Anya.

"I won't be long," he promised.

When she stepped inside, shutting the door behind her, his shoulders slumped, and he let out a strained breath. "Thank you," he whispered with gratitude. "A little longer. I know I am being preserved for a reason. I know not what it is, but please reveal it to me soon. By Idumea's hand, make it so."

He gazed up at the stars again, his eyes full of tears. "Whatever your will is, I will do it. Make it known to me. Help me see it. Please."

Then, taking a breath, he turned and began to walk back to the doorway. When he was gone, Eilean released the magic. Her heart ached for him.

And she knew that *she* was the person he was waiting for.

One of the wisest mastons from the ages said that no one is guilty who is not guilty of his own free will. For too long I have excused my actions. I have pardoned my supercilious thoughts. Justification was my ally then. Like bricks in a wall, I have separated myself from feeling anything but smug self-assurance or withering anger. That wall is gone, and guilt scours me like Ardys's helpers in the kitchen take to their pots and pans. Every day I am tormented anew by memories of the injustice I visited unto others.

Today I am harrowed by memories of the girl Eilean. She was the first to begin to breach the wall. And I condemned her for it. She trusted me—no, she trusted the Medium. And I fear I will never see her again to proclaim my guilt or her rectitude.

Every guilty person is his own hangman.

—Sivart Gilifil, Aldermaston of Muirwood Abbey

CHAPTER FOURTEEN

Aldermaston Kalbraeth

When the púca returned Eilean to the mouth of the cave, Gropf and Sergeant Nimrue instantly charged toward them. Gropf was so furious she had to calm him for fear he would do the creature harm. It snickered in the shadows, reveling in the trouble it had caused. Did it always make that noise, or was it a sign that it delighted in teasing mortals?

"Don't touch it again," Gropf ordered, pointing a finger at her with a scowl that matched his intensity.

"It took me to Cruix Abbey," she explained to him and Sergeant Nimrue. "It is not very far. Much closer than you feared. A little more than a day's journey. I can lead us in the right direction. And I also saw the Aldermaston. I was supposed to go."

The hunter snorted, shook his head with a disgusted look, and then stomped off.

Nimrue scratched the back of his head and offered her an apologetic look. "Indeed so, my lady. Nevertheless, you gave us a fright and have been gone too long."

She offered an apology for worrying them and then returned to the shelter of the cave and knelt down on her bedroll by the crackling fire. Rubbing her hands before it, she began to warm up and then, after she was comfortable again, burrowed down and fell asleep.

She awoke to the smell of sizzling meat and was surprised to find Celyn cooking something over the fire. Although the cave was still dark, sunlight streamed in from the opening, revealing that day had already come.

"What are you making?" Eilean asked.

"Gropf caught a boar and skinned it. I offered to cook it. I was so tired yesterday. Sorry I fell asleep and missed your adventure." She lifted her eyebrows, a silent invitation to share what had happened.

Eilean recounted the frantic ride to the abbey and the scene she had witnessed between the Aldermaston and his wife on the balcony. She shared her certain knowledge that the Aldermaston was dying, and Celyn's mouth gave a sad twist.

"I wish Mordaunt were there to heal him," she said.

"I imagine he's already sought a Gift of Healing," Eilean replied. "I don't think it's the Medium's will."

Celyn nodded, prodding the sizzling meat in the skillet. She added some spices to it, and when it was done and sliced up, the soldiers gathered around and ate the hot pieces. Several of them even licked their fingers.

"Well done, lass," complimented Nimrue.

Celyn smiled at the praise, and Eilean helped her clean the skillet while Gropf put out the fire. They cleaned up camp, then left the mountain cave and resumed their westward journey toward the abbey she had seen.

Before midday, they could see Cruix beneath the jagged peaks of the Peliyey. Even from the distance, they could see the road cut into the trees leading up to the heights. Several eagles soared above the trees, reminding Eilean of her journey with the púca.

They spent the rest of the day walking closer to it, the land rising steadily, which made the journey more difficult. There was a village at the base of the mountain, so thankfully they wouldn't be bedding down in the wilderness.

Nimrue worried that their Hautlander speech would raise suspicion, so Eilean suggested that Celyn ask for help in Pry-rian first. If no one understood her, she could try the language of Moros, which was similar. The soldiers wouldn't have to speak, nor would Eilean need to drain her strength by using magic.

Celyn had success at an inn called the Gladstone and secured two rooms for the night. The innkeeper spoke multiple languages and was familiar with the tongue of Moros. They ate a delightful meal of fresh salmon, potatoes, honeyed carrots, and a strange dish made of strings of boiled dough covered in shaved cheese. It was wonderful.

As he had in Fenton, Gropf sat apart from the others so he could keep an eye on the room and monitor those coming in and out. The inn was crowded, and she heard a variety of different languages. She started when a man cried out *"Pethet!"* and a row started between two burly fellows, which quickly settled down before it got ugly. Neither man was Mordaunt, but hearing the word made her miss him. She patted the satchel with his tome still strapped to her side.

We're getting closer.

After spending time in the common room, she felt weary again, and she and Celyn went to their shared room. A key had been provided to lock the door, and they both changed their clothes and fell onto the mattresses.

The next morning, they breakfasted with the other patrons in the common room, much less crowded than it had been the night before.

They ate a delicious breakfast of eggs, fruits, and another strange dish of boiled dough cut into little shapes and again sprinkled with cheese. Celyn spoke to the host and returned with information.

"There is a group of pilgrims heading to Cruix this morning," she said. "The host offered to introduce us."

Gropf looked from Nimrue to Eilean. He arched his eyebrow inquisitively. "We're coming too. The prince said we should stay with you until we're certain you're safe."

"I need to speak to the Aldermaston to see if he can help me translate the tome," Eilean said. "If he can, I may be staying here for a few months. You can't stay for that long, not when you'll be needed in Isen."

"What about the Apocrisarius?" Nimrue countered. "If he tracked you to Fenton, he could track you here."

"It will take him time," said Gropf. "I'll keep watch."

Nimrue's brow furrowed. "I could leave some of the men here. But maybe we are being premature. We don't even know if he *can* help translate it."

"Doesn't matter. I'm staying," said Gropf. He shook his head, implying he was not to be swayed.

"There is not much you can do at the abbey," Eilean told the hunter. "We have another way to escape if needed. The púca can fly us to safety one at a time."

The hunter folded his arms over his chest with a stubborn air. "I'm not going to the abbey. I'm going to stay around here and wait for him."

She knew what he meant. He wanted revenge on Captain Hoel. For reasons she didn't care to contemplate, the thought made her stomach tighten with dread.

"I think you should go back to the prince," she said softly.

Gropf shook his head.

Nimrue sighed, then held up his hands. "Let's not be hasty. Some of us will go with you to see the Aldermaston," he said to Eilean. "Either he knows the tongue, or he doesn't. If the best course is for you to stay, and we all agree it seems safe, we'll come back down the mountain and return to Isen. I can't justify lingering here for months when our land is under attack."

"I agree," Eilean said. "You've been a good escort. Thank you."

"We'll see you there," Nimrue said.

Having settled on a plan, Nimrue brought two soldiers with them and left the others under Gropf's command to remain in the village. The host arranged for them to travel up the mountain with the pilgrims, who were from Dahomey. One of them was a lady's maid named Kariss, who immediately approached Celyn and peppered her with questions in the common language of Moros. Kariss wore a very fashionable dress in the Dahomeyjan style and had a choker around her throat with a stone pendant. Her easy manners and friendly smile were inviting, but Celyn—calling herself Holly—shared very little about the purpose of their journey and even less about where they were from, Pry-Ree.

But hearing they were from Pry-Ree only intrigued the girl more. Kariss asked question after question about the land and abbeys there, including whether Holly had been to Tintern. She was delighted to hear the answer was yes and assumed that they had been learners there.

Eilean was relieved when the slope of the road leading to Cruix made conversation impossible. Eilean's legs burned with the strain of the climb. There were two pack mules to carry their gear, but Eilean didn't trust anyone other than Celyn with the satchel. Partway up the mountain, she asked if her friend wanted her to carry it.

"I'm your maid," Celyn whispered back. "It should be me anyway. I can do it."

Soon the trees became sparser, the road rockier. The mules brayed at the climb, but they persevered. As they neared the lower walls of the abbey, it became easier to talk again. Kariss explained that the lady she served, Lady Montargis of Dochte Abbey, was studying at Cruix and liked to send her down to the village for gossip, news, and to send messages to her husband. Kariss complained about the constant back and forth and wished there were an Apse Veil down in the village to make the journey easier.

"You have heard about the Naestor attacks, no?" Kariss asked breathlessly.

Celyn nodded but said nothing about what they'd faced in their crossing from Hautland.

"I don't understand why the High Seer doesn't punish them. It's not as if she cannot humble Hautland *and* Naess, no?"

"I should think," Celyn said with a shrug.

"You are from Pry-Ree. You don't see these things. In Dahomey, we see them. The Dagenais family . . . very powerful in the Medium. You'll see. Can defeat both. No problem."

As the girl spoke, Eilean felt a growing sense of uneasiness. Kariss was pretty and expressive, but there was something beneath that surface that belied the smiles and easy manners. Eilean felt that Celyn sensed it too, for she was more guarded than usual. More determined not to engage in conversation.

Kariss was acting one way while secretly she was another. In a word, she was a *pethet*.

At last they reached the gates of Cruix Abbey. Eilean strained her neck to look up and felt a tingling sensation down her spine. The Medium radiated from the abbey walls. A porter welcomed them at the gate and said that some wretcheds would be sent down to carry their baggage. The man spoke to them in Dahomeyjan, and when he learned that Eilean and Celyn were visiting from Pry-Ree, his gaze brightened.

"Well met, then! Aldermaston Kalbraeth is from Pry-Ree!"

Kariss flashed them a smile. Was this why the girl had taken such an interest in them? Did she hope to curry favor with the Aldermaston?

"Do you speak Pry-rian?" Eilean asked the porter in that language.

The man looked at her in confusion. "If you asked me if I know the tongue, I don't. He rarely speaks it, for his wife is from Mon. Still, I'm sure he will rejoice that a native of his land has come all this way."

"I look forward to meeting him. May my escort wait for me here at the gate?"

"Of course. We have a hostel down here. They can stay as long as needed. Many come in and out every day."

"Thank you," Eilean said. She turned to Sergeant Nimrue and dropped her voice lower. "Wait here at the hostel. If all is well, we'll tell you."

Nimrue nodded.

Almost instantly, Eilean heard Kariss whisper to Celyn, "Are your guards Hautlanders?"

Celyn excused herself without answering the question, and when she got Eilean's attention, she shook her head at the girl's prying.

A bell was rung, and wretcheds arrived to carry the baggage. One of the teachers arrived next, wearing an amulet bearing the maston symbol. He greeted the pilgrims, addressing Kariss by name, and then introduced himself to Eilean and Celyn and offered to escort them to meet the Aldermaston.

✳✳✳

There were so many steps to climb that Eilean found herself wishing the púca had left her there when she had visited before. The master introduced them to the Aldermaston's wife, Lady Anya, whom Eilean recognized from her previous visit. Well-spoken and friendly, she asked about the hardships of their journey and offered them a repast of cool water and fruit. When the Aldermaston finally arrived, she excused herself. Eilean saw the crinkling at the edges of his eyes and knew he was in constant pain. But he suffered it almost invisibly.

"I understand you are from my native land," he said, hand on his heart, greeting them both in Pry-rian. He looked frailer in the daylight. Eilean could see a waxy pallor on his skin. Was she noticing because she already knew?

"I'm grateful to be here," Eilean replied as formally as she could.

"What is your name? Maybe I know your family? Although, I must admit, I have been away from Pry-Ree for many, many years."

"I am Gwenllian. This is my maid, Holly."

He bowed slightly to both of them, looking at them as if they were equals in his eyes. "A proper Pry-rian name. Gwenllian. It means *fair and blessed*, and so you are. I feel the Medium strongly in you, my dear. You have not passed the maston test." He stated it as a fact.

"I have not," she answered.

"Naturally, or you would have crossed through the Apse Veil to come to Cruix. If you traveled this far, daring such risks, something important has brought you here."

"We come seeking knowledge."

The Aldermaston looked closely at her. "I will assist you as best I can. What knowledge do you seek?"

Eilean unlatched the satchel and removed the page with the characters she had copied. Her heart was on fire with curiosity and a little fear. How would he react when he saw the writing?

An Aldermaston's authority was supreme inside his abbey. Would he help them? She thought he would. In fact, she *knew* he would.

"Do you recognize the language of this writing?" she asked him, showing him the page.

He took it and gazed at the page with searching eyes. Then he slowly lowered it. "This is from the Sefer Yetzirah," he said bluntly. "A copy perhaps?"

Eilean was startled, but she controlled her expression. "Can you read it?"

His hand, holding the paper, began to tremble. "Who sent you?"

She wasn't sure what to tell him. It would be unwise of her to speak openly of Mordaunt or Utheros. "Do you recognize the language?"

"I do. Years ago, when I was a learner, I met one of the greyfriars who had a special tome." He gazed into her eyes in wonder. "You have it. You have the Sefer Yetzirah. Did a greyfriar give it to you?"

Hadn't Mordaunt appeared to Utheros as a greyfriar? It required no stretch of the imagination to guess the same was true of this Aldermaston. After all, Mordaunt's púca had brought her directly to him.

Choosing her words carefully, she said, "A druid gave it to me, Aldermaston Kalbraeth."

He was perplexed, his eyes serious but not accusing. She waited for a reaction from him. "The druid who advised the King of Moros?"

"Yes."

"And he taught you some of the words of power, didn't he? I can feel how *strong* you are in the Medium."

She reached out and touched his arm. "I know you are dying."

He didn't deny it. In fact, he looked a little chagrined. "I am," he said softly, "and you are the reason I'm still alive."

A sniffling sound. Eilean glanced to the side and saw her friend wiping away tears. The Medium was strong, so thick in the air it made her heart tremble.

"If I am to teach you that ancient tongue, then you must be a maston first. You will take the test. Today."

When I was young and scorned by the wealthy and beautiful, I rose above the marks of disdain by hard work, perseverance, and—as I now discover—pride. Though I craved acceptance, I put myself above my fellows. I said with my mouth that I did not care for their approbation, but I was pretending all along. Secretly, I craved that my peers would see my worth, that the young maiden I admired would see beyond my ruddy hair and freckles.

My successes multiplied. I was respected if not admired. And I passed the maston test in my fourteenth year, ahead of all my fellows. Courage prevails. Yet success allowed my pride to grow unchecked. I learned that by giving, instead of hoping to receive, I could draw everyone to my will.

I did not seek the Medium's will. I sought my own success. Until the whispers stopped, and all that remained in my mind were the croaks of silence. That was my grave. Unending silence.

—Sivart Gilifil, Aldermaston of Muirwood Abbey

CHAPTER FIFTEEN

The Harbinger

The wretcheds had been provided a learners' room. There were two small beds, the head and footboards made of polished ash wood with vines carved into the ridges. The window overlooked the valley below, thick with gorse and trees, and allowed them glimpses of the village where they had stayed the night. Celyn searched for a place they could conceal the tome in the small room, and they ultimately crammed it onto the top shelf of the small closet.

At Cruix Abbey, the floors of the abbey itself comprised the highest rungs of the mountain abode, with the Aldermaston's dwelling sharing the lowest of these. Just below the abbey proper was a residential level for prominent visitors. The learners' quarters were the next rung down, and all the wretcheds lived lower still. The walls were made of pale granite, quarried from the cliffs themselves. The abbey's chief industry was architecture and stone masonry. In fact, she believed that the master stonemason who had designed and constructed Muirwood had come from Mon.

A soft knock sounded on the door. Celyn's eyes widened, and she hastened to shut the closet before answering. Had that nagging girl Kariss discovered where they were staying? But when Celyn opened the door, it was the Aldermaston's wife, Anya.

Draped over her arms were robes made of pale flax. She recognized the cloth of the fabric immediately from her time at Tintern Abbey. In fact, it was a wretched's kirtle. Her stomach plummeted.

"This is for you," Lady Anya said, offering her the kirtle and a pair of slippers.

Eilean touched the fabric and then took the robe, confused by the gift.

"Don't be taken aback, Gwenllian," said Lady Anya. She spoke to her in the language of Moros but with an accent from Mon. "Yes, this is a wretched's dress, but it is part of the maston test. You need to wear supplicant robes, and my husband says that every maston, at least once in their life, should wear the garments of a wretched. It will help put you in the right mindset. Pride in any of its forms is abhorrent to the Medium. Put on the dress—my husband says it's called a kirtle in Pry-Ree—" she added with a gentle smile, "and meet me in the foyer at the end of the corridor."

Eilean held the dress to her bosom, relieved that her true identity had not been revealed.

"Yes, my lady," she answered.

The Aldermaston's wife shook her head. "Just Anya will do." She clasped Eilean's hands, rubbed them gently, and then left.

Celyn sighed with relief. "*Shaw*, that was a surprise."

"Indeed," Eilean muttered as she examined the dress. Even the stitching was Pry-rian. It had been brought from far away. Wretched garments as supplicant robes . . . she'd never heard of such a thing.

At Tintern, the learners wore white when taking the maston test, and their heads were veiled to disguise their identities. As a little girl, she had seen them walking in rows, heads bent, following Aldermaston

Gilifil to the abbey for the rites. Her memory of him caused a pang of sadness. She had admired him then.

Celyn helped her change, and when her own dress and boots lay folded on the bed, Eilean looked down at herself, smoothed the kirtle, and felt like a pretender. A feeling of nervousness tugged inside her, making her a little giddy. Was she truly to become a maston?

"I'm so nervous," she admitted, trying not to tremble.

Celyn gripped her arm and looked at her with conviction. "You can do this, Eilean. I know it. You've always been strong at taming Leerings."

Eilean swallowed and then straightened her shoulders. "I hope I can."

"I *know* you can. I love you. Now go."

The two friends embraced, and Eilean left and walked down the corridor to meet Anya. She moved so quietly, she doubted anyone heard her pass. The older woman smiled at her in greeting, then escorted her deeper into the building, not to the doors leading outside.

They reached a doorway with a Leering poised over it. Anya stood before it, and Eilean felt a pulse of thought. The Leering's eyes flashed, and then the stone door opened, revealing a dark tunnel carved with stairs leading up.

"Would you light the Leerings?" Anya asked her, gesturing for Eilean to enter.

Eilean sensed the Leerings carved into the walls, and with a thought she illuminated them. The stairs were steep and rose at a sharp angle, as if they were carved out of the mountainside itself. As they both climbed, Eilean felt her breath quicken with the exertion. Finally, after a second set of stairs, they reached another door, also protected by a Leering.

Eilean tried to open it with a thought, but the door remained fast.

"The learners do not know the password," Anya explained. "This tunnel is for the teachers to pass through. You will normally be walking the grounds and using the steps out there."

"Oh," Eilean said. "I'm sorry."

"It's all right. You didn't know. Which region of Pry-Ree are you from?"

"The borderlands, near Bridgestow."

"Ah. That's close to Tintern Abbey. Your kirtle was made from the flax that grows there."

"I thought so," Eilean said, feeling strange again at the coincidence.

Anya released the Leering, and they entered the upper part of the grounds. With Anya in the lead, they soon reached the arched doorway leading to the abbey itself. Aldermaston Kalbraeth was already there, wearing his cassock and giving her a kindly smile, although she saw the pain festering in his eyes.

"Will you join us?" he asked Anya.

"Thank you," she accepted.

With hands clasped behind his back, he walked to the door, and the stone slab opened before him. The interior of the abbey shone with daylight, although the light actually came from dozens of Leerings carved into the pillars. At Muirwood, the abbey was longer than it was tall, for there was plenty of space on the grounds. This abbey had been built vertically, so each floor was smaller than the last. The Aldermaston led her past a beautiful oak carving depicting a tree with fruits of various shapes and sizes. People had gathered about it, and a path appeared to lead to the tree.

"This is the Rood Screen," explained the Aldermaston, gesturing to the carving. "It represents the Garden of Leerings with its many fruits. After the First Parents were expelled, the garden was empty. This screen symbolizes how we may return from that error. The bar"—he pointed to the line she'd thought a path—"is the Medium, showing us the way back. Follow me, please."

They entered another archway, which led to a series of stairs that brought them deeper into the abbey. The feeling of the Medium grew more powerful as Eilean ascended.

On the next level, the walls were covered in intricate mosaics, the angular nature of the artwork interesting and precise.

"This level represents the fallen world," explained the Aldermaston, gesturing toward the walls to either side of them. "Begin at this panel," he said, walking to it. "This depicts the days of the Fallen Empire, ruled by the dark empresses. This one has two faces. It is symbolic."

Eilean gazed at the depiction of a woman on a throne, holding two scepters. Indeed it did look as if she had two faces. One of her profiles was made of shards of ivory, not stone. Kneeling men surrounded the throne, some holding swords, some spears, some shields. They wore tunics that went to the knees and sandals. Her gaze darted back to the empress, and she noticed that her crown bore the symbol of the kystrel.

"There were many dark empresses," the Aldermaston said. "Some were poisoned. Some died of old age. But they ruled the empire for over a thousand years. Although many sat on the throne, only one individual truly wielded power. The demoness Ereshkigal. The ivory face represents her. With her loyal followers, she corrupted every kingdom, forcing their leaders to kneel before her. Those who refused were dispatched through the cunning of her champions, the kishion."

As Eilean stared at the image, she recoiled from the sensation of being watched by the small bead-like eye set in the ivory.

"This way. This next panel represents the coming of the Harbinger."

The next panel over showed a woman making the maston sign. A group of men surrounded her, and Eilean quickly counted their number: twelve. One of them, a fleshy man with dark hair, stood out to her. Mordaunt! He leaned on a staff and had a sword belted to his waist.

"The Harbinger went to the city-state of Hyksos. There was an emperor there who tried to rule justly despite the wickedness of Ereshkigal, which dominated the kingdoms. The Harbinger instructed the emperor about the maston order, describing it as an order that would end poverty, corruption, and pride. The Twelve were chosen and given charge to help the emperor-maston perpetuate the order within Hyksos."

Eilean felt her heart tingling at the words. She knew parts of the story just from growing up at an abbey. But there were details that had never been explained to her. The things she'd heard fascinated her, and part of her longed to reach out and touch the mosaic stones.

The Aldermaston was sharing something meaningful with her, though, and to the next panel they went. It showed a city floating over a vast mosaic ocean. Safehome. She knew this part of the story already. Every child in their world did.

"The Harbinger departed with the new emperor-maston to return to Idumea and travel to other worlds. Some of the Twelve went with them. The rest remained behind, waiting for the Medium to manifest its magic more broadly in our world."

He led them to the fourth panel starting on the other wall. It was an image depicting a great celebration. The Whitsunday feast. There was even the image of a maypole there. The Medium was represented as a great wind.

"The remaining members of the Twelve went forth and began to teach our kingdoms. Some were converted sooner than others. Miracles were performed. Those who embraced the maston order thrived, although there was naturally some resistance. Ereshkigal and her servants, the hetaera, tried to seduce and destroy the maston order. They mingled among the people, known to each other only by charms they wore around their necks, shaped after the image of the dark empress's crown. Some of the Twelve were murdered by kishion. Some were executed. But always new ones were chosen to replace those who had fallen. In time, there was a great battle between the last of the Twelve and the Dark Empress Ereshkigal. The demoness was banished."

He led Eilean to another mosaic depicting Mordaunt facing the two-faced empress. Oh, how she wished she had known this before! She could have asked him about it.

"After the empress was freed from the demoness, she proclaimed the maston order throughout the empire and completed the rites herself. Many hetaera were captured, although some continued to practice their malevolence in secret. Many of the kishion, the butchers, were destroyed, but not all. One by one, the kingdoms unified and made a covenant for a holy empire. An empire that still awaits the return of Safehome, whereupon the rightful emperor-maston will rule to the end of time."

He stopped the speech and turned to his wife. "If you please, give her the warning."

Lady Anya gave Eilean a pointed look. "Ereshkigal was banished. But she is not destroyed. There must always be opposition—it defines us. Without dark, what would light mean? Neither can there be love without hatred, selflessness without greed, meekness without pride. So Ereshkigal and her hetaera seek our downfall. Before she left, the Harbinger warned that the day would come when evil is proclaimed as good, when falsehood is touted as truth, when pride will enter the maston order itself, and when Ereshkigal would rise again with another face."

A shiver went down Eilean's spine. "This is that day," she whispered.

The Aldermaston glanced at his wife and back to her.

"I believe so. If that is true, then Ereshkigal is already among us. The Harbinger promised that another of her kind would be sent to help save the maston order from destruction. The Medium will choose that person. It will help guide them with visions of the future."

The Aldermaston took his wife's hand and squeezed it. "I think that person may be *you*," he said to Eilean.

They both looked at her with hope.

But she knew they were wrong.

Too brief is man's life. Too small is our nook of the world where we live. Brief, too, is fame. The lives of the great Aldermastons of the past are no more, and all that is left to attest that they ever existed are faint scratchings on metal. Every life is buoyed only by a succession of other poor human beings who will very soon perish—ones who know little of themselves, much less of someone who died long ago.

As I stare into the void of my despair, knowing I must either kill myself and be done with it or bow my knee in submission, I wonder: Is it death that I should fear, or should I fear never having lived? What is death, anyway? Is it a dispersion into realms of glory, or is it annihilation? It must be one or the other. Either extinction or change.

How the tomes have tried to teach us this. Now I'm beginning to understand the counsel I've long ignored. "Let us prepare our minds as if we'd come to the very end of life. Let us postpone nothing. Let us balance life's ledgers each day. The one who puts the finishing touches on their life each day is never short of time."

—Sivart Gilifil, Aldermaston of Muirwood Abbey

CHAPTER SIXTEEN

The Knowing

I n order for you to be reborn in the Medium," said Aldermaston Kalbraeth, "you must first shed the taint of this world."

He stood before an arched doorway they'd come to by climbing another set of stairs. The Leering engraved atop it was fashioned not into the face of a living person but the grinning face of a skull. It startled her instantly, for she'd never seen its like. But it did not radiate fear or danger. It was just another aspect of the mortal condition.

"Before you take the maston oaths, you must face your own mortality. I can give you no assistance except at the very end, when it is time to cross the Apse Veil. Once you have crossed it, you will no longer be your old self. You will be reborn."

He smiled at her, but she saw the pain in his eyes, the slight curl of his lips as he used his willpower to keep from buckling to the agony he felt. His wife stood there too, watching Eilean.

"You will succeed," she told her. "I have never met a learner who had the Medium with her more strongly than you do."

"Maybe *one* other," said the Aldermaston. "But that was years ago. It may seem like this is the end of a journey, Gwenllian, but it is only the beginning. Proceed when you are ready."

She looked from one face to the other. "Will you be able to see what happens inside?"

The Aldermaston shook his head. "No. We will await you on the other side." Then the two of them went back down the staircase they'd ascended. Certainly, there must be another way to the Apse Veil.

When she could no longer hear them, she approached the grinning skull. The Leering's magic washed through her as she stepped forward, and the portal opened with the loud grinding of a stone. She stepped into the opening and found herself in a windowless chamber. There were eight sides, each constructed of pale granite polished to a smooth shine. Light came from several Leerings set into the ceiling, illuminating the Leerings centered on the walls. Some had animal faces, including that of a serpent, while others had human faces carved with varying looks of fear. One, interestingly, was a plant—a grapevine that reminded her of the vineyards in Pry-Ree. She sensed meaning in the symbolism.

The Medium thrived in all living things.

At the center of the room was a stone ossuary, set into the floor. The lid was open, and within it lay a folded garment, the kind of shift that could be worn beneath a kirtle. She felt drawn to the ossuary and moved toward it, her slippers scuffing on the polished stone floor. At the far end of the room, another set of Leerings formed a barrier.

Eilean walked around the chamber, looking at each of the Leerings in turn. Nothing happened, so she went to the ossuary and retrieved the shift. She saw the maston symbol embroidered into the fringe in silk thread. The idea that she should wear it beneath her kirtle came to her as a whisper, so she quickly undressed and then dressed again, feeling a little self-conscious with the stone eyes of the Leerings gazing at her. When she was garbed, she looked down at the ossuary and knew she needed to lie down in it.

An ossuary symbolized the death of the flesh. A box had been prepared for Celyn's bones, and if not for Mordaunt, her friend's body would have been burned and buried. *He* had sent Eilean here, and she needed to complete her mission.

Hesitant still, she lingered by the edge of the ossuary. But there was no going back, so she took a deep breath and then lay herself down on the hard stone.

As soon as she was settled, she stared up the light Leerings, wondering what would happen next.

Darkness.

The light vanished, leaving her totally engulfed in blackness. She could not see even her hand in front of her face.

Terror began to wriggle inside her stomach.

She tried to calm her breathing, but it quickened instead as she lay in the dark. Strange snuffling noises came, and she sensed the presence of the Myriad Ones. It had been a long time since she'd felt their presence so powerfully. The Myriad Ones were the spirits of unborn demons, the essence of evil. The thought of one of them brushing against her foot in the dark made her mind panic. She gripped the sides of the ossuary and began to sit up, but felt a warning not to.

Be still. They cannot harm you. They are drawn to your power.

A mewling sound came to her ears. She squeezed her eyes shut, even though there was only darkness. She clenched her hands into fists, her throat dry and hard as a walnut shell.

The presence of the Myriad Ones thickened, and she felt them prowling around the ossuary. Hatred and fury pummeled her, and thoughts that weren't her own scored her mind like claws.

Who was she to take the maston test? She was nothing, no one, insignificant. Her life was nothing but a spark from a campfire, lasting but a few bright moments, hanging in the air before quenching after it struck the dirt. All life was meaningless. Temporary. Even a mountain, in time, would be carved into nothingness by wind and rain. Hopeless.

There was nothing in her future but an empty void of nothingness. Extinction. Abyss. Coldness.

And then she saw a spark of light coming from one of the Leerings high above. It was just a little glimmer at first, then the ceiling began to glow with pricks of light, shaped like the stars and constellations she'd watched all her life, some brighter than others. They shifted and moved, spinning over her. She felt the power of the Medium rise from beneath her, welling up from the ossuary like a bath.

The sparks brightened.

No! No! The darkness prevails! No!

The thought-screams in her mind began to falter, like shouts in the wind. And then a brilliant dazzling light engulfed her inside the stone tomb.

Rise.

Hope filled her breast. She obeyed the command and stood inside the ossuary, feeling as if she were leaving a husk behind. That spark of hope grew around and within her. And she felt love, the same deep, caring compassion she'd felt in the Bearden Muir when she had gone there to learn for herself about the Medium. It was a feeling of connection, of belonging, of assurance that she was not a worthless wretched.

She was precious.

The Leerings whispered to her then, each one pleading with her to make a pact, a promise to obey the guidance of the Medium in her life. Everything they asked of her felt so insignificant compared to the joy and rapture she experienced that she agreed with hardly a thought.

Yes, gladly. The Leerings fell silent.

Above her, the small pinpricks of light continued to swirl. Her understanding opened, as if a key had been turned inside a lock in her mind. Those glimmers were other worlds—worlds that had been made by the same power as this one, and they were all bound together.

In that moment, she understood that the druids, like Stright, were part of the same order as the mastons. And that there were others like them who lived in worlds with dragons made of smoke and ice, worlds where massive waterfalls clashed and people heard the whispers but called them by another name. They were connected, and she was part of the web. The Medium was just another name for the same magic.

The only way she could articulate it was in a single word: Knowing.

With that thought, her heart nearly burst with emotion. She knelt down in the ossuary and began to sob, feeling so loved and connected and *accepted*. This wasn't the maston test others experienced. She knew it instinctively because her mind was connected to the power of the Knowing. She had been chosen, not because of who her parents were, but because of who *she* was.

Power thrummed inside her. She realized that wearing the chaen, which all mastons wore, helped her contain the power. There was magic in certain oaths, and her promises had allowed her access to something she hadn't been able to grasp before.

Rise.

Although her bones felt weak from the rush of power, she easily lifted to her feet. She was no longer limited by the abilities of her mortal body. She had access to a vast spring of magic that existed beyond herself. The Myriad Ones she'd sensed earlier had been bound to a Leering, captured by an intricate weaving of the Knowing's power. They quivered in their terror of her.

It was then she saw that invisible words of power had been written in the stones around the ossuary. She recognized the shield rune from her lessons with Mordaunt—*gheb-ool*. She'd been protected against them inside the ossuary when they'd been released. And that same shield rune was part of the chaen she now wore. No Myriad One could ever enter her body to seize control.

That knowledge filled her with sweet relief.

There was never a need to fear the dark again.

The light Leerings on the ceiling returned to their natural brightness, and the swarm of stars vanished. The far wall had opened during the ceremony, revealing a fluttering silk screen. Next to it, she saw a transparent stone, as if glass, within the alcove.

Lift it.

Eilean stepped out of the ossuary and approached the alcove. She felt impressed to lift the object, and when she did, she saw a word shining in the center of the surface.

Gwenllian.

The name that Mordaunt had given to her before she left Muirwood. It was not a false identity, but a true name. And it wasn't Mordaunt who had given it to her, it was the Medium. *Fair and blessed.* Another sign that she was where she needed to be on her path.

She spoke her name aloud, and when she did, the glass stone flared white-hot and burned her hand. Instinct made her want to cast it away, but she clenched it instead. The stinging pain receded. and when she set it down, there was a crescent-shaped blemish on her hand.

Returning the stone to its alcove, she approached the veil. She could see the shape of a figure standing on the other side.

"What do you seek?" asked Lady Anya.

She knew the answer in her heart. "To be a maston."

"What do you desire?"

Eilean thought for a moment. "Idumea." The world where the magic of the Medium came from.

"And what is your name?"

She felt excitement well inside her. "Gwenllian."

Anya reached through a gap in the Apse Veil, and Eilean took her hand. As soon as their hands touched, she felt a throb from the Medium.

Anya pulled Eilean through the gap and into the final room of the maston test. The chamber was a comfortably appointed space, with couches and billowing curtains and vases of fresh flowers. The smell of roses and daffodils filled the air.

"Congratulations. You are a maston," said Lady Anya gently.

Wonder filled Eilean as she stared up at the vaulted ceiling, at the soft light coming down from the Leerings higher up.

Anya released her hand and then embraced her. She brushed her thumb against Eilean's cheek. "I'm proud of you. I know the Medium is too."

"Thank you," Eilean said, feeling overjoyed. "I've always dreamed of coming this far."

"It is only the beginning," said Anya. "A maston can cross the Apse Veil to other abbeys. It is a draining experience, and it makes some queasy, but it is one of the blessings of the Medium."

"Where is the Aldermaston?"

"He . . . was very tired," said Anya, some concern in her eyes. "He wanted to be here for this moment, but he needed to rest. It is tradition that the Aldermaston gives you a Gifting after you pass the test. He will do that in his study later when he feels stronger."

"Thank you," Eilean said.

She felt a swelling of the Medium's power and then one of the other curtains of the Apse Veil ruffled.

Lady Anya turned, her eyebrows lifting. "A maston is coming through from another abbey. Watch."

There was a slight dimming of the Leering lights, and then Captain Hoel passed through the Apse Veil. He was holding a golden orb in his hand, wearing his hunter leathers, and armed with two gladiuses and his bow strapped across his back. The orb cast a slight glow over his features, highlighting his high cheekbones, his strong jaw.

Their eyes met, and a look of vindication throbbed in his hard gaze. He hadn't followed her across Mon. He'd known she would be at Cruix, so he'd crossed from another abbey to head her off.

Eilean gripped Anya's arm.

"My lady, stand away from her," Captain Hoel said. He pointed to Eilean. "That young woman is a hetaera."

"Hoel, what are you doing here?" Anya asked. "What are you talking about?"

"Where is Father?" Hoel demanded, his eyes still fixed on Eilean as if he expected her to flee.

And it was only in that moment, after sensing his emotions, that Eilean recognized the subtle similarities in the two men's faces. The familial resemblance.

Aldermaston Kalbraeth was Hoel's father.

The interior of Muirwood Abbey is nearly complete. It is a singular thing to witness something born out of stone. But an abbey is nothing without the authority to perform the rites. Only the High Seer, or someone delegated by her, can empower the Leerings that authorize the maston rites to be performed.

Word has reached us that the Naestors have attacked Hautland, Pry-Ree, and the northern shores of Moros. This is the Blight that Mordaunt warned us would come to pass.

With death's grim visage before me, I must stand firm. Whatever the cost to me personally, I must see that my people are safe. I will do my duty as best I can until I am removed from my office.

I felt the first stirrings of the Medium today. And I wept.

—Sivart Gilifil, Aldermaston of Muirwood Abbey

CHAPTER SEVENTEEN

The Hetaera's Brand

Y our father is unwell," answered Lady Anya. "But we will see him directly." She frowned at him. "I'm astonished at your accusation. This young woman is not a hetaera."

Hoel lowered the golden orb and tucked it into a pouch hanging from his belt. His eyes glittered as he stared at Eilean, and she felt her skin prickle with gooseflesh. As he took a step forward, she saw the muscles in his cheek flinch with suppressed pain. A slight limp revealed much—he was still injured from his fall out of the inn window.

"I have proof," Hoel said. "Or, rather, she does. There is a brand on her left shoulder, a ring of serpents. She doesn't wear a kystrel, I know that. Someone else wears hers, probably the druid that she traveled with."

"I am not," Eilean said, shaking her head. She stared at Hoel in confusion, wondering why he was saying such outlandish things when he had to know they weren't true. It wasn't like him to tell such bald-faced lies.

"By the authority of the Apocrisarius, I must bring her to Avinion."
As he approached, Eilean took a step back. Hoel looked as if he meant
to grab her by the arm and drag her through the Apse Veil right then.

Claim the right of sanctuary.

The whisper came as a flash of thought. Only a maston could claim
the right of sanctuary in an abbey . . . and now she was one.

She lifted her eyes to Hoel's and said as calmly as she could, "I will
not leave with you. I claim the right of sanctuary."

"Only a *true* maston can claim that right," Hoel said. "Utheros is
no longer qualified to—"

"She passed the test just now," Anya interrupted. "She *is* a maston."

Confusion contorted Hoel's face. Eilean lifted her chin a little
higher. "You cannot take me by force," she said. "Nor would I let you."

Hoel's anger was apparent in his furrowed eyebrows. "Has my
father accepted her claim?"

"I suggest we go to him at once," Anya said. "You must explain
yourself."

"*I* must explain myself?" he said with agitation. "I'm an officer of
the High Seer. My accusation alone should be enough."

"Not even Aldermaston Utheros could be compelled to leave sanctuary," Anya reminded him. "I see you are upset. Let us talk to your
father."

Eilean saw the determination and frustration in Hoel's eyes, but he
nodded to Lady Anya. He had believed his journey was over, that he had
ensnared Eilean at last. Once more, his intention had been thwarted.
She sensed he still desired to wrest her away from his mother and drag
her to the Apse Veil, but she was prepared to block such an attempt.

"We will go to the Aldermaston," Eilean said. "And then you will
see I'm no hetaera. I've been accused of it before, but it's not true."

"We shall see," said the hunter. He reached to take her arm, but
she backed away from him. "Do not touch me, Captain," she warned.

"I'm not letting you out of my sight," he said.

"I understand. But I'm not your prisoner. Do not touch me."

Hoel gave her a venomous look and gestured for her and Anya to lead the way. Lady Anya hooked arms with Eilean, giving Hoel a look of reproach, and then led them through a doorway and down some interior steps heading deeper into the abbey. They continued the descent to the lowest floor of the abbey proper.

Hoel's steps were noiseless as he followed them down the Leering-lit stairwell, but Eilean smelled him, the scent of his leathers and skin bringing back vivid memories that tangled her thoughts. She still felt the Medium pulsing inside her, however, giving her strength she knew she would need.

They went through interior passageways to the living quarters, and Eilean was lost from all the twists and turns. Then they reached another doorway, blocked by a Leering, and Anya dispelled it with a thought, allowing them to enter another hallway. The furnishings were beautiful, and one of the paintings made Eilean nearly gasp—Tintern Abbey and a field of blossoming flax. She paused when she saw it, struck with memories that filled her with physical pain and longing.

Anya paused, looked from her to the painting, and then nodded in understanding. Peering over her shoulder, Eilean saw Captain Hoel's expression had softened a little. Tintern was where he had taken the maston test.

Anya brought them to the Aldermaston's study, but he wasn't there.

"He may be resting. This way," she said.

The next corridor they passed through had windows facing out, and daylight streamed in through the curtained windows. They went to a double door, fastened on iron hinges, and Lady Anya opened it. Beyond it was a chamber with a large bed, several couches, and another door leading to a balcony. The curtains were open, and Eilean recognized it as the one the púca had brought her to.

The Aldermaston lay asleep on a couch, a knit blanket covering him, his brow furrowed in sleep.

She noticed the look on Hoel's face transform when he saw his father lying there, his eyes softening with concern. It said much for him that he cared for his father—for the man whose kindness had already transformed her life. Hoel had declared himself her enemy, but she felt herself warming toward him. How could she not?

"He never rests," Hoel whispered.

Lady Anya turned to look at him. "He's been more tired of late."

"Who's there?"

The Aldermaston sat up on the couch, tugging aside the blanket, and looked up at them in confusion. "Son?" He tried to rise to his feet but fell back in pain.

Hoel was at his side instantly, kneeling by the couch. He clasped his father by the hand, an act of such tenderness that it surprised and moved Eilean.

"Why have you come to Cruix?" asked the Aldermaston.

"You are ill?" Hoel asked, ignoring his question. "You didn't tell me."

"I'm very tired."

"You're in *pain*."

The Aldermaston hung his head. "I cannot deceive you. Not with your training. But you did not come through the Apse Veil to look after your father, did you?"

Hoel shook his head. Still grasping his father's hand, he turned and looked at Eilean. "I came for her. I've been commanded by the High Seer and Lord Nostradamus to bring her to Avinion. I've been hunting her for months with the Cruciger orb, but she's been in Hautland, protected by the heretic. The orb brought me here. I just crossed from Fenton."

The Aldermaston looked from his son to Eilean. "You hunt her because she knows where the Sefer is."

"Indeed so. She fled Muirwood Abbey, and I pursued her. Father, she's a hetaera. You've been deceived."

Eilean's stomach clenched at this outrageous accusation from a man who'd invaded her dreams and her thoughts. And if the Aldermaston believed the accusation—

The Aldermaston's brow crinkled. "The Medium brought her here. I am certain of that."

Bowing his head, Hoel shook it slowly. "The working of their power feels very similar to the Medium. You must trust me in this, Father. I know she is one. She has a brand on her left shoulder that will prove my words."

"I do not," Eilean said adamantly. "I am a disciple of one of the Twelve. One of the *founders* of the maston order. The tome wasn't stolen. It belongs to *him*."

"Father, please," Hoel said. "I must do my duty."

The Aldermaston glanced at his wife.

"She has claimed sanctuary," Anya said, "after passing the maston test."

"Let me see your hand," the Aldermaston said, gesturing for Eilean to approach him.

Hoel released his father's hand and stood, looking at Eilean with accusation. She came forward and held out her palm. The white sphere had left a small burn.

Hoel shook his head and muttered in disbelief.

"Are you a hetaera?" the Aldermaston asked her softly, with no ill will.

"No," Eilean answered. "He's lying. I have no mark on my shoulder."

"Prove it," Hoel snapped in challenge.

"Right now? In front of everyone?" Eilean asked, her cheeks getting hot.

Hoel held up his hands. "I know what you are," he said with malice. "And I warned you."

She met his bold gaze. Lady Anya had approached them. She had a worried look as she reached for her husband's hand and squeezed it.

Eilean sighed. Then, facing Captain Hoel, she tugged at the bodice of her kirtle and the chaen and exposed her left shoulder to him.

161

He stared at her unblemished skin in disbelief.

Turning, Eilean showed the spot to the Aldermaston and Lady Anya. Then she pulled the dress back up to cover her shoulder again.

"I am not what you say I am," she said triumphantly. "I've never worn a kystrel, nor will I. But I will say this since we're making accusations. A kishion with a kystrel tried to murder Prince Derik and me in Hautland at Yuletide. He was dressed like an Apocrisarius. If anyone should be explaining themselves, it is *you*, Captain Hoel."

The Aldermaston's brow furrowed with concern. "Son, you made a false accusation against this young woman."

Hoel was still reeling. By the look on his face, he had believed his accusation. Either he had been told an untruth and accepted it, or there was another reason for his false certainty. The chagrin was obvious, and he seemed astonished that things hadn't been as he thought.

"I . . ." But no words would come. Hoel shut his mouth, shaking his head, and then grimaced. "I did not deliberately mislead you, Father."

"It appears that way," said the Aldermaston with just the hint of a rebuke.

Hoel looked beaten. "It is my duty to bring her back to Avinion."

"That may well be," replied his father. "But for now, she is under my protection. She's claimed the right of sanctuary, and I accept it."

Hoel tightened in pain. "Father, if you shield her, the High Seer will punish you. I've seen what's happened in Hautland. Let me take her to Avinion. If I bring the tome back, I think I can persuade the High Seer to forgive her trespasses."

Eilean snorted in anger.

The Aldermaston pursed his lips, thinking it over. "Lady Dagenais is a powerful woman from a powerful family, but I am more interested in doing the Medium's will than hers."

The Aldermaston shook his head. "I've granted her request of sanctuary. Let us explore this matter more fully. I will do what is right, not what is expedient."

Eilean was relieved to hear the words. She felt terrible for Hoel but was grateful she'd been vindicated.

***

When Eilean returned to the room she shared with Celyn, she found the other girl, Kariss, sitting on her bed. The maid rose, regarding her with a look of wonder. "You passed the maston test already?" she asked. "But you only just arrived!"

Celyn looked relieved to see Eilean. She hugged her friend and then pulled back, looking at her inquisitively.

"I did pass," Eilean said.

"Incredible," Kariss said and then laughed with delight. "Well done!"

"Are you tired?" Celyn asked, her tone prompting Eilean to say yes.

"I am."

Kariss made a little twirl and went to the door. "I shan't intrude, then. Wait until I tell my lady!" Then she was out the door and off to gossip with someone else.

Celyn sighed. "I couldn't get her to leave. She just kept talking and talking, asking questions, trying to find out more about us."

"We have bigger problems than her," Eilean said with a frown. "Captain Hoel is here."

Celyn started, reaching out and gripping Eilean's arms.

"We're safe, for now." Then she quickly explained the events of the day, how she'd passed the test with an incredible outpouring of the Medium's power and then crossed the Apse Veil with Lady Anya's help, only for Hoel to immediately pass through another veil from Fenton. She described the accusation of the hetaera brand on her shoulder and how shocked Hoel had been to see she had none.

Celyn was just as astonished as Eilean had been.

"Why would he falsely accuse you?"

"And he did it in front of his *father*. Oh," she added, "I forgot that part. Aldermaston Kalbraeth is Hoel's father."

"You're joking!"

Eilean shook her head. "I wish I were. I had no idea before we came. And he seems just as principled as his son, so neither one will yield to the other." She shrugged. "I thought it only a matter of time before Hoel caught up to us. But now he cannot take me away by force."

Celyn clapped her hands and laughed. "So we have more time. And Aldermaston Kalbraeth knows the ancient language. You can finally start translating the tome."

"For a little while. I'm sure Hoel will go back to Avinion and try to get an order from the High Seer."

Celyn winced. "Would he do that, knowing his father might be condemned as Utheros was?"

"I hope not!" Eilean said. She bit her lip and thought. "Instead of hurrying to Avinion, he might try to persuade his father to revoke the protection."

"Is that likely?"

"I don't know. There is no honorable way for him to force me to leave Cruix Abbey."

Celyn began to pace. "We need to find a better place to hide the tome. He could try and steal it and then leave you stranded here without it."

Eilean hadn't thought of that. "You're right. He used some orb to find me. I saw him holding it when he crossed the Apse Veil. He called it a Cruciger orb. I've never heard of it before."

"One of us needs to have the tome at all times," Celyn said. "We can't leave it in this room unguarded."

"Agreed. My mind is still whirling. I need to change out of this kirtle."

Celyn grinned. "It makes me think of long ago."

Eilean had to smile. "The Aldermaston has a painting of Tintern Abbey in his living quarters. Oh, Celyn, it looked so beautiful. Sometimes I wish we'd never left."

The two embraced, and Eilean took off the kirtle to put on her gown. It felt strange to be wearing the chaen, and Celyn gazed at her in it with admiration.

"I knew you would pass," she said softly, making Eilean smile again.

After changing clothes, she went to the window and stared down at the valley below. The village was barely visible from this height. The majesty of the mountains made her feel so tiny.

But she also felt full of purpose, of certainty that the Medium had guided her to Cruix Abbey. It wasn't an accident Hoel's father was the Aldermaston here and not in an abbey in Pry-Ree. Or that he was sick, maybe even dying. The Medium had brought them together to translate the tome, yes, but were there other reasons too?

Only . . . why had Hoel thought she was a hetaera? The one explanation she hadn't considered, until that moment, was his Gift of Seering. Had Hoel seen something in a vision? Had that vision persuaded him to believe that Eilean would become a hetaera?

It is not that. Do not be concerned.

Eilean sighed in relief. Then another thought came to her mind as she stared at the expanse down below.

There is wisdom in climbing mountains. For they teach us how truly small we are.

Sometimes even to live is an act of courage. But I am finally ready to do so. I have sent a message to be delivered to the High Seer that I will not obey her desire to release Mordaunt. I have granted him sanctuary at Muirwood Abbey.

—Sivart Gilifil, Aldermaston of Muirwood Abbey

CHAPTER EIGHTEEN

The Coming Storm

The rumble of thunder and the tapping of rain broke through Eilean's sleep. When she opened her eyes, it was early dawn. The sun was still hidden by the mountains to the east, wreathed with clouds both orange and pink, but the western sky showed an approaching storm. In that direction, the clouds were dark, angry, and another ripple of thunder announced trouble.

Celyn was asleep on the other bed, her face tranquil in the morning light. Eilean lifted herself up on her arm, grateful for the refreshed feeling brought by a night of sleep. Rising from her bed, she looked in the mirror. The fringe of the chaen could be seen beneath her bodice, and memories from the maston test flooded her mind.

Another deep growl of thunder came, and the rain began to tap impatiently at the window. A shadow blotted out the light, and when she turned, she saw the púca straining against the pane, tapping its small claws against it. Eilean hurried over and undid the latch, swinging it open. The púca scampered inside, its pelt glistening with raindrops, and it snickered as it bounded from the table to her bed and then burrowed into her blanket. The wind howled against her as she pushed the window shut again.

"Is it raining?" Celyn asked sleepily, sitting up and rubbing her eyes.

"It's just started. A storm is on the way."

Eilean sat on the edge of the bed and stroked the púca's large ears. It snickered in delight.

Celyn yawned, stretched, and then smiled at the little creature. "I wish it could talk," she said. "Maybe it knows how Stright is doing?"

"I could ask the Aldermaston," Eilean offered. "Maybe there is news from Hautland."

"Thank you," Celyn said, her brow furrowing. "How I miss him. I worry about him every day. But I know the Medium wants us to be here."

A knock sounded on the door. Celyn rose and answered it while Eilean covered the púca with the lower part of the blanket to hide it, lest it be visible to the newcomer.

The servant at the door, a wretched, looked from Celyn to Eilean. "The Aldermaston asked me to wake you. He'd like you to join him for breakfast in his study. He said he'll begin teaching you today."

A throb of relief came to her heart. "Thank you, I'll be right there."

"I'll wait for you outside," said the girl and left.

"I'll stay with the púca," Celyn said with a smile. "But let's get you dressed, my lady."

Soon, Eilean was wearing one of her fancier dresses, an outfit she'd gotten during her stay with Prince Derik. She brushed out her hair and then brought down the satchel with the tome and slung it over her shoulder. She brought her cloak, for Anya had told her the learners did not typically use the inner tunnels to travel through the abbey.

Upon opening the door, she found the girl leaning against the wall, talking to Kariss. There she was again. Eilean felt a frown tug on her mouth, wondering why the gossiping young woman was still hanging on. Was she simply curious about where they'd come from?

"Lady Gwenllian," said Kariss with a meek bow. "I heard news last night that I thought you should know. A village in Pry-Ree was attacked by the Naestors. It was a massacre. I'm so sorry. I assumed you probably hadn't heard since you only arrived yesterday."

A gasp escaped her. "When did it happen?"

"Several days ago. It was a village by Krucis Abbey. Is that near where you're from?"

"No," Eilean said. "That's terrible news."

Kariss looked genuinely grieved by the information she'd shared, but again, Eilean detected another layer to her actions. She wasn't sharing the information as a kindness—she was doing it to win favor.

"I have to go to the Aldermaston now," Eilean said. She nodded to the wretched to escort her.

"Be careful," said Kariss. "A storm is coming. But, as they say in Dahomey, 'After the rain, all is well.'" She flashed Eilean a pretty smile as she walked away.

The wretched led Eilean to the outer doors, and they hurried across a small courtyard to a series of stone steps leading up two levels. Thunder boomed, the sound echoing from the mountains, and the wind tugged violently at Eilean's cloak. They rushed up the wet steps, and rain began to pelt them viciously before they reached the safety of shelter.

Eilean recognized the corridor they entered, and shortly thereafter, they reached the study that she'd stopped by the day before. The wretched knocked, waited for the invitation to enter, and then opened the door for Eilean.

"Thank you, Accorsa," said the Aldermaston, who sat at his desk with a tome already open before him. Captain Hoel stood against the far wall, where bookcases stored various books and tomes, his arms folded, his eyes and mouth brooding as he watched Eilean enter and startle at finding him there.

Aldermaston Kalbraeth leaned back in his chair, massaging his temples. Once the door was shut, he gestured to the chair next to him.

"I have a few questions for you, Gwenllian. Or would you prefer to be called Eilean?"

He spoke to her in Pry-rian. It was comforting to hear its familiar cadence.

"Gwenllian is the name Mordaunt gave me," she said, "but Captain Hoel knows me by the other name."

"My son informed me that you were originally a wretched from Tintern Abbey and were brought to Muirwood by Aldermaston Gilifil. You were assigned to be Mordaunt's servant, he says, and you quickly became loyal to him. This is true?"

"It is true, Aldermaston." She felt a throb of anger. "Did he also tell you that Aldermaston Gilifil cannot use the Medium? That his pride has choked off his connection to it? And did he tell you that I took lessons from Mordaunt on the Aldermaston's orders?"

"He did say as much," said Kalbraeth patiently. "He knows that you are sincere in your beliefs, but according to him, you've become a heretic by your association with the druid Mordaunt."

Eilean felt a jolt of displeasure. "Did he also tell you that Mordaunt is one of the Twelve?" she said, giving Hoel an arch look.

He returned it, unflinching. "I know *you* believe him to be one of the Twelve."

"I know it from the Medium," she said.

He shook his head slightly, looking down, but said nothing. Her gaze shifted to the Aldermaston, who seemed interested by her words, though she could not tell whether he believed her.

"My son believes that you are an imminent danger to Cruix Abbey," he said.

"Why?"

"He said the words of power you know can engulf this abbey in flames. Is that your intention in coming here, Eilean?"

"No!" she said in shock. That Hoel should accuse her of such a thing incensed her. "I came here to learn how to read the tome. It *is* the Sefer Yetzirah."

"And you brought it with you?" His gaze shifted to her shoulder. "Is that it?" While still under her cloak, the satchel was not completely covered.

"Yes," she answered.

Hoel looked at it, then at her, and she felt his urge to yank it from her and flee to Avinion with it. She gripped it tightly, warning him with her eyes that he'd better not try.

"Can I see it?" the Aldermaston asked.

"I don't trust your son at the moment."

Hoel lifted his eyebrows. "I won't try and take it from you, Eilean. I remember what you did to Aisic and those soldiers at the stables behind the Pilgrim. What you did to *me*. Nor do I wish to see my father harmed."

"I'm not a hetaera," she said to him boldly.

Hoel sighed. She could almost hear the thought he expelled with the breath.

Not yet.

This had something to do with his Gift of Seering. She opened her mouth to ask about it, but the Medium bid her not to. His own father didn't know his secret.

"You proved that yesterday," said the Aldermaston. "It was wrong of my son to accuse you. I believe he was persuaded it was true. The Apocrisarius are naturally suspicious and are trained to unmask those trying to deceive. By your previous interactions with him and your connection with a druid and a condemned heretic, he believes you are on the wrong path."

"I know he does," Eilean said, "but he's the one who's wrong. Did he have an explanation for the kishion who tried to kill me?"

The Aldermaston shook his head. He was about to speak, but Hoel interrupted. "I know nothing of it, as I told you. An imposter most likely. Someone who wanted to imply corruption in Avinion."

"There *is* corruption in Avinion," Eilean said hotly.

"And you've been there?" he challenged. "You know this yourself? Or only by what Mordaunt told you?"

The Aldermaston raised his hand to forestall more argument. "Arguing drives away the Medium. It would be best if we remain civil." He gave his son a scolding look. "I have granted her sanctuary here at Cruix. I do not believe she poses a threat to me or to this abbey. And I know for myself that money was the chief motive that brought Tatyana Dagenais to her role as High Seer. I've been to Avinion and seen the opulence. For many years it has troubled me."

Hoel clenched his jaw and shook his head in disbelief. "Father, *please.*"

"I speak the truth, even if it is unpopular. Integrity is everything, Hoel. So I've taught you."

"My duty commands me to bring the tome and the girl to Avinion."

"She's not a girl, Hoel. She's a woman. And she is just as strong in the Medium as you are."

The fury smoldering in Hoel's eyes betrayed how much those words had stung him.

"Furthermore, the High Seer cannot read the tome herself. She would likely have needed to bring it to Cruix anyway. I will work with Eilean to begin translating it. You may go back to Avinion and tell the High Seer yourself that both the tome and Eilean are safe here in Cruix. She is under my protection, and the rights of sanctuary shield her from being *forcibly removed.*"

In a direct way, the Aldermaston was warning his son that he'd be excommunicated from the abbey if he tried to take Eilean away.

Hoel did not look chagrined. He looked impatient, aggrieved, and upset with his father's decision. "I tried to warn you," he told his father. Then he shot Eilean a glare and walked out of the study.

The Aldermaston leaned back in his chair, steepling his fingers together, and let out a weary sigh. But he did not speak.

"I'm sorry," Eilean apologized. She touched his arm in sympathy.

"There is a certain kind of pain that only comes within a family," he said, with a tight smile. He stared off into the distance, reliving memories of the past. "He was such a *diligent* boy. If I gave him an assignment, he would see it done. There's always been a trust between us. A special bond."

Eilean could sense it and respected it. She could also sense, from his unspoken thoughts, that he was silently grieving his own death, which would sever their long-lasting relationship. It made her throat thicken.

"I can't even imagine what he was like as a boy," Eilean said with a small laugh, pulling her hand back.

Aldermaston Kalbraeth chuckled. "When he was twelve, he acted like a man grown. He was a sober child, not involved in the sort of pranks common at that age. His mother died after he went to study at Tintern, but he refused to come home because he knew it was his duty to finish his studies. He claimed that she would have wanted him to finish the year." He glanced her way. "He was the one who encouraged me to marry again. But I decided to give up the rest of my life to the Medium's will. I renounced my claim to the throne and was made Aldermaston of Holyrood Abbey. Instead of coming to my abbey, Hoel stayed at Tintern, determined to own his success without any hint of suspicion it wasn't earned. And he was so talented, he visited and trained in other abbeys as well."

Eilean swallowed. She looked at him earnestly, interested to hear more about Hoel's childhood. Her heart softened in compassion toward both of them.

"He passed the maston test a year early," said his father proudly. "And he took a position with the Apocrisarius instead of accepting the offer to serve my brother, the king. I think Hoel was the youngest to ever earn the rank of captain. He's very disciplined, very conscientious. And he's done well . . . a natural leader." His lips pursed. "Now comes the greatest test of loyalty. Will he be true to the Medium? Or will he be true to a title?"

"He doesn't know you're dying," Eilean whispered softly.

He stared at his desk and then brushed a few tears away. "No. He doesn't. I haven't told Anya yet either. It may be several months away still." He smiled at her and patted her hand. "Not to worry. I will."

She nodded, feeling nothing but sympathy for all of them. Some of her anger toward Hoel faded, for she could easily imagine him as the brave, stoic child described by his father, and she knew how much grief it would cause him to lose his only remaining parent. There was a lovely fondness between father and son, and it hurt to think of them being parted.

"Can I see the tome?" Kalbraeth asked.

Eilean nodded and unstrapped the satchel, hefting the great tome out by the rings that held the pages together. The Aldermaston's eyes widened with awe as it was laid before him. Eilean gently handled some of the pages, opening it before him.

"The Sefer Yetzirah," he murmured in reverence. "The Book of Creation. This is the story of how the Essaios made the world. The Garden of Leerings. The tree of life and transfiguration. How the foundations of Safehome were laid." He gasped as he looked at the scrivings and reached out with a finger. "It was written in Glagolitic," he said. "A language not spoken in centuries, very similar to Calvrian, dating back to the days of the Harbinger. I wondered, at the time, how the greyfriar had come by his knowledge, though I was pleased he'd chosen to be my teacher. He told me not to share the knowledge I'd learned from him until the Medium brought to me someone who needed it."

She gave him a pointed look. "The tome was hidden with a few other items, Aldermaston. One of them was a set of greyfriar robes."

He studied her for a moment before nodding. "I think he taught me for this very occasion. Once you've learned the alphabet and can pronounce the words, a Gifting of Discernment will help speed your learning."

"Please," she said, her stomach thrilling with excitement.

I came across this quote from one of the Twelve today. I've read it before, but it has new meaning to me now. This is why tomes are more valuable than the metal they are made from. "Blinded as they are to their true character by self-love, every person is their own flatterer. That is why they welcome the flatterer from the outside, who only comes confirming the verdict of the flatterer within."

I have been guilty of this for too long. Choosing to surround myself with those who would praise my strengths and be too afraid to point out my faults.

The mind is not a vessel to be filled with praise. It is a fire to be kindled to do the great work the Medium has for us.

—Sivart Gilifil, Aldermaston of Muirwood Abbey

CHAPTER NINETEEN

Wills Colliding

Eilean knew the story of the creation of the world. Even the lowliest of wretcheds had been taught that the Essaios had formed the world to be balanced and self-sustaining. Light was birthed from darkness. Rock and earth were separated from sea by Leerings, which were then used to make streams, rivers, and mighty waterfalls. Seeds and animals were brought from the other worlds maintained by the Essaios, creating different varieties for different climates, followed by plants, trees, fruits, and flowers. How these varieties had been transported, however, had been a mystery up until now.

From the Sefer Yetzirah, the Book of Creation, Eilean and Aldermaston Kalbraeth learned the truth about creation.

Through the power of the Medium, portals could connect the worlds together in a similar manner to how the Apse Veils connected the abbeys. The word of power used to create this connection was *"mar-ah shaw-ar."* With the power of *xenoglossia*, Eilean understood the words to mean *mirror gate*—a reflection of sorts between two worlds that allowed passage between them. As they translated the tome, her understanding of the concept grew. A mirror gate was a natural formation of stone, hollowed out over long eons of time by wind, rain, or the sea. These natural arches existed on land and sea and could be used to connect to arches in other worlds. The Essaios had carved Leerings imbued with those words of power to provide passage between the worlds, and they'd used the arches to bring giant whales as well as other creatures of the deep.

As she and Aldermaston Kalbraeth read the story of creation within the tome, she recognized other words of power she already knew. For example, as the world was created, a great mist came and watered the new growth. *Vey-ed min ha-ay-retz.*

The legend itself taught the words of power. Mordaunt had taught her the words using different symbols from another alphabet, but they were pronounced the same.

Eilean and the Aldermaston made sure to use the null sigil so they wouldn't inadvertently work magic by the act of reading the tome.

After they spent the bulk of the day together, minds connecting, Eilean found herself exhausted, and they had only read the first few sheets of aurichalcum. But just those pages were enough to open her mind to endless possibilities.

Utheros had suggested that Mordaunt had shared the story of the high king for a reason, and perhaps he was right. Perhaps Mordaunt had intended for her to make the crossing between worlds and approach the high king for help. The idea seemed far-fetched, yet hadn't she seen the impossible made possible time and again? And Mordaunt had explicitly told her the tome would help . . .

Dare she hope the location of that mirror gate was disclosed in the tome?

"I've spent much of my adult life as an Aldermaston," said Kalbraeth after she closed the tome and tucked it into her satchel. "I gave up the opportunity to serve my brother, the king, in favor of a higher cause.

Sometimes I have wondered if I would regret that decision." He turned and looked at her, his eyes filled with wonder. "I wouldn't trade what I've learned today for anything this world could offer. Thank you for coming to Cruix Abbey, my dear Gwenllian. I thank you wholeheartedly." He leaned back against his chair, his shoulders slumping with fatigue.

"Thank you for teaching me," she said. "There is still much to learn."

"Agreed, but I'm impressed with how quickly you've picked it up. You have a sharp mind, and the Gift of Xenoglossia was clearly at work. Are you not tired after using the power of the Medium for so long?"

"I have felt so much stronger since taking the maston test. In the past, I might have lasted an hour, but we've been going most of the day." She yawned suddenly and realized that she would sleep well that night. And yet, she hadn't fainted or even come close to it.

"The learners all eat together in the commons," said the Aldermaston. "When you go back down, get some food and then rest. We can meet again first thing in the morning. I can only work with you half the day tomorrow. But we'll make the most of it."

"Thank you again. I hope you rest well."

She rose, slid the satchel around her arm, and then left his study. With no assistance, she found the door leading to the outer balcony, which would take her to the stairs leading to the learners' quarters on the lower level. She was excited to tell Celyn about some of her discoveries. Her mind was still whirling with the ideas she'd learned.

The storm had passed already, leaving wet marks on the granite. In the east, she could see the storm clouds still raging while the wind at the abbey blew her hair across her face. She ran her hand along the railing as she climbed down. Halfway there, she caught sight of Captain Hoel on the balcony beneath her, standing at the edge of the wall and gazing at the distant storm. Her gut clenched, but he'd heard her steps and slowly turned his head. His dark look confirmed he was still angry with her.

Without slowing her pace, she reached the bottom of the steps and started toward the doors.

"Eilean."

His command halted her. She squeezed her hands into fists and turned to face him, feeling the wind blast her again. Her stomach growled with hunger, and she felt a little light-headed. Still, she could show him no weakness.

"You're not going to try something foolish, are you, Captain?"

He approached her soundlessly. His cloak was damp, attesting that he'd been out in the storm himself.

"I thought you'd be gone already," she said.

"I am going back to Avinion. I have a duty to report the situation to Lord Nostradamus, the head of my order."

"And he will tell the High Seer, no doubt. Is that what you want?"

"What I *want*," he said, his eyes flashing with anger, "has been thwarted once again. By you. This will not end well for you, Eilean. I don't care how strong in the Medium you think you are, you won't survive an ordeal, and I don't wish to see you destroyed before my eyes." His mouth twisted with suppressed emotions. He was envisioning her fate, the fate of a heretic.

"The Medium has guided me thus far," she said.

A look of disgust screwed up his face. "I know you believe that. But I promise you, you are deceived."

"And so is your father?"

"In this . . . for now . . . yes! I'm convinced of it."

"Don't you think it strange, Hoel, that you, who have known him all your life, could not persuade him of that? Have you not considered that *you* may be on the wrong side?"

He snorted. "You truly believe *I* am on the wrong side?"

She stepped closer to him, wishing she could make him understand. Despite everything, he was a good man. One she admired. "Can't you see the corruption in the maston order? You've been trained to notice subtle details. To discern when men and women are lying. Am I lying to you right now? Would I be risking my life like this unless I absolutely knew what I was fighting for? I am a wretched. Why would the Medium have chosen me for its purposes if the order itself were not poisoned?"

"It didn't," he answered, but she sensed a struggle within him. He loved his father and trusted him. That his father had taken Eilean's side so quickly was disturbing to him. He shook his head as if to jar their connection loose. "You could have been part of the Apocrisarius. I saw—" He stopped himself from speaking, clenching his jaw. There was something else. Something she didn't understand. His feelings were powerful at that moment but still veiled from her.

She reached for his hand, looking into his eyes, but he jerked it away and stepped back from her as if he didn't trust himself or his resolve. "What did you see?" she said softly. "We both know the Gift you have."

"I won't tell you. You are my . . . my enemy."

The words lacked conviction, but they still hurt. She didn't want to be his enemy. The more she knew of him, the more she understood him. The more she understood why they needed him to support their cause. He was good. And noble. And, beneath his bluster, kind.

But he would not yield.

"I'm not," she said, shaking her head. "Why haven't you told your father the truth?"

"The Medium has ordered me not to," he answered with growing desperation. "And now you'll tell me that you know better?"

Eilean shook her head. "I don't know anything about that. You do what the Medium has told you to do. Just as I must do the same."

"Even if the High Seer comes and removes my father from his place? If she puts in a new Aldermaston, your right of sanctuary will end if the new Aldermaston chooses not to honor it."

"I suppose that could happen."

"You suppose? Eilean, it's *going* to happen! I don't want to see my father ruined. I don't want to see him tried, like Utheros, as a heretic." His expression was livid. "Nor do I want to see it happen to you!"

"Is that why you haven't gone yet? I'm here because the Medium compelled me to come. This was the only place, I think, where I could learn the language of the tome."

"And you've been reading it," he said, looking even more concerned.

"It's wonderful!" she exclaimed.

"And not for your eyes!"

"It was given to me. Mordaunt told me where to find it. He entrusted it to me."

He took a step closer to her. They were very close now. She could smell the dampness of his tunic and the mint on his breath. "I don't want you to get hurt. Just . . . give it to me!"

She sensed his emotions in that moment. He was angry, yes, but it masked deeper feelings. He was enthralled with her, but he struggled against those feelings, his devotion to duty stronger than his own desires.

"I can't give you what you want," she said and watched him flinch. The look of pain in his eyes made her want to weep.

"You can't, or you *won't?*"

He is your protector. Your guardian.

She heard the whisper of the Medium distinctly. He *had* always tried to protect her, in spite of them being at cross purposes. Even when the Fear Liath attacked him, he'd worried for her. But his stubbornness and pride prevented him from discerning the truth.

She looked down at the flagstones and then back to his eyes, which were regarding her with desperation and confusion.

"Hoel, please. The Medium brought me here. It brought you here as well. I know, without any doubt, that it also brought us together."

"I will not forsake my oaths. Not for you. Not even for my father."

She wanted to speak, but her stomach was quivering with fear. He wouldn't give in. He refused to believe her. Still, she needed to try.

"Not for me, then. For the Medium. Please, find out for yourself. Remember that day you and Twynho discovered me in the Bearden Muir? When you carried me back to the abbey?"

She saw the muscle in his neck tighten. He swallowed and nodded.

"I went into the Bearden Muir to seek an experience with the Medium. To find out for myself if what Mordaunt said was true. All my life, I'd believed in Aldermaston Gilifil. But he relied too much on his reputation. He lost his power to tame the Medium." She looked him in the eye. "The same thing is happening to you. You will lose your connection to the Medium, just as he did, if you remain against me."

"Against you? What you are saying is the most grievous of blasphemies. You claim the High Seer has fallen, but the Medium would not allow that to happen."

"It was not the Medium's will that it did. If pride were not such a dangerous failing, why would the tomes mention it so many times in warning?" She paused, deliberating. "If you find out that she or Lord Nostradamus ordered a kishion to murder Prince Derik, is that what it would take for you to believe? Could you possibly justify that? The mastons hunted down the kishion long ago. Are they but a means to an end now?"

"That's conjecture," he scoffed. "I don't believe the kishion came from the Apocrisarius."

"Why was he dressed like one?"

Hoel chuffed. "By Cheshu, I knew you wouldn't see reason."

"You are supposed to be my guardian. My protector. The Medium told me this, just now."

He looked up and held out his hands. "I didn't hear anything."

She looked him in the eye. "But you already knew it. You've known all along. Please, Hoel. Your visions. Trust them."

"I did," he snapped. "They've brought me nothing but confusion. I saw you burn down this abbey, Eilean. I saw the brand on your shoulder." As he said it, he gripped her by that shoulder, his fingers squeezing. She felt a strong tingle go down her arms. He looked, for an instant, as if he might kiss her. They were close enough.

"But you know I don't have one," she said. "Tell me of your vision."

"No!" He recoiled, let go, and backed away from her. "You know too much already. If you do it, Eilean. If you hurt my father. I swear . . . I will *live* to watch you burn."

"I'm not going to hurt him, Hoel. And I would never burn an abbey. I promise you that is not why I'm here. Stay. Learn with us. Be my protector."

He lifted his hand to his forehead and kneaded his brow. "I can't," he whispered. "I won't. My visions are usually of the future. It's how I knew you'd be at that oak tree near the Fear Liath. It's how I knew you'd be here, at Cruix Abbey. You may not be a hetaera yet, Eilean." His face was grim. "But you will be."

She felt a warning throb in her heart not to believe him. He had misunderstood his vision.

"I wish so much that I could make you see the truth," she said with a sigh.

"Your truth?"

"There is one truth, Hoel. You are meant to be my guardian. You will protect me when the Medium bids me leave this place."

"And where will you go?"

"I don't know yet. I'm supposed to be here now."

"And the Medium took you to Hautland?" he asked, his expression making it obvious how little he believed her.

"Of course. It brought you there too."

"Because I was hunting *you*, Eilean," he said, obviously frustrated. He ran a hand through his hair. "And the only thing stopping me right now is my sense of honor and duty. Utheros was found guilty of heresy.

Your presence with him does not help your standing. You will see, when this is over, that you allowed yourself to be deceived. That you gave yourself an air of importance because a bizarre man was lonely and bored and convinced you to trust him. You've always wanted to *be* someone you are not and never will be."

His words wounded her. But they did not undermine her conviction. His look softened after he said it, and he seemed almost embarrassed. The accusation was beneath him, and he knew it.

She let his words hang in the air. "Is that the problem, then, Hoel? You're *offended* the Medium chose me, a wretched, and not *you* to save the maston order from destroying itself. But doesn't it make sense? Wouldn't it choose someone more teachable than a man who's been raised to privilege and is convinced he knows everything already? It gave you your Gift for a purpose." She gazed into his eyes. "That purpose was to help *me*. The Medium is leading us to each other."

She shook her head, her heart aching for him. He looked at her with startled shock, confusion, and even a tinge of horror. The wind blew her hair across her face again, and she brushed it aside as a scattering of raindrops fell on them.

"Open your eyes, Captain. Before it's too late."

He came again to see me. I wish I could say his real name. I wish I could find the tome that has the binding sigil preventing us all from speaking or writing it. If I did, I would destroy it.

He asked if I'd had a change of mind, a change of heart. I told him that I had, unequivocally, and believe he is one of the Twelve.

Mordaunt is no longer my enemy. He asked for freedom to roam the abbey grounds. I granted it. Then he asked if I would destroy the Leering that binds him to Muirwood. I told him I would have one of the lads get a hammer and smash the face off it. He said no. He said I could destroy it with my mind when I was ready.

—Sivart Gilifil, Aldermaston of Muirwood Abbey

CHAPTER TWENTY

Lady Montargis

Day after day, page after page, Eilean and Aldermaston Kalbraeth read Mordaunt's tome. It contained the history of the world, from the First Parents to a great Blight that flooded it. The tome contained the records of kings and queens, of wars and contentions, and of how the Medium had intervened in crucial times and seasons, often in small and subtle ways. It told the story of great harbingers who had come, warning of the future or teaching of the past.

Throughout the record, Eilean continued to learn new words of power, and each one opened her mind further.

By the fifth day of study, she came across her favorite passage of all. It did not translate well into her language, but the gist of it was clear. It was a story about Ilyas, a special harbinger who'd prophesied the building of Safehome, the city that was taken up to the clouds. It was clear that Mordaunt had copied Ilyas's record into the tome, for there were little asides that interrupted the flow of the text.

The passage they were studying read thus:

"*Way-yo-mer, se we-amad-ta.*"

"'Go stand on the mountain and look for the Medium,'" Eilean repeated, the finger of one hand touching the runes as she translated, her other hand forming the null gesture to prevent summoning the Medium's power.

"Go on," encouraged the Aldermaston. They'd gone through it once already.

"*Lip-ne, Metavékh. We-hin-neh, Metavékh ober keraunos.*" She paused and felt the Medium swirling through her. ". . . and a great and mighty storm came."

She looked up. "*Keraunos.* 'A storm.'" Saying it again, she felt the ripples of magic down her arms, but the null gesture prevented the word from summoning any clouds.

"Yes . . . and?" prodded the Aldermaston.

"*Keraunos me-pareq harim. Shawbar se-la-im.*" She smiled. "The great storm broke in pieces . . . it *shattered* . . . the stones of the mountains." She looked at the Aldermaston. "It could destroy a Leering too. Just that one word. '*Shawbar.*'"

"Correct," agreed the Aldermaston. "But I wonder if it could also be used to shape the stone. What do you think?"

"It's possible," she agreed and then eagerly continued. "It's poetic too. *Harim* and *Se-la-im.* They rhyme."

"That is the nature of the old speech. Its purpose is not just to convey words but to convey them meaningfully. Reverently. See the next line: *Lo keraunos Metavékh beraunos.* 'But not in the great storm was the Medium.' Even though the Medium has power over storms, it is not the storm itself. Even the Glagolitic word for the Medium, as you've seen over and over—*Metavékh*—conveys that idea. It means *middleman.* Intermediary, advocate, peacemaker." He entwined his fingers together. "That which brings everything together."

"I love this passage," Eilean said.

The Aldermaston nodded. "As do I. It is one of my favorites so far. I've seen a different translation of this story in another tome." He stared off in contemplation. "An earthquake followed the storm."

"*Ray-as,*" said Eilean.

"The Medium was not in that either. After it came a raging fire."

"*Thas.*"

"Exactly." His mouth made a small twist. "A raging fire! Which is why there are also words of power for smaller fires, lest you summon an angry one and destroy everyone around you! Boundaries, limits, conditions—all of these are necessary to invoke these powers! But the Medium was not in the raging fire either, was it?"

"No. After the fire . . ." She looked past to the next runes. "*Qo-wl, de-ma-mah, de daq-qah.*"

"So poetic," whispered the Aldermaston. "*Qo-wl.* After the fire, a *voice*. Still and small. A whisper. And *that* is where the Medium was. *That* is where Ilyas found it." He massaged his eyes and leaned back in the chair. "This passage teaches us words of power that could raze a civilization, yet it offers the wisdom that simply because such things can be done does not mean they should be. It does not mean they are the Medium's will. We must listen for those whispers if we are to wield the Medium's power. And sometimes it is hard to hear them." He sighed, a look of regret in his eyes. And she knew his thoughts as clearly as if they'd been whispered to her.

"You're grieving for your son," she said.

He rubbed his mouth and then rested his hand against his lips. "I wish he were here with us, learning this for himself. I taught him to trust the Medium. To let it guide him in all that he does. And he's prospered. But he trusts too much in himself now. In his training, his instincts. In the many Gifts of the Medium he naturally possesses." He gave her a sidelong look. "He's forgotten to trust that whisper."

Hoel had tried once more to persuade the Aldermaston to revoke the sanctuary protection for Eilean. When his father had refused,

Hoel had left the abbey through the Apse Veil. He had been gone for three days, and every day Eilean feared he would return with more Apocrisarius and maybe even the High Seer herself.

Worry would get her nowhere, though—all she could do was learn, and in the days that Eilean had worked with the Aldermaston, she had begun to master Glagolitic.

She didn't know every word or every nuance, but she knew the alphabet and how to pronounce words, and with the invocation of *xenoglossia*, she understood what the words meant. The Medium had amplified her learning abilities, and with a week gone by, she was well on her way through the tome.

There was a knock on the study door, and Lady Anya entered the room and went to the Aldermaston, smoothing his hair. He caught his wife's hand and kissed it. "You've been in here all day," she said. "Some of the learners have questions I can't answer."

He smiled at her. "Send them in. I still have strength."

"Thank you, Aldermaston," Eilean said. She rose from her chair and gently shifted the aurichalcum pages closed before returning the tome to her satchel.

"That tome is precious," he said to her, his tone reflective. "Imagine what horrors could be done, in the Medium's name, if the wrong people acquired it."

"I made a promise I would safeguard it," she answered. "I will not give it to the High Seer."

The Aldermaston pursed his lips and then nodded. Squeezing his wife's hand, he announced, "I'm ready to see some learners."

Eilean escorted herself back down to the lower level, but she encountered Kariss on the stairs.

"Oh, it's you!" said the other girl with a friendly smile. "I was just on my way to find you."

"I'm very tired," Eilean said. "Perhaps we could talk later."

"Holly will tell you this when you return, so I may as well pass along the message. My mistress, Lady Montargis, wishes to be introduced to you." She did a graceful curtsy. "Her invitation is for you to join her for dinner in her suite. Can I tell her you will come?"

Eilean had been looking forward to a moment to relax her mind, but she didn't want to offend the Dahomeyjan noblewoman by spurning an invitation. She knew from Mordaunt that those from Dahomey were very sensitive to slights.

"I would be honored," Eilean said. "I should change first."

"Of course! I know my lady will be pleased."

Kariss went off in another direction, and Eilean returned to her room. Celyn was there, practicing reading from a tome herself. She glanced up with a rueful expression. "You've been invited—"

"Yes, I know. I ran into Kariss on my way here." She huffed out a sigh as she lowered onto the bed. "I'm exhausted."

"Are you sure you want to go?"

"I should. I don't want to cause offense."

Celyn helped her prepare for dinner, and then Eilean left the satchel and tome in her friend's possession. Although she knew the Dahomeyjan lady resided in one of the suites on the floor above the learners, she had to ask for directions after she arrived. Finding the appropriate door, she drew in a deep breath and knocked.

Kariss answered it, giving a pretty smile as she stepped aside and motioned for Eilean to enter.

"Lady Gwenllian *de* Pry-Ree, *me delaine*," Kariss announced in Dahomeyjan.

Lady Montargis was a striking woman, middle-aged, wearing a violet dress with sable fur lining. Her golden hair was braided on each side, the braids wrapped into coils covered in silver netting stippled with pearls. She had a vast jeweled necklace, dangling earrings, and her face had been powdered to make her look younger than her actual years, with a heavy smear of rouge on her lips.

"Entrez, demoiselle," said the lady with a fluttering of her hand.

"Xenoglossia," Eilean whispered under her breath.

The maid, Kariss, turned her head sharply when she heard it, and her eyebrows narrowed with confusion.

After having used the Medium so much that day, Eilean was already weary, but she worried about surviving the conversation without a decent command of the language.

"Do you speak the tongue of the blessed kingdom?" asked Lady Montargis in Dahomeyjan.

"Passably so, my lady," Eilean answered, matching her tone and dialect. She curtsied to the older woman.

A table had been set between the two chairs, and Lady Montargis gestured for Eilean to take the other seat. Servants holding pitchers stood nearby and commenced producing food from various chafing dishes set off to the side. One of the dishes was eel, which tasted awful. Eilean smiled through the bites and hoped she wouldn't gag. The two ate in silence, for it was rude to talk while enjoying food. From what Eilean had learned from Mordaunt, who had taught her the ways of many different kingdoms while she was in Muirwood, there would be several rounds of dishes brought out, so she paced her appetite and always left something uneaten on her plate to signal she was sated. It was during the intervals between dishes that conversation happened.

"You know our ways," complimented Lady Montargis with a prim smile. "I shall confess some surprise considering Pry-Ree is so far away from the blessed kingdom."

"I had a good tutor," Eilean said evasively. "How long have you been at Cruix, my lady?"

"Several months. Like you, I am a scholar. I teach ancient languages at Dochte Abbey. Have you visited that wondrous edifice?"

"I have never been to Dahomey."

"Sad. You would be most welcomed there. A native of Pry-Ree would be an interesting diversion. Please say something in your native tongue. I should like to hear if it lives up to its reputation."

"What would my lady like me to say?"

"Something innocuous. For example, 'Aldermaston Gilifil is a heretic and a traitor.'" She gave Eilean a dark smile. "Yes, say *that*."

For a lady from a society of individuals who easily took offense, she certainly knew how to cause it. Eilean's brow furrowed.

"Have you not heard the news? You seem surprised?"

From the corner of her eye, Eilean saw the servants bring another tray of food.

"I don't know what you mean," Eilean said.

The lady sniffed with a superior air while the servants arrived with an assortment of melted cheeses and cut bread, with small pokers for them to dip the one in the other. The two ate silently. Lady Montargis kept her eyes on Eilean all the while with a reproving look, as if she were somehow culpable.

Eilean ate very little from that course.

When Lady Montargis finished, her servants, without a gesture, began clearing away the small plates.

"Aldermaston Gilifil of Muirwood Abbey is originally from Tintern Abbey in Pry-Ree. He was entrusted by the High Seer to acquire a certain artifact of great and inestimable worth."

Eilean felt her stomach churn.

"As I understand it from my contacts in Avinion, he not only failed in his duty, but he has openly declared himself against the High Seer. Now, as I see things, so has Aldermaston Evnissyen. While he prefers to use his given name, his family name is of far more import. Two Pryrians, revolting against the maston order. How interesting. So I ask you, Lady Gwenllian, will you declare one of your own a heretic? Whose side are you on?"

Eilean wiped her mouth on the napkin and then set it down on the table. Aldermaston Gilifil had rebelled as well? Like Utheros? She had never thought it possible, but a surge of respect filled her breast. Relief too. She had always respected the man, before she had learned his secret. Perhaps she could do so again.

"I will not listen to you any longer," Eilean said, pushing away from the table.

"Stay," said Lady Montargis in a tone of command. A flash of silver came into her eyes, there and then gone.

Eilean looked at the woman's face, then subtly lowered her gaze to her collar and necklace. She thought she saw smudges or bruises on the skin beneath the wreath of glittering gemstones connected within silver bands. She also thought she saw another chain beneath them, sinking into the bodice of the woman's gown.

Fear crept into Eilean's heart. She knew the power of kystrels.

"You've offended me, Madame," Eilean said, rising. "And I will go."

"But there is so much to talk about still," said Lady Montargis with a gleam in her eye. "You have it, don't you?"

A messenger arrived from Tintern with a warning. I'm grateful for the loyalty of my friends there. The High Seer is going to Cruix Abbey, where Eilean, as it turns out, has sought sanctuary. The Aldermaston of Cruix is Kalbraeth Evnissyen, a man who sacrificed his worldly ambitions and his claim to the throne of Pry-Ree in order to become a teacher. His son, Hoel Evnissyen, was captain of the hunters here at Muirwood.

If I understand the situation, the High Seer is not only facing my refusal to obey her but also Aldermaston Kalbraeth's rebellion. This puts Lady Dagenais in a difficult position. The attacks from the Naestors have impacted the soldiers sent to punish Hautland, many of whom wish to return to defend their homelands. The more towns along the rivers and coasts being threatened, the more the kings rage to bring their soldiers back to defend themselves.

The question is—will the High Seer be able to "see" the truth of the situation? Will she realize that she is the cause of the Blight?

—Sivart Gilifil, Aldermaston of Muirwood Abbey

CHAPTER
TWENTY-ONE

The Pig Keeper

E ilean looked Lady Montargis in the eye. Was she a hetaera? She did not know for certain, but the other woman was certainly attempting to dominate and frighten her. Just as Mordaunt had taught her, some people were drawn to rivalry—to the establishment of an order that put others beneath them.

"Whatever do you mean?" Eilean said, putting her hands firmly on the table. Standing, she was in a position of looking down on the other woman.

"I think you know very well what I refer to." The woman's eyes flashed with malice.

Eilean stared her down. "I came here with the same purpose as you, Lady Montargis. To understand ancient languages. If all the nobles in Dahomey are as rude as you are, I have no desire to visit."

Eilean heard a little gasp from Kariss, but she did not turn and look that way.

Lady Montargis's lips pressed into a firm line. "Our friend is rather sure of herself."

To whom was she speaking? Eilean or Kariss?

"Further discussion is pointless," Eilean said. "I do not like you."

"You are wrong if you think I care for your regard. Making me your enemy only hurts *you*."

Eilean straightened, smoothing her dress. "You wear too much jewelry," she said. "It isn't seemly. A sign of your vanity. Farewell."

"Sit down," commanded the older woman.

Eilean felt a throb from the Medium. Not a warning, but a compulsion. It caused an uncomfortable wriggling feeling in her chest. For a moment, she thought she might faint.

But Eilean kept her feet, gave the woman a dismissive snort, and then turned and walked to the door. On her way out, she passed Kariss, who was staring at her with wide eyes and what looked like respect. The maid bowed her head slightly in farewell as she opened the door.

Once Eilean was alone in the corridor, she walked swiftly away. After turning a corner, she leaned back against the wall and sighed with relief. What had caused those conflicting feelings? Was she fighting against the power of Lady Montargis's thoughts, or had a kystrel been involved? The woman's eyes had appeared to flash silver, but had it truly happened, or had her fear conjured it? Would the noble have used her ill-gotten power so nakedly at Cruix Abbey if she had one?

She was determined to tell the Aldermaston of her suspicions. With a firm stride, she walked back to the upper level but discovered there were several learners still waiting to speak to the Aldermaston. Not wanting to bother him, she decided to return to her room, where she found Celyn enjoying her supper.

Her friend's brow wrinkled. "How did the visit go? You're back early. I thought Dahomeyjan meals lasted for hours."

"She was very rude to me. On purpose, I think. She knows about the tome."

"Kariss has said the lady she serves is a domineering woman."

"She wasn't lying." Eilean sighed. "I'm tired but restless. I think I will read for a while."

Sitting on her bed, by the window, she opened the satchel and removed Mordaunt's tome again. She opened it to the pages she had been reading earlier, the story of Ilyas visiting the mountain and witnessing the power of the Medium.

The story of Ilyas reminded her of Mordaunt. But Ilyas had struggled to remind the people about the power of the Medium against a kingdom, which no longer existed, ruled by a weak king and a cunning wife. Her name was Yzevel, and she was an incarnation of the Queen of the Unborn, Ereshkigal. The conflict between Ilyas and Yzevel went back and forth with many fascinating manifestations of the Medium's power.

Eilean read them, her knowledge of Glagolitic helping her to decipher enough of the story, even though she was weary from using the Medium all day long. The night came on slowly, and she lit one of the Leerings in the room to provide light.

Soon, Celyn went to bed and fell asleep. Outside, the first stars began to glitter in the sky. Still, Eilean turned the pages. Ilyas was banished from the kingdom as other followers of the Medium were hunted down and destroyed by Yzevel.

And then something unexpected happened.

Ilyas was unwearying in his efforts, and while he'd failed in their world, the Medium had taken him to Idumea. He was given a piece of fruit that granted him immortality. Then he was sent to another world through a mirror gate to teach those people about the power of the Knowing.

As she read, she grew more and more interested. Sleepiness fled from her eyes. In the back of her mind, she sensed her back was aching and her legs needed stretching, but the story of Ilyas's journey to another world fascinated her. The people of that world didn't know what he was, so he told them to call him a Wizr.

In the other world, there were rivers and massive waterfalls. Most of the landmasses were surrounded by rough seas, which crashed against the shores. The people worshipped and lived near the water, so Ilyas called the Knowing something different in that land. He named it the Fountain.

Page after page, she kept reading, unable to stop. Ilyas traveled back and forth between the two worlds, waiting for some time before returning to Eilean's world so that Yzevel's power would ebb and he could begin teaching the people again. The years passed by in this manner, long and wearying, until he began searching for someone who could take on his mantle, who would replace him so that he might, eventually, be able to rest.

Hour after hour passed as she kept reading deep into the night. She had no hunger, no thirst, just an insatiable desire to absorb the truths in the tome.

Ilyas continued to travel between the worlds. And then a young emperor rose to power in what had previously been the most wicked kingdom in Eilean's world, the island kingdom of Hyksos. She recognized his name and felt giddy to be reading it. He was the one who would form the maston order.

But he wouldn't do it alone. He needed an impetus to make the change.

Ilyas sought the Medium's will to determine who could help the emperor change the culture of his people. He sat near an oak tree in a crevice of stone by a fountain of water, in the very place where the mountains had been cracked by an earthquake and the great winds had blown, and there he held a vigil that lasted for forty days. That was when he gained his answer.

The oak tree had a Dryad.

Eilean stiffened and held her breath. The description matched the place she had visited in the Bearden Muir. It was the first time the tome had referenced a place she felt she knew. Ilyas met the Dryad and learned that she was ending her life cycle. She needed a daughter to take her place at the tree, to continue holding the memories of the past. Ilyas knew this. In turn, the Dryad felt compassion for Ilyas, whom she'd fed during his days of banishment, when Yzevel sought his life.

The two immortals joined in marriage and sired a daughter, a Dryad-born whom they named Gwragith Annon.

Eilean stopped again, staring at the name. It sounded familiar to her. It sounded very familiar. What did it mean? She summoned the word of power *xenoglossia*, spoke the name aloud, and then she comprehended the meaning.

Lady of the Fountain.

The Dryad-born was bestowed a blessing, the Gift of Seering. She was the famous Harbinger who would one day help the Emperor of Hyksos.

Eilean blinked rapidly, excited by everything she'd read. As the Harbinger grew up, she abandoned the cleft in the rocks for a time before bonding to the mother tree as Dryads must do. She wandered the lands of Moros, Mon, Paeiz, Avinion, and chose twelve people from among the lowest classes of people, including a teenaged pig keeper named Maderos.

Eilean saw the name, clear as day, but when she tried to whisper it aloud, her lips froze and her tongue clove to the roof of her mouth.

Her mind opened. Mordaunt's true name was Maderos!

She read on, rapt. Maderos followed the Harbinger, the Dryad-born, and she taught him and the others about the wonders of the Medium, just as her father, Ilyas, had taught her. And then they went to Hyksos to meet the emperor, and they established the maston order.

Blinking with wonder, she smoothed her hand across the cool metal page, her heart in her throat.

He had been a pig keeper, yet he had become one of the Twelve.

She couldn't stop reading. If anything, her desire to know his story had only bloomed.

The Harbinger had not left on Safehome; the maston tradition had gotten that wrong. Or perhaps the truth had deliberately been concealed. The Dryad-born had returned to her tree in the kingdom of Moros, to take her mother's place.

It was Maderos who'd escorted the Harbinger back. He knew her secret. Ilyas met him there, and he offered him the same mantle of responsibility he had borne for years. He could become an Unwearying One, untouched by death, if he desired it. Ilyas taught Maderos about the mirror gates and took him on his first journey through them.

Because he was still a mortal being, there were rules and covenants he needed to follow in order to use them. He could only stay in the world of the Fountain for a set time. If he did not return, the mirror gate would be destroyed, severing the connection between the worlds.

Maderos traveled from kingdom to kingdom, helping the rest of the Twelve establish abbeys, teaching the people the ways of the Medium. Men like Ovidius were his friends and companions. Ereshkigal and her minions sought to destroy them, to purge the budding maston order from the earth. But the dawn had come, and the miracles they performed with the Medium's magic persuaded all that the violence and evil of the Myriad Ones could be bound, trapped, and contained.

Even Ereshkigal herself.

Once the city of Safehome had been built and every last vestige of the Myriad Ones was purged from humanity, no longer able to infiltrate living bodies, the Twelve's work was done. The emperor-maston and his city departed to spread the faith to other worlds, promising to return someday.

Maderos was the only one of the Twelve who stayed behind. When he was middle-aged, after years of proving his willingness to follow the Medium's whispers, he was allowed to partake of the fruit of immortality.

Even the Gift of Immortality came with conditions, however, and there was a tree in the mortal world that could strip his immortality away. He would know it because instead of leaves, its skeletal branches would be filled with poisonous insects, spirit creatures masking as beautiful butterflies with blue wings. If he tasted one of those insects or the dust that came from their wings, he would be rendered mortal once again.

And then he could be killed.

She understood the importance of the tome and its knowledge as she read those words. This was why the tome had been so carefully safeguarded in a dead language so few even knew.

Relentlessly, she read on and learned about Maderos's visits to the other world. As had been done in her world, he'd tried to encourage the founding of a kingdom that would model the order of the Fountain, preparing it for the eventual coming of Safehome. Many generations later, Maderos had become the Wizr of the most powerful king, Ulric, King of Leoneyis. But the king's ambition had been overcome by his lust for a fellow ruler's wife.

She stopped again, her heart beating fast. This was the story Mordaunt had told her at Muirwood. Page after page she turned before she felt a soft glow on her neck. The sun was beginning to rise. Her back and shoulders ached after reading all night long. The mystical fog, the seducing of the wife, the siring of a child.

Andrew. That was the child's name.

"Have you been reading all night?" Celyn asked with a yawn. She sat up, rubbing her eyes, looking incredulously at Eilean.

"Yes," Eilean said hoarsely. She was thirsty. She was tired.

Celyn rubbed her eyes again. "I can't believe you did. You must be exhausted."

"Not really," Eilean said. "I want to keep reading. I can't wait to tell you what I've learned. I know Mordaunt's true name!"

"You do?"

"I cannot speak it. None of us can. This tome is so incredible."

A soft knock sounded at the door.

It was early for visitors. Celyn slipped off the bed and opened the door.

Kariss was there, already dressed, her hair done up finely. Eilean had the tome in her lap still. She grabbed the satchel and covered it quickly.

"What do you want?" Eilean asked, past the point of politeness with the Dahomeyjan noble and her intrusive maid.

"The High Seer has come," she whispered, her eyes looking over Celyn's shoulder. "She brought the Apocrisarius with her. My lady is meeting with Lord Nostradamus now. I think you should go." Her eyes looked worried. "Before they come for you."

A Naestor ship struck a village near Bridgestow. Many fled and survived. Many were massacred. Some women and children were carried off in their longboats, we think as slaves. The sheriff's men who patrolled the inlet leading to Muirwood Abbey said they saw one ship pass by, but they did not venture upriver. It's only a matter of time before they come for us.

The abbey is not empowered, so we cannot use the Apse Veil to escape.

As they say in the tomes, we suffer more often in imagination than in reality. I don't think that will be the case in this instance. These Naestors fear us not. They come bringing the Medium's vengeance against our pride.

—Sivart Gilifil, Aldermaston of Muirwood Abbey

CHAPTER
TWENTY-TWO

The High Seer

Eilean had to ask herself why Kariss had brought the news. She didn't trust Lady Montargis's maid. But at least the information she'd brought was useful.

Celyn looked worriedly between the two.

"Thank you for telling us," Eilean said. "I'm not sure why you did."

"Just because I serve my mistress doesn't mean I'm loyal to her," Kariss answered. Her expression was guarded, her normal gossiping attitude gone. In fact, Eilean thought she looked a little fearful.

"But why would you help us?" Eilean asked.

"I came to warn you, nothing else," Kariss said. "Do as you please." She shot Celyn a worried look and shut the door.

Celyn wrung her hands and started pacing. "Should we flee? Gropf is still waiting down in the village. If we leave now, we could get down there before—"

Eilean held up a hand, cutting her off. "I don't trust her. Maybe fleeing is exactly what she intends for us to do. I've been granted sanctuary."

"Unless she replaces the Aldermaston."

"That will take time. I'm not leaving without talking to him first. But you're right, we should be prepared. Maybe the púca can help us one at a time?"

Celyn grinned. "I'd forgotten."

Eilean walked to the window and opened it, which brought a wave of fresh-smelling mountain air. Stright had the power to summon the púca with his talisman, a power she lacked. But the Medium worked on the same principle—thoughts could summon such creatures. They responded to need. Gripping the edge of the window, she stared into the mountains and sent out the thought.

Come, púca.

The fastest way out of Cruix Abbey was through the Apse Veil, which was a path Celyn couldn't take because she wasn't a maston, but the púca could bring her friend down to the village, probably even directly to Gropf.

A snickering sound came from the window, and then the fox-bat spirit creature scrambled over the upper part of the window and entered the room, grinning at them with its pointed little teeth.

Eilean was pleased it was nearby and had come so quickly. "Thank you for coming, púca. You are so swift. The swiftest of them all!"

The púca seemed to grin at her and then nuzzled her palm.

After paying it some attention, she turned back to Celyn. "Put the tome in the satchel. I'm going to talk to the Aldermaston if I can, but you should wait here. If Captain Hoel comes and tries to take it, grab the púca's pelt and have it bring you to Gropf. Stay together, and I'll find you both."

"How will you get out?" Celyn asked. "Will you use the Apse Veil?"

"I have a plan," she assured her. "If I don't find you in three days, then go back to Utheros. Bring the tome to him, and I'll meet you in

Isen." She considered sending him a message about the translation but thought it unwise in case of trouble.

"Eilean, I'm worried about you!"

"I'm not afraid of the High Seer." A tingly feeling suffused her heart. "I think the Medium wants me to confront her." As she said the words, a shiver went down her spine. That confirmed it to her.

Celyn gripped her hands. "Be careful."

"I'm worried about you," Eilean said, "but all will be well. If we need to flee again, we will. And the Medium will tell us where to go."

Celyn nodded and put on a brave face.

After returning the tome to its satchel, Eilean prepared for the day as if nothing were amiss. Her stomach was agitated with worry, but she swallowed her fears and patted the púca atop its head. It snickered at her, giving her a yearning look for her to touch its back so it could take her on another wild flight.

"Not now," Eilean said, patting its head. "Stay nearby in case we need you."

Another snickering sound came from it.

Eilean embraced her friend and then left the room. A few of the other learners were out in the corridor now, and Eilean saw Kariss talking to one of them with animated eyes, but her voice was too low for her to hear any words. Kariss glanced at Eilean, and they held eye contact for a moment before the maid returned to her conversation, continuing to talk to the other girl. Eilean walked the other way, heading outside. In case Captain Hoel had assigned any Apocrisarius to keep an eye on her, she thought it best to remain out in the open.

She was fatigued from the all-night reading of the tome, but the threat of the High Seer's arrival had driven away any sleepiness.

The fresh morning air outside reinvigorated her, and she climbed the steps to the upper level, where the Aldermaston's residence was located, along with the main part of the abbey. A few clouds swirled around the upper peaks of the mountains, and they glowed with different shades of gray in the morning light. The sight filled her with regret. She had loved being at Cruix and didn't want to leave so soon.

At the doorway leading to the Aldermaston's residence, she saw a man in hunter leathers and a cloak standing guard. Her heart jumped until she got a better look and saw it wasn't Hoel. His hand gripped the hilt of his gladius as he regarded her with suspicion.

She knew he was going to challenge her, so she thought to forestall it with a question. "Is Captain Hoel here?"

The man's brow furrowed. "Aye. Are you the lass assigned here?" He had a Paeizian accent.

She was close to him now, and although she hadn't expected his question, she understood the intent of it. He was expecting a female Apocrisarius, but he didn't know what she looked like.

Kariss.

The insight struck her instantly. No wonder Kariss had brought the news. She *had* been purposefully infiltrating their room all along. Hoel had left knowing that Eilean would be watched by one of their own.

Eilean gave him a smile, inclined her head, and the hunter let her in. "They're meeting in the Aldermaston's chambers. He's unwell."

"I know," she answered and passed him on her way inside. She walked to the Aldermaston's chamber and found the doors guarded by two more hunters. They watched her with wary looks as she approached. Both were strangers.

"Captain Hoel is expecting me," she said as she stopped in front of them.

One hunter looked at the other in confusion. "He didn't tell us," he said.

"I was already here," she said, being as vague as possible.

The hunter gave her the universal halt gesture and then entered the room. He came back a few moments later and motioned for her to enter.

Eilean heard the High Seer's voice. The two had met, briefly, at Tintern Abbey when Tatyana Dagenais had come to enlist Aldermaston Gilifil to oversee the construction of Muirwood. She recognized her voice and also her tone. She was agitated.

"With all the troubles facing us right now, these evil Naestors plundering and looting our shores, we do not have *time* for such trivialities, Aldermaston!"

"One can hardly call the violation of sanctuary trivial, High Seer," Aldermaston Kalbraeth spoke patiently.

"You defy my authority."

"I respect your authority, but how many other Aldermastons must stand before you begin to listen?"

As Eilean entered the room, she saw the Aldermaston and his wife, Lady Anya, sitting on the small couch. The Aldermaston looked haggard, but he sat up straight and spoke in calm and deliberately conciliatory tones. The High Seer, in her cassock bedecked with glittering gems and a rich sable trim, stalked the chamber. She looked older than Eilean remembered, her faced lined with age and her features sharp with bridled anger.

Captain Hoel stood in the background, hands clasped behind his back, but shock flashed in his eyes when he saw Eilean enter. Shock and a flash of . . . was that regret?

An older man with streaks of gray in his goatee stood near him. A gladius was belted to his tunic, but instead of hunter leathers, he wore a decorative jerkin and high boots. Lord Nostradamus. She recognized him from a brief visit he'd made to Muirwood long ago. His eyes came to her next, and his brow wrinkled. He nudged Hoel and then pointed at Eilean.

Lady Anya noticed Eilean's arrival as well, and she clutched her husband's arm and squeezed it.

"Do you think, Aldermaston, that I would have come all the way from Avinion if this were no important matter? The tome is here. It does not violate the girl's claim of sanctuary if it is remanded back to where it was stolen from."

"It was *not* stolen," Eilean felt prompted to say as she strode forward.

The High Seer gave her a dismissive look at first, which quickly altered to an expression of surprise. "It's you!"

The Aldermaston, seeing her for the first time, struggled to rise from the couch. Lady Anya came up with him, holding his arm to steady him.

Eilean continued, "'Stealing' means *to take something that does not belong to you, without permission*. The tome of the Sefer Yetzirah *belonged* to the man who took it. It was entrusted to him by Ilyas himself."

The High Seer's face betrayed her growing outrage at being confronted by a young woman a fraction of her age. "Look at you," she said, her lips quivering with contempt. "I hardly recognized you without your wretched garments. But I know you. We've met before, child."

"I am no longer a child," Eilean said. "And just as Ilyas entrusted the tome to my teacher, so did my teacher entrust it to me."

The High Seer was struggling with her emotions, but she mastered them, restraining them to her fiery eyes. "And which heretic master do you refer to? The druid Mordaunt or the false Aldermaston Utheros?"

"You know whom I speak of, my lady," Eilean said boldly. "And you also know that Mordaunt is not his true name. I know it now, although I cannot speak it. Because of you."

The Aldermaston gave her a kindly look. "Lady Dagenais, I scarcely believe that I'm the only one who perceives that the maston order has deviated from its purpose under the Dagenais leadership. I was surprised, frankly, to learn that Utheros was excommunicated for heresy, given it was not revealed what his heresy *was*. Surely the truth can abide scrutiny."

The High Seer turned on him. "You criticize *my* leadership? Do you not recall that it was my leadership that converted the kingdom of Moros? They joined us willingly, without further war. This is progress."

"But surely, my lady, you can also appreciate that the conversion of Moros and the construction of new abbeys have strained the coffers in the other realms. There is much pageantry and spectacle in Avinion. It is not pleasing to the Medium since so many of the poor suffer."

"We care for the poor! We shelter the wretcheds!" She glared at Eilean again, her eyes daring her to contradict the words.

The Aldermaston sighed. "My lady, this confrontation serves no purpose. The young woman is under my protection. She passed the maston test, and—"

"I am the High Seer of the maston order," Lady Dagenais proclaimed. "You are here because I put you here, Kalbraeth."

The Aldermaston's expression altered to one of disappointment. "At the time, my lady, you assured me it was the *Medium* that had chosen me. I see no further point to this conversation. I am very weary from my illness. This is taxing me greatly."

"Then clearly it is time you were replaced," snapped the High Seer. "I had hoped you'd be open to reason, Kalbraeth."

"My lady, surely even you can see that the coming of the Naestors to plague our shores is a Blight. The order has turned against itself, and we are being punished for it."

"Even I? How condescending, Aldermaston."

"I will not give you the tome," Eilean said. "Nor will I let you take it hence. I've spoken to Utheros. I spent the winter with him in Hautland."

"Pfah, you convict yourself!" the High Seer snorted.

"He was only guilty of speaking the truth," she said. "The order is corrupt, and the Medium will not suffer such hypocrisy. It begins to withdraw."

"Insolence!" the High Seer snarled.

Eilean could feel the woman's seething emotions. She was so wrapped up in layers of pride that she could not allow others, whom she considered beneath her, to proclaim that she was wrong, that her actions had been driven by selfish motives.

Eilean took a step forward. "What I said was not rude or disrespectful. You should have compassion on Aldermaston Kalbraeth. He serves the Medium despite suffering great pain. Pain he has not even revealed the full extent of to his loved ones. Have sympathy, High Seer."

Her brow flashed with fury. "A heretic deserves no pity. And what do you think this little speech will avail you? Through trickery and deceit you came here and took the maston oaths, yet you are nothing but an insignificant child plagued by her own delusions."

Eilean didn't feel hurt by the words. The Medium swirled within her, reassuring her that she was worthy, that she was loved.

"I am a wretched," she said. "But that makes me no less precious. A kishion tried to kill Prince Derik and me. Who hired the man, High Seer? Who gave him a kystrel?"

"Are you accusing me of plotting murder? That's an outrage!"

"If you did not, who did?"

As she said the words, she experienced a ripple of worry coming from someone in the room. She turned her gaze and looked at the man standing next to Captain Hoel—a man who was staring at her in disbelief and with glittering eyes. A man who wondered how she knew.

And Eilean had the feeling that a great secret was about to be exposed.

"My lady," Aldermaston Kalbraeth said firmly. "I intend to summon a conclave of the Aldermastons here at Cruix Abbey. Our authority, together, is equal to yours. And I will invite Utheros to take part in it. Return to Avinion and await our verdict."

The High Seer's jaw opened in rage.

The villagers by the river are frightened. We have not received any funds or supplies from Avinion since the last shipment. This is a result of my letter to the High Seer stating my qualms about her leadership. We are on our own to face our enemies. And yet, a suspicion has been needling my mind. When the dark druids attacked Muirwood last year, they knew about the underground tunnels leading from the abbey to the castle. Captain Hoel was never able to determine who had given them that information. He investigated the matter, but there were so many deaths that it seemed likely that whoever had done it had been killed.

What if it was one of Captain Hoel's men?

—Sivart Gilifil, Aldermaston of Muirwood Abbey

CHAPTER
TWENTY-THREE

Schism

Hope brightened in Eilean's heart. Aldermaston Kalbraeth was a respected and trustworthy man. Others would heed him. He had given up a chance to be a high-ranking official in the court of Pry-Ree, possibly even king himself someday, to devote his life to the Medium. She glanced at Hoel and noticed the look of dread on his face as he regarded his father.

"A conclave?" snarled the High Seer when she could find her voice again.

"It is fitting and proper under the circumstances. It is the only way, other than death, that *you* can be removed from your position."

The High Seer was not cowed. Not in the least, and the little spark of hope in Eilean's breast withered.

"Do you not *think*, Kalbraeth, that Utheros tried that approach? A conclave indeed. It is not proper under the circumstances, not in the least! He was convicted of heresy. Excommunicated. And this girl, this pathetic wretched, visits him and then brings his heresy here to Cruix. It appears I must make examples of both of you, and that *fool* at Muirwood as well! I will not let you bring disorder. We have enemies enough, prowling like wolves."

The Aldermaston's shoulders slumped, and Eilean sensed his pain and torment. "It is within my rights as—"

"A pox on your rights!" interrupted the High Seer, her nostrils flaring. "I will not be disregarded any further. My authority is paramount. Lord Nostradamus, arrest the Aldermaston and this foul spark of heresy—this *child*—and bring her and the tome to Avinion at once." The High Seer turned her contemptuous gaze on Eilean. "You will share the translations you have made thus far, and you will do it willingly, or those you care so much about will suffer in ways you cannot yet comprehend." She turned to the man standing next to Hoel. "Now!" she thundered.

Lady Anya clutched her husband's arm worriedly, her face contorting with fear and desolation.

Lord Nostradamus nodded in affirmation and pointed at them. Hoel looked conflicted. It was his own father he had been commanded to apprehend. But after a moment's hesitation, he made a sharp whistle between his teeth, summoning the guards stationed at the doors.

He came toward her, hand on his gladius.

Eilean felt the Medium surge through her. Even though she had been up all night and had used the power constantly the previous day, she felt fresh and renewed, empowered by her determination to prevent injustice. A word came to her mind, one she had learned through her readings with Aldermaston Kalbraeth. The Medium was not a storm, but it could summon one.

"You will not touch him," Eilean said with a throbbing voice and held up her hand in the maston sign. She uttered the word of power. *"Be-ray-keem."*

It was the word that summoned lightning.

At her utterance, she was sheathed in a shaft of brilliance that crackled with energy and blinded those in front of her. Although she was in the middle of the bolt, she felt no pain, only the prickling of the hairs on her arms and neck as they stood. Her heart thrummed with the rushing of power.

The High Seer cowered from her, shielding her face with her arm, and so did Hoel and Nostradamus. In fact, the older man fell to one knee and raised both arms to cover his eyes.

"If you touch any of us," Eilean said, her voice booming like thunder, "the Medium will smite you. You will die."

The High Seer, although straining against the brilliance of the light, looked as if she still wanted to attack her. "This is druid trickery," she accused. "Heresy!"

Captain Hoel, who'd been staring at Eilean with an inscrutable expression, seemed to awaken. He grabbed the High Seer by the shoulders and propelled her out of the room. The Apocrisarius stationed at the door opened it, and they all fled, leaving Eilean, the Aldermaston, and Lady Anya alone.

As soon as the door shut behind them, Eilean felt the rushing of the magic intensify. Her heart began to throb painfully. She released the spell, and the bolt of lightning that had engulfed her vanished. Dizziness made her sway, and then she felt blackness crashing down on her. She sagged down to her knees, fighting to stay awake.

"Help her."

That was the last thing she heard from the Aldermaston's lips before she fainted.

***

It was a dream. It had to be a dream.

Eilean was kneeling at the Dryad tree. She could hear the chirping of birds and the rustling of the leaves in the wind, could smell the rich earth, the turf, and wet stone from the babbling headwaters. She no longer sensed the Fear Liath in its lair, the cave wedged into the rocks.

It had to be a dream. But it was so *real*.

She heard a woman's voice. "Do you remember my name?"

It was the Dryad. She sensed power coming from the oak tree. Eilean looked down, willing herself not to look. To look would be to lose her memories.

"I believe you are Gwragith Annon," she answered, smoothing her skirts. They felt like clouds to her, soft and insubstantial.

"Where is the tome?" asked the Dryad.

Eilean felt a panicked feeling. "I left it with Celyn. My friend."

"You have a stewardship to protect that tome," said the Dryad. "It is your burden, not hers. Visions of the future are written into it. Maderos wrote them down, but I was the Harbinger who spoke them."

It confused Eilean that the Dryad was able to speak his name, yet this woman was otherworldly. Perhaps the restrictions on mortals did not apply to her.

"Yes, my lady," Eilean whispered. "I will be more careful."

"It is *your* burden," the Dryad repeated. "Yours. A burden you will-ingly took. If you serve the Medium, you also serve the Lady of the Fountain."

She felt a hand brush against her hair. A word of power was spoken. *"Anthisstemi."*

The word of rejuvenation.

Eilean gasped and came awake. She sat up, bewildered anew by her surroundings. She'd been lying on the Aldermaston's couch, and a blanket had been draped over her while she slept. Soft afternoon light came from the gauzy curtains overlooking the balcony.

Afternoon already? Looking off the couch, she saw the floor rushes had been scorched from the lightning that had surrounded her when she stood before the Aldermaston and his wife.

Her energy and strength had been completely replenished. It felt like the most wonderful sleep she'd ever had. After stretching, she pulled the blanket away and then stood and looked around. No one was there.

Worried about the others, she hurriedly left the room and went down the hall to the study. She found Aldermaston Kalbraeth there, talking with two of the abbey's teachers. He had a troubled look on his face.

"Ah, you're awake," he said.

"I'm glad to see you here."

The Aldermaston's lips pursed. "The only reason I am is because of you."

"I've been asleep for too long."

"Your maid said you didn't sleep at all last night."

Her heart raced at the mention of Celyn. "Is she all right?"

"Yes, she came to check on you."

"Did she have the satchel?" Eilean asked worriedly, fearful that Celyn may have left it unguarded.

"She brought it with her to give to you, but you were unconscious. She said that you sometimes faint from the Medium's power." His lips quirked into a smile that reminded her painfully of Hoel's. Surely he was lost to them now. "I can see why."

"Where is she?" Eilean asked.

"In your room. She'll want to see you now that you're awake. That was, shall I say, an impressive event." He turned to the two teachers. "You have your instructions. Get on your way."

"Yes, Aldermaston," said one, nodding, and the other bowed in respect.

"Are you sending them through the Apse Veil?" Eilean asked after they'd both gone.

"I cannot," Kalbraeth responded. "When the High Seer left Cruix, she put the Apse Veils under interdict."

Eilean was confused. "What does that mean?"

"She magically revoked her authority for anyone to use them," he explained, his eyes flashed with suppressed anger. "We cannot travel from abbey to abbey that way now. She's trying to prevent me from calling a conclave. One she *knows* she will lose."

Eilean was saddened by the news. "Does that prevent her from using them too?"

"No. She can authorize agents to travel through them, which means she can spread news faster than we can. I'm sending some of my teachers to travel by land. One to Hautland to tell Utheros what's happened. Another to Muirwood to warn Aldermaston Gilifil and then on to Tintern to share the news with my brother, King Daveth."

"And all the while, the Naestors continue to attack us," Eilean said, growing even more concerned.

"Yes. It's not safe to travel by ship, but without the Apse Veils, we have no choice. It's the only way to get word to Moros or Pry-Ree. Paeiz is on the other side of the mountains. I've sent a messenger to the holy emperor as well, asking him to intervene."

"Lady Dagenais helped put the emperor in his position," Eilean said. "He'll be loyal to her."

"Maybe not. He is beholden to her, true, but I'm sure it cost him and continues to cost him. He may welcome the chance to be free of her power. Also, let's be honest. She no longer represents the Medium's will. Her pride and ambition are everything we preach against in the order. She wasn't even trying to hide it."

"How can she still use the Medium, then?" Eilean asked.

"How, indeed?" said the Aldermaston with a grave look. "I've been giving that some thought. If she ordered a kishion to murder you and

Prince Derik, then we face a similar risk. Aldermaston Gilifil will also be in danger. I wish the abbey were not so vulnerable."

Eilean thought of Gropf instantly. "I may be able to help in that regard. A hunter came with me from Hautland. Prince Derik sent him to escort us."

The Aldermaston brightened. "That is good news!"

"I could have Celyn find him and bring him to the abbey," Eilean suggested.

"Would you? There is so much to do right now. Letters I must send to warn possible allies what is happening. I cannot act as fast as Lady Dagenais, but I must do what I can." He winced and clutched his chest.

She looked at him with compassion. "I'm sorry, Aldermaston."

He panted for several minutes, trying to regain his strength. "I fear I don't have much time." He gave her a sorrowful look. "My son is ensnared in this mess. He's loyal to the High Seer. I'm afraid he sees all of us as a threat now."

That unleashed a deeper anguish within her. They needed Hoel, and having him on their side would have helped enormously. He was conflicted, though. She'd seen as much in his eyes.

"Did he leave with the High Seer?"

"Yes. I think he feared you were going to set the abbey on fire and wanted to rush Lady Dagenais out quickly, lest she be endangered. All the Apocrisarius are gone."

"What about Lady Montargis and her maid?"

The Aldermaston frowned. "What do you mean? Lady Montargis left for Dahomey this morning."

"And her maid?"

"I presume she left with her."

"Her maid was part of the Apocrisarius," Eilean said. "That's how I made it past the guards to get into your room. If she's still here, she's working against us."

The Aldermaston scowled and then nodded. "That's good to know. I'll have someone look for her."

"Thank you," Eilean said, patting his arm. "I'm sorry I fainted. I'm surprised that I was still able to use the Medium at all after last night."

The Aldermaston gave her a tender smile. "Actually, it's not surprising in the least."

Eilean inclined her head, silently requesting an explanation.

"There was an ancient practice with the earlier mastons," he said. "They called it a 'vigil.' If you sacrifice something we all need—sleep—the Medium honors the sacrifice with an extra Gifting of the Medium's power."

Eilean blinked with surprise. "I've not heard of that."

"Not many practice it anymore. Whether or not you knew what you were doing, you gained the blessing of it. The power you demonstrated was the kind Ilyas had. The kind we read about in the tome. I think you are the one whose coming was foretold by the harbinger of old."

She wanted to tell him that it was his son. But she felt the constraint of the Medium not to.

"Thank you, Aldermaston. I read the tome all night. There's so much you'll want to know. There's another world, connected to ours. Mordaunt had already told me about it. Utheros and I wonder if *they* might be able to help *us*."

He leaned back in his chair, touching his fingers together. "Only the Medium knows."

She smiled at him and then hurried to find Celyn.

After descending back to the lower level, she went to the room and found her friend inside, gazing out the open window.

Turning, Celyn shouted her name, and the two ran to each other and embraced with strong affection.

"I'm so glad you're safe!" Celyn said joyfully.

"Did they tell you what happened?"

"Yes, Lady Anya did. I wish I'd been there to see the looks on their faces. When people learn what happened here, everyone will know the High Seer is corrupt."

"She's afraid of losing her power, her position. This . . . this could cause a schism."

"What's that?"

"It's like a rock splitting in half. It cannot be made whole again. A Blight will engulf all of us. Given what we've heard of the Naestors, it sounds like it's already started."

"But change needs to happen, and hopefully others will realize it too before it goes too far," Celyn said. "Maybe Stright won't have to masquerade as a greyfriar anymore. He can be a druid out in the open, without risking persecution."

Eilean squeezed her friend's hand, seeing how much Celyn missed him. "I hope so." She looked around the room for the satchel. "Where's the tome?"

"I hid it under the mattress," Celyn said. She lifted it up and revealed the satchel. Eilean pulled out the satchel and was reassured by the weight of it. She slung it around her shoulder, remembering the Dryad's warning.

"Was there a lot of commotion?" she asked.

"Oh yes," Celyn said. "Kariss came to tell me that Lady Montargis was fleeing back to Dahomey. She gave me a hug and said I should be careful. She didn't want anything bad to happen to me."

It sounded uncomfortably like a threat. "And did she go too?"

"I think so. I paced around the room and felt so worried I was sick. Then I hid the tome under the mattress and lay down on it for a while. I think I dozed, but then one of the teachers came with a message from the Aldermaston that you'd fainted. I brought the tome with me when I came to you."

"Thank you," Eilean said, relieved. She sat down on the edge of the bed and undid the straps. Now that she was so refreshed, she wanted to finish reading it. She'd learned so much the night before. "When it's sunset, we need to get Gropf. I was thinking you could take the púca down to the village and look for him and then fly back here."

"Me?" Celyn said worriedly.

"It's not *that* terrifying," she said with a small smile. Then she opened the satchel and pulled out the tome. A gasp escaped her.

It was a tome.

It just wasn't Mordaunt's.

What is deservedly suffered must be borne with calmness. When the pain feels unmerited, the grief is unbounded. Yet much of what we suffer, fair or not, tests our character. It is not fair that those who chose to come to Muirwood may suffer the unimaginable. Yet as I look at the abbey, shining before the coming sunset, I know I must face the unknown with courage. Even if the worst happens.

—Sivart Gilifil, Aldermaston of Muirwood Abbey

CHAPTER
TWENTY-FOUR

Away

The look on your face—something's wrong," Celyn said, her expression twisting with worry at the look of shock that must have been apparent in Eilean's countenance.

"It's gone," Eilean whispered. She opened some of the pages, running her fingers along the smooth edges. Even the rings in the binding of the tome were shaped differently. It was written in Dahomeyjan, a translation of the tome of Mestrius, one of the Twelve.

"You're frightening me," Celyn said, her voice quavering.

Eilean's heart had already dropped. She began to tremble. The vision of the Dryad had been a warning—a warning that had come too late. Panic rippled inside her, followed immediately by scorching anger. It was the Dahomeyjan maid, Kariss, who had stolen it. The Apocrisarius who had infiltrated Cruix Abbey.

Eilean looked at her friend, feeling the urge to vomit. "The tome's gone. This isn't the same one. They *stole* it!"

Celyn gaped in disbelief, then her brow furrowed, and she began to pace. "It was with me the whole time. I didn't leave it; I swear on the Medium!"

"I know, Celyn. I know you didn't." Eilean shoved the tome aside and rose from the bed, covering her face with her hands. Then she squeezed them into fists. "It was Kariss."

"How? When?"

"When you fell asleep. I had it before then. I *should* have taken it with me."

"But I would have woken if she'd tried to take . . ." Her voice trailed off. She reached behind her neck and rubbed a spot. "I remember . . ."

"What?"

"I remember a little sting when she hugged me. Just a little prick. Then I was so tired, I had to lay down at once." Realization dawned on her face, and her eyes widened with horror.

"She must have drugged you," Eilean said. "You were totally unconscious when she switched the tomes, and I was gone. I should have taken it with me!"

Celyn covered her mouth and started weeping. "I'm sorry . . . I'm so sorry!"

"They have it," Eilean said angrily. "And Lady Montargis has been studying ancient languages. I wonder which?" Her stomach shriveled further. "I have to get it back. I have to."

Celyn shivered. "You can't go to Avinion."

"I think I *must*," Eilean said. "They've taken control of the Apse Veil, and I will not let that woman have Mordaunt's tome. No, I *have* to get it back."

Celyn began sobbing in earnest. Eilean felt tears in her own eyes, but they were tears of rage. She saw everything so clearly now. After warning them to flee, Kariss had lingered in the corridor, talking to someone, keeping an eye on the door. She'd seen Eilean emerge without the satchel. She'd *known* that Celyn was alone with it.

Despite her self-recrimination, Eilean strongly suspected that if she'd brought the satchel with her, Kariss would have pursued and attacked her instead. She still would have taken it.

The coming of the High Seer had been nothing but a ruse, a way to divert attention from the plan of theft.

Hoel must have been behind the whole thing. The dishonesty of the deed was appalling. But what else could she expect from someone who served the High Seer? That woman would ruin many more lives unless she was stopped.

Eilean was determined to stop her.

Approaching her friend, who had sacrificed so much already for her, she cushed her, squeezing her tightly, and stroked her hair.

"Shhh, it's all right."

"It's my fault! I f-feel horrible. I f-failed you."

"No. Shhh. You've done everything to help me. But I have to retrieve it. And you have to go back to Stright."

Celyn choked on her tears. "I can't leave you!"

"The Aldermaston is sending one of his teachers to Hautland to tell Aldermaston Utheros what has happened. You could go with him and cross the mountains. I have to go to Avinion. They must have taken it there."

"But Eilean, please! Let me come with you!"

Eilean squeezed Celyn even harder. "You can't. I can disguise myself. I can even be invisible. But I can't do it for both of us."

"What if you faint?"

"I'm stronger since taking the maston test." She pulled away and gripped Celyn by the shoulders. "I want you to go back to Hautland. You've done everything you could. This next part, I must do alone."

"You shouldn't have to," Celyn whimpered. "Please don't leave me."

Eilean lifted her hand and brushed a tear away from Celyn's cheek with her thumb. "I wouldn't have made it this far without you."

"Are you going to take the p-púca to Avinion?"

Eilean pursed her lips and then nodded. "That is the fastest way there now. I'll talk to the Aldermaston. Get yourself ready."

Celyn looked totally miserable, so Eilean hugged her again. "I'll be all right," she said soothingly. "And I'll feel better if you're with Stright again."

"I'm so sorry, Eilean. It's my fault."

Eilean shook her head, feeling her lips firm into a line. "No. It's *her* fault."

***

The Aldermaston was distressed by the news, but he gathered himself and agreed to send Celyn with the teacher and learner who would be traveling to Hautland. The teacher had grown up in the Peliyey Mountains and knew the way through the passes. The learner was also going in case anything happened to the first. More than one witness was needed for each contact. The Aldermaston also said that Celyn would be helpful because she was known to Prince Derik's men and pretty fluent in the Hautlander tongue. She could also help find the secret entrance to the prince's fortress—the postern door they had left from.

Eilean had disclosed to Aldermaston Kalbraeth what she'd learned from the tome before losing it, especially the information about the High King of Leoneyis, along with her theory that Mordaunt intended for them to approach the ruler for help. The Aldermaston was wary about seeking help from another world, but he thought it worth sending an emissary. The problem was finding the location of the mirror gate.

Before the sun went down, Eilean and Celyn bid their farewells to each other, and the small group started down the mountain toward the village. Celyn promised to look for Gropf and tell him the news and ask him to report to the abbey.

Eilean's appetite had dwindled since losing the tome, but she forced herself to eat. She would need strength for her journey. She prepared her pack by herself, including food that had been generously provided by the abbey's cook, and considered her plan. The island kingdom of Avinion was south of Mon, on a narrow stretch of land. The High Seer's palace was on the northern tip of the island. Its strength came from the support it had from Paeiz, Mon, Dahomey, and now Moros. It was the smallest kingdom but very influential, with a sizable treasury. Mordaunt had taught her that it was a beautiful city, with a wide waterfall along a river that had come into being after the land was split by an earthquake. Several bridges straddled the river.

Eilean gripped the straps of her pack and gazed out the open window at the setting sun. She would fly with the púca at nightfall. Could she reach Avinion by dawn, or was the journey too far for even the púca to accomplish in one night? She opened the window to summon the spirit creature, but she felt a throb from the Medium not to.

Releasing the straps of her bag, she rubbed her arms against the cool breeze coming in from the window. The sun was creating a whorl of colors as it set. Although it was beautiful to behold, it saddened her too. It felt like all the light was seeping out of the world and the coming darkness was going to last for a very long time.

She glanced at Celyn's empty bed, feeling an intense longing for her friend. A lump formed in her throat. If not for Mordaunt, she wouldn't have Celyn at all. In her mind's eye, she could see him in the little room in the upper floor of the castle. She missed him too, but there was no way she could have faced him in that moment. She'd failed him.

But she would get the tome back from the *pethets* who had stolen it.

She heard the sound of running footsteps approaching, and then a knock sounded at the door. Who had come seeking her? She had already bid farewell to Aldermaston Kalbraeth and Lady Anya and told them how she'd be leaving.

Eilean went to the door and touched the handle cautiously. Was she in danger? She thought of a word of power to defend herself and then twisted the handle and opened it.

It was a young woman, one of the Aldermaston's wretcheds.

"The Aldermaston asked for you. H-he told me to run!" The girl was gasping, out of breath.

Eilean left her pack and hurried to respond to the summons, rushing up the stone steps to the higher level. She was out of breath herself by the time she reached the Aldermaston's private chamber, where she found him on the couch, shoulders slumped, Lady Anya stroking his back.

Hoel stood across from them.

Eilean gaped at him in shock and disbelief. She nearly uttered the words *"kozkah gheb-ool"* to fling him violently back across the room. Instead, she stood there in silence, panting to catch her breath as she gazed at him with scorching anger.

"Hello, Eilean," he said, his eyes also intense. He had the posture of a man expecting to be attacked.

"Tell her the news," Kalbraeth said, wheezing slightly.

"Lord Nostradamus is dead."

Eilean blinked with surprise.

"Murdered."

She felt a chill go down her arms. It was so unexpected she didn't know what to say. "I-I'm sorry," she stammered.

Hoel put his hands on his hips. "When I went to Lord Nostradamus's office with the list of men I wanted, I found him with a dagger in his lower back, slumped over his desk."

"How awful," Lady Anya whispered. "Who else knows?"

"It was one of the Apocrisarius; it had to be," Hoel said. "I told the High Seer about the murder, and she went as pale as snow in shock and fear. There's a kishion loose in Avinion. Maybe more than one."

Eilean looked him in the eye. "Lord Nostradamus is the one who hired him."

He frowned. "And how do you know this?"

"How else? The Medium."

Sighing, he shook his head. "I have the same suspicion. Since you told me a kishion attacked you and Prince Derik, that he was *wearing* the armor and had the weapons of an Apocrisarius, I asked Nostradamus to investigate the matter. He had a malady of the throat and could only write messages, but that didn't prevent him from being dismissive. Overly so. And he forbade me from telling anyone else for fear of causing distrust within the order."

Aldermaston Kalbraeth's lips were a firm line of disgust before he spoke. "It's like the proverb I told you as a boy, about the lad who picked up the snake that bit him."

Hoel couldn't help a small smile. "*You knew what I was when you picked me up,*" he said, reciting the fable's ending, no doubt. Eilean looked from father to son, her heart hurting from the conflict between the two.

"I don't believe the High Seer knew," Hoel said. "Nor do I think she would have approved such a course. I have to assume that some of the kishion have infiltrated the Apocrisarius. I'll have to root them out, one by one."

Eilean sensed his emotions. She could feel the burden he was shouldering. And horror shuddered through her because the Medium revealed to her what he had not.

"The High Seer chose *you*," she said softly.

Kalbraeth looked at her in confusion, and then realization struck, and his eyes widened.

"You're the new leader," he said.

231

Hoel sighed. "I am, Father. And being one of the youngest captains in the order isn't a mark in my favor. There were many others more capable than me."

Eilean didn't think so. Part of her was proud of him for having been chosen. Another part of her was horrified.

"So you didn't come to arrest me?" she asked.

"No, I came because I'm concerned for your safety," he said, looking first to her and then to his father and stepmother. "For all of you. I'm leaving three hunters to protect Cruix Abbey."

"What if one of them is a kishion?" the Aldermaston asked.

"They aren't."

"How do you know?"

He glanced at Eilean. "They aren't," he repeated firmly. "I escorted the High Seer to Paeiz through the Apse Veil. She feels safer at the emperor's court. I need to fix this problem, but I have other issues equally pressing." He turned to Eilean again. "While I didn't come to arrest you tonight, I *have* been ordered to gather enough men to capture you. Your display of power frightened us all. The High Seer wants you and the tome. You've already seen she's willing to violate sanctuary. I tried to warn all of you—"

"The tome is gone," Eilean interrupted him. She stared into his eyes. "It was stolen."

He looked at her in confusion.

"It was stolen by one of *your* people. Lady Montargis's maid, Kariss. She's one of you."

The stunned look on Hoel's face said a great deal. He was usually less demonstrative than this. "Stolen?" he asked incredulously.

"Then you didn't know that," Eilean said, her own voice trailing off. Relief wrapped around her like a warm blanket. He hadn't tricked her by using Kariss against them. Her respect for him grew again.

Hoel reached into the pouch attached to his belt and withdrew the golden orb that she'd seen him wield earlier. He gazed at the sphere, concentrating. She heard his thoughts as clearly as if he'd spoken them aloud. Was this a manifestation of the Gift of Discernment? It had to be.

Where is Mordaunt's tome?

The upper part of the orb began to whir and spin. A gentle throb of the Medium's power came from the orb. Hoel lifted it, looking at words that had suddenly appeared on the lower half.

She could hear his thoughts as he read the words in his mind.

Dochte Abbey in Dahomey.

He came to kill me at midnight. It was Captain Cimber all along. His eyes glowed silver with unholy power while he came at me with a dagger, intending to plunge it into my chest. I asked why. He didn't know. All that mattered was the order had come, and I was to be removed. He didn't see Mordaunt behind him. He didn't see the crooked staff that struck him in the skull. I removed the kystrel from his neck, and Mordaunt helped me carry him down to the dungeon, where we disarmed him of weapons and locked his wrists in chains.

Now we wait for him to revive. We wait for answers as to why a kishion was protecting Muirwood.

—Sivart Gilifil, Aldermaston of Muirwood Abbey

CHAPTER TWENTY-FIVE

Twisted Fates

Hoel's expression darkened with anger, and he stuffed the orb back into the pouch. "It wasn't taken at my command."

"Then who ordered it?" Eilean countered.

Hoel sighed. "Probably Lord Nostradamus." He looked at his father and bowed his head. "But I will go retrieve it."

"No!" Eilean warned, feeling a premonition of dread.

Aldermaston Kalbraeth rose shakily from the couch. "Son, surely you must see that such duplicity is contrary to the Medium's will."

"Didn't you teach me deference to proper authority?" Hoel shot back. "I serve the High Seer *and* the Medium."

"You straddle a chasm that is only getting wider with each step. You risk falling."

"Please listen to him," Eilean implored.

Hoel's eyes flashed with anger and determination. "I came to warn you that you might still change course before it's too late." He gave Eilean a serious look. "The next time I come, it will be to arrest *you*."

"Son, please," the Aldermaston said mournfully.

"I cannot obey you in this, Father," Hoel said. "Farewell." He turned and started for the door.

Eilean looked at the grief-stricken father, the kindhearted step-mother, and she hurried after Hoel.

"Hoel, stop!" she said, watching his strides speed up as he went down the corridor.

He ignored her and turned the corner.

Eilean raced after him. When she turned the corner, she heard a door shut. There was no sight of him in the hall. She wondered where he'd gone so quickly and then remembered the inner passages in the abbey, the ones that were only to be used by the teachers. After reaching the door, she noticed the Leering set to guard it. She didn't know the password.

"Anoichto," she muttered, invoking the word of power that opened things.

The Leering obeyed and released its grip on the door. She opened it and noticed that the light Leerings were already illuminated within. She heard the faint scuff of boots jogging up the steps.

"Hoel, wait!" she called and started up the stairs herself.

Her legs burned as she rushed up the steps, catching a glimpse of his cloak as he raced her to the top. He hadn't slowed his pace at all—if anything he was bounding up the steps two at a time. Was he afraid of her? Worried she might use words of power to stop him? Eilean wasn't sure—she only knew she wasn't about to slow her pace either, and she put everything she had into the pursuit.

To her own surprise, she caught up to him just as he reached the door at the top of the stairs. His hand was gripping the handle.

"*Tychos,*" she said, conjuring an invisible wall to block him from leaving. He tried to open the door, but it wouldn't budge. He turned and gave her a menacing look.

She leaned against the wall, gasping for breath, hands on her knees. Looking up at him, she said, "*Shaw,* I just want to talk. Give me a moment . . . please."

"Open the door, Eilean," he warned.

"I will. I promise. Just . . . hear me out."

He sighed and mirrored her position, leaning back against the wall and breathing fast. He hung his head and muttered something.

"I just wanted to talk to you," she said.

"I don't want to hear it," he countered.

"Please. Please don't do this."

He gave her an exasperated sigh. "I have to, Eilean! Can you not see that?"

"It feels wrong, and you know it," she said, coming up the final steps to be on the landing with him. "Your father is an honorable man. It's well within his right to call a conclave. The High Seer is abusing her authority."

"She is," Hoel agreed. "We have no argument there."

"Then why are you—?"

"Because it is my *duty* to obey her commands!" he shouted at her. "Look at what's happening, Eilean! We have heresy, the Naestors, and now the kishion. If we don't stand together, any one of those threats could destroy the maston order. We need unity right now, not division. Now open the door."

He was so stubborn it infuriated her. "And might not these things also be a sign that the Medium has forsaken her? You know the tomes, Hoel; I shouldn't have to teach you. Pride is anathema to using the Medium's power."

"I don't need you to school me in the tomes, Eilean," he said, his voice raw.

"Because I'm a wretched?"

He clenched his fists, and his nostrils flared. "No. It was never because of that."

"Why, then? You must know what I'm saying is true. The tome was entrusted to me. If you bring it to the High Seer, then there will be terrible consequences. For all of us." She reached out and touched his arm. "There are things in that tome she *shouldn't* know. Things she can't know, for all of our sakes. Please, Hoel. Don't do it."

"The tome isn't in Avinion," he said.

"Obviously," Eilean said. "Because you came back to persuade me to let it go. You didn't know she'd already taken it. It's probably in Dahomey right now with Lady Montargis."

If she'd hoped for a reaction, she didn't get one. His expression was indiscernible. "I won't tell you where it is," he said.

Rather than tell him that she already knew the answer from his own thoughts, she looked him in the eye and said, "I think Lady Montargis is a hetaera."

The anger was draining from his face. He looked miserable now, conflicted. "Why do you suspect her?"

"Because she summoned me to her room. The way she spoke . . . the way it made me feel. It reminded me of the dark druid who attacked me in the kitchen in Muirwood. Do you remember?"

"I do," he said.

She'd been so afraid that her bladder had drained. It was a humiliating moment, but he was kind enough to have never mentioned that detail again.

"Her eyes flashed silver, just like his did. Hoel, the kishion who attacked me in Hautland wore a kystrel too. Are they not the tokens of a hetaera?"

"There is much written about the hetaera in the archives at Avinion," Hoel said. "They used to influence the emperors of old. They persecuted the mastons."

"I've passed the maston test, Hoel. I know of them too."

"The maston test says very little," he said. "There is much more about them in the archives." He folded his arms, and the motion reminded her she was still touching him. She lowered her hand. "I don't think Lady Montargis is one. She couldn't be."

"She wore enough jewelry. If she had a kystrel, you'd never see it."

"Yes, but her maid would know. You're right. Kariss *is* one of the Apocrisarius."

"Does Lady Montargis know that?"

Hoel shook his head. "No. Kariss's role is hidden from her. Lady Montargis is a notorious gossip. She's one of our major connections at the Dahomeyjan court. Why am I telling you this?" He chuckled to himself, looking frustrated by his indiscretion. "Maybe because I want to convince you that I know what I'm doing. That I know things about what is happening that you don't. I don't know *why* they took the tome to Dahomey, but it's easy enough to find out."

"Please don't go," Eilean said, shaking her head. "But if you must, take me with you."

He smirked. "You realize that if you leave this abbey, you forfeit sanctuary?"

"I trust you," she said and meant it. "If you promised not to arrest me until we find the tome, I'd believe you."

"My duty is to arrest you," he said, clearly frustrated. "I cannot in good conscience make that promise. If you came with me, I would arrest you the moment we passed the Apse Veil. And you cannot pass through it now anyway, for it's under interdict."

Her stomach shriveled. Every question or suggestion she made was met with an immovable wall of self-control.

"Will you make me another promise, then?" she asked.

"You must admit that you've made it difficult for me to do *anything* for you."

"I'll worry about you while you're gone. I don't have a good feeling about you going alone. Will you come back and tell me that you succeeded in taking it from them? That you are well?"

His brow furrowed. "I *am* coming back, Eilean. I already told you."

"Yes, but you're coming back with other hunters. I just want to see you."

Despite all his self-control, he couldn't conceal his reaction completely. She saw him swallow. Saw his hands tighten into fists. Then he nodded.

"I won't bring the tome with me," he said. "I can't trust you that much."

"I didn't ask that of you. I knew you'd never agree."

He gazed down at her. The conflicted look on his face grew more intense. She hoped he would relent. Her thoughts burned at him to do so. *Help me,* she pleaded with him silently.

But the Medium would not compel someone to feel or to act against their conscience, and his conscience had been forged in steel.

He was standing so close she could smell him. The urge to cush him was powerful. She wanted to bury her face against his chest and hold him so tightly that he would choose not to leave her.

He lowered his head, and she thought, in a moment of total surprise and delight, he would try to kiss her.

But no. Their foreheads touched. He took her hand. She felt powerful emotions swirl inside her. His. Hers. She closed her eyes, her skin tingling with anticipation.

His lips brushed her hair. "Open the door, Eilean."

She removed the barrier with a thought.

"Be safe," she whispered, her throat too thick.

He opened the door and stepped into the hall of the abbey proper.

Eilean waited for him to go before invoking the word of power that would make her invisible.

"Sahn-veh-reem."

✶✶✶

Weariness hung across Eilean's shoulders as she walked back down the interior stairwell. She had followed Hoel to the Apse Veil unseen. At one point, he'd stopped and turned around, as if he'd heard something. She had remained perfectly still, admiring his sense of hearing or whatever instinct had driven him to halt before proceeding to the room with the veils. Again, she had followed him. She'd watched him stand before one of them, his head bowed in concentration. He hadn't even spoken the word to allow him passage, but she'd heard it in his thoughts.

Bicci.

At first she'd thought it was a word of power, but it wasn't the right language. No, it was some sort of password allowing him to circumvent the High Seer's interdict. It was a simple enough word to remember, so she allowed herself to watch as he crossed through the Apse Veil. She felt a rush of the Medium's power, and then his presence disappeared from the chamber.

After descending the steps, she returned to the Aldermaston's private room and found him sipping from a goblet.

Lady Anya turned and looked at her as she entered.

"He's gone?" she asked.

Eilean nodded. "He just left."

Aldermaston Kalbraeth sighed. "I didn't think you'd be able to stop him. But thank you for trying."

"He's very stubborn," Eilean said, smiling.

"He is. It made him an excellent learner. Because of his acuity, he was transferred to several abbeys during his training so he could pick up additional languages. I think Lord Nostradamus had his eye on him for many years." He frowned after speaking the other man's name. "And now he's replaced his master. I fear for him."

"You must gather the conclave quickly," Eilean said.

"It will take weeks for the messages to travel. Time we cannot afford."

Eilean smiled. "I followed Hoel to the Apse Veil. I know the password."

Lady Anya started with surprise. "He told you?"

Eilean shook her head. "He didn't even know I was there. The password is *bicci*."

Aldermaston Kalbraeth chuckled.

"You know it?" she asked him.

"That's the name of the bank the Dagenais family founded a century ago. The source of wealth that allowed her and some of her predecessors to become High Seer." He glanced at his wife. "Rather heavy-handed choice if you ask me."

Lady Anya smiled. "That means we can send mastons to the other abbeys."

Eilean tilted her head. "That thought had crossed my mind. I did try to persuade him first. Either way, I was determined to find out how to cross the Apse Veil, with or without his consent."

The Aldermaston set down his goblet and chuckled. "He'll be furious."

"I imagine so," Eilean agreed. "The tome was taken to Dochte Abbey."

Kalbraeth's brow wrinkled, and he turned to his wife again.

"That abbey is the foremost one in Dahomey," Lady Anya said. "It is built on an island off the coast. It's only accessible at low tide or through an Apse Veil."

There was also the púca, but Eilean didn't mention that. "I'm going to cross over myself," she said. "If he succeeds in getting the tome, I'll get it back from him."

"You mean you'll wait by the Apse Veil for him to return?" the Aldermaston asked.

"Yes. I can't let him bring it to Avinion or to the High Seer. He will not like me very much, but I, too, have a duty to live up to." She didn't wish to anger him. No, she wanted the very opposite of that. She needed Hoel, and not just because he was the harbinger. They were meant to do this together. The Dryad had said as much in her vision.

"I feel I should give you a Gifting," the Aldermaston said. "Would you take one at my hand?"

Eilean nodded, pleased, and approached his chair and then knelt in front of it, clasping her hands before herself. Aldermaston Kalbraeth gently placed his palm atop her head. When he did so, she remembered Hoel kissing her hair and felt her cheeks flush.

"Gwenllian Siar, through the Medium I invoke this Gifting of Sagacity. You are an instrument in the Medium's hands. It will guide you in your journeys ahead. I Gift you with the ability to see clearly and to understand your feelings. To discern what is light and good and what comes of the dark." His voice began to thicken. "You will be a light to many others. Watch over my son. Tell him, for me, that it is not his office for which I love him, but for his noble character and integrity. Tell him . . . tell him to watch over you as the Medium commands him to do. By Idumea's hand, make it so."

By the time he finished, he was weeping. As he lowered his hand, Eilean gazed up at him, tears welling in her own eyes. They were connected in that moment, thoughts flowing freely between them. She respected and admired him, and he felt the same for her.

And they both knew the same truth.

Hoel would never see his father again.

She reached out and held the Aldermaston, giving him a parting hug since his son would not.

During the time of the dark empresses, one of their famous battle commanders said that an empire can survive its fools and even their ambitions. But it cannot survive treason from within. An enemy at the gates is less formidable, for he is known and carries his banner openly. But the traitor who moves freely within the gates? His sly whispers will rustle through all the alleys, heard in the very halls of government itself.

Captain Cimber would say nothing. He glared at us with hatred. But he did not need to speak to divulge what he knows. Mordaunt has a special Gift from the Medium. He can hear the thoughts of others, which is why Captain Cimber always stayed far away from him. He knew of Mordaunt's ability. And because he knew of it, he choked himself to death with his own chains as soon as we left the chamber.

We do not know all. But we know much. The hetaera of old have returned. Ereshkigal has taken human form again.

—Sivart Gilifil, Aldermaston of Muirwood Abbey

CHAPTER
TWENTY-SIX

The Perilous Abbey

Eilean unfolded the wrappings of the sword she'd found with Mordaunt's tome at the Dryad tree in the Bearden Muir. She examined the raven symbol engraved on the metal collar at the throat of the scabbard, called the locket. As she closed her hand around the hilt of the blade and gently tugged it loose, a jolt of power shot up her arm. She slid it back, her heart hammering in her chest.

Weaponry was not something she had trained in. Her words could cause more damage than any sword. She wrapped the blade again, wondering about its origin, and then cinched off the ties that bound the wrapping and added the bundle to her pack. She didn't know how long she would be gone from Cruix Abbey. But there was no time to waste. She had to cross the Apse Veil to Dochte and intercept Captain Hoel.

She slung the pack around her shoulder, smoothed the blankets over the empty beds, and left the room. She had already dismissed the púca and told him to catch up with Celyn and watch over her until she reached Stright. The púca's chuckling noise had been plaintive, and she'd been tempted to touch its fur for one more wild ride. Its toothy maw had seemed to grin at her before it flew off in search of Celyn.

Pacing in the corridor outside her chamber was the hunter Gropf. As soon as their eyes met, he strode up to her with a forceful expression. But he said nothing, he just ground his teeth and glared at her.

"You can't come with me," she told him.

Those were probably the words he'd expected. His frown and narrowed eyes showed he wanted to argue with her. But still, he said nothing.

"The Aldermaston needs you here for a time," she told him, touching his arm in a friendly way. "There may be a kishion at the abbey. In fact, I think there probably is. You must protect him."

His lips wrinkled with distaste. He didn't like anything she'd said so far.

"I've orders to protect *you*," he reminded her.

"And you've done your duty. I'm not traveling by land or sea. I'm crossing from abbey to abbey. Your skills would be better served here. Celyn told you about the conclave. Prince Derik and Aldermaston Utheros may be coming here very soon. This is where you should wait until then."

His brow wrinkled, and he swiped this thumb across his nose to relieve an itch. He shook his head and sighed, his look softening just a bit. Then he nodded.

"Thank you," she said. She took his hand and squeezed it, endeared by his taciturn nature.

"What should I tell the prince?" he asked. "About you?"

"Tell him I lost Mordaunt's tome and I'm going to get it back."

"He has it. Doesn't he?"

She knew who Gropf meant.

"He doesn't have it now, but he's going after it. I'm going to stop him."

The intense look came back to Gropf's eyes. A grudge still existed between the two men. Gropf shrugged and backed away from her. His expression showed he still wanted to come with her, that he was begging her to ask for his help. But he wouldn't insist on it. Or invite himself.

Eilean closed her eyes, petitioning the Medium to know its will.

If he comes, he will die.

Eilean opened her eyes again. She gently shook her head no. Adjusting the weight of the pack on her shoulder, she walked down the inner corridor and then went to the stairs that would take her to her destination.

***

Lady Anya was waiting for her at the Apse Veil. She had a forlorn look in her eyes, but she brightened when Eilean came.

"I'm glad to have met you," she said, embracing Eilean tenderly. It wasn't exactly a cush, but it was close, and it made her heart hurt to be reminded of her childhood parental figures, Ardys and Loren, the cooks first at Tintern and then Muirwood. In a strange way, Kalbraeth and Anya had stepped into the role of parents for her. Even though Eilean hadn't been there long, she felt great admiration and respect for both of them.

Eilean kissed the other woman on her cheek. "I will return as soon as I can."

"I have a feeling it won't be soon," said Lady Anya. She stroked Eilean's arm. "Be careful. And if you can . . . save Hoel from himself." She swallowed. "He could have served his uncle the king. He was *wanted*. But he followed Kal's path instead, and . . . there's a bit of a stubborn streak in him, you know."

"Oh?" Eilean said playfully.

Anya lowered her head. "The only advice I can give you is to follow the Medium. You are a special young woman. I sensed that about you from the start."

Eilean felt unworthy of such praise. But she felt the stirrings of the Medium inside her. A strong compulsion that she needed to go soon.

"Thank you for all you've done. Thank Aldermaston Kalbraeth for me as well." She didn't share her premonition. It would do no good.

Eilean mustered her courage and walked to the Apse Veil. In her mind, she thought of Dochte Abbey. But she didn't want to be seen if there was the chance someone might be lying in wait for her.

"*Sahn-veh-reem,*" she whispered.

And then she gave the password that would allow her to bypass the interdict and stepped through the veil.

The power of the Medium swirled through her, and it felt like she'd taken a step off a cliff, as if there were no ground on the other side of the veil, and she were falling, falling, falling. A spasm of panic arrested her, but the rushing sensation ended abruptly, and her foot touched stone on the other side. Dizziness washed over her, and she nearly lost hold of her invisibility and pitched forward, but she stopped herself from sprawling on the ground.

She knew at once it had worked, for she was in a completely different location. This abbey's decor was far more ornate than Cruix's, more marble than granite. Light shone from Leerings set into the walls, each one carved into a different aspect of the Medium. But one was more prominent—the aspect of the serpent.

There were two women in the chamber, both wearing white cassocks, and they were staring right at her. Eilean held her breath, wondering if they'd heard her stumble upon entering. One said something to the other in Dahomeyjan.

"*Xenoglossia,*" Eilean whispered so lightly her voice couldn't carry. Immediately, she understood their words.

"I saw the veil ripple too. But no one came."

"That is odd."

"Isn't it, though? There was no shadow behind it either."

"How strange. Let's look closer."

Thankfully, Eilean was still invisible. She quietly stepped aside, moving slowly around the perimeter of the room. The two women approached the veil and stared at it with curiosity.

"One of us should tell the Aldermaston."

"I agree. I can do it."

After their brief discussion, one of the women walked away, leaving the other alone to guard the veil. There were several cushioned seats arranged around the room, along with plinths topped with marble vases full of fresh lilies and tulips. It was so quiet that Eilean felt she needed to stay stock-still so as not to accidentally draw the other woman's attention toward her. But maintaining the invisibility would also drain her strength. She'd hoped to stay there at the portal, waiting for Hoel to come back.

Unless he already had?

No.

The answer came before she even asked for it. A feeling of urgency continued to coil inside her stomach. Her plan to wait by the Apse Veil had to change. But where should she go? Should she try to find Kariss and the tome, or should she look for Hoel?

There was no prompting or direction provided to her. All she could discern was that she shouldn't stay put.

Eilean quietly completed the circuit around the chamber and exited into the corridor the other woman had used to leave. More decorative urns lined the way, and she noticed they were carved with the design of the two-faced woman she'd seen in that mosaic during the maston test. Was it symbolic or was it a sign of something darker? Her stomach continued to clench with dread.

At the end of the corridor was a door protected by a Leering. As she approached it, she felt impressed to wait.

Soon afterward, the Leering's eyes flashed, and the stone door opened, revealing the woman who had left, as well as a man Eilean assumed to be the Aldermaston. His cassock was black and white, such a startling contrast in color that she gaped at it. Judging by the thinning stubs of hair atop his head and jowls about his neck, he was probably fifty years old.

Eilean stood aside so they could pass and then felt the urge to hurry down the corridor before the door closed again.

"Thank you for summoning me. Very strange indeed," the Aldermaston said.

As soon as the stone door shut, she could no longer hear either of them speaking. The Leerings set into the polished marble walls were lit, so she hurried down the steps. Small strips of carpeting were centered on each step, which absorbed the sound of her footfalls as she quickly went down.

At the bottom of the stairwell, she exited and found herself in a tall corridor that was opulently appointed with stained-glass windows and velvet drapes. Everywhere she looked, there were subtle nods to the dark empresses of the past.

It felt offensive to her that such lavish windows—each panel painstakingly crafted—should be constructed in an abbey when so many went hungry in the streets. Aldermaston Kalbraeth was right. It wasn't conscionable for money to be spent on such things when so many were poor.

As she passed a door, she felt a nudge that she should open it. Doing so, she found another stairwell going down. Although she knew little about Dochte Abbey, she did know that it was built on an island, and the abbey itself was the crowning feature of the island, with a giant spire pointing to the sky. It made sense, then, that she would need to descend before reaching the living quarters. She decided to release the invisibility so that it did not continue to strain her, even though she felt much more resilient since passing the maston test and donning the chaen.

When she reached the bottom steps, she heard the door above her open and voices echo through the marble tunnel. Eilean wasn't dressed in the Dahomeyjan fashion, so she knew she'd stand out.

"Mareh," she said and used her memory of Kariss to disguise herself as the other woman. Looking down at herself, she saw the impact of her transformation. Her dress altered, her hair became darker, and she suddenly had jewelry.

Eilean knew this was risky because she might be recognized by someone, but she didn't hesitate before opening the door and entering the corridor.

A throng of people were walking in unison down the hallway. Their manner of dress and speaking was very refined. They were young, most of them ranging in age from twelve or so to eighteen, and although they spoke many different languages, the majority of them conversed in Dahomeyjan. The Dahomeyjans were the most marvelously dressed, the most refined in manner, and displayed the most wealthy assortment of jewelry.

"Kariss!" one of the young noblewomen squealed. She rushed up to Eilean with three shorter girls and grabbed Eilean by the arm.

"You must dine at our table tonight!" implored the beautiful young lady, who was probably no older than fourteen.

"Oh please! You must!" echoed her hangers-on.

There was recognition and regard in their eyes, and Eilean realized that Kariss was quite popular among the learners.

"I would love to," Eilean answered in Kariss's voice, "but I have to go."

Disappointment wrinkled their features. "Are you seeing Captain Evnissyen? He's so handsome!"

"He's gorgeous," gushed another girl, fanning herself.

"I must go, I told you," Eilean said, disengaging her arm. Her tone was sharper than intended, but she didn't like hearing him spoken of like that. "I'll find you later on."

Which would cause a problem, of course, because the real Kariss wouldn't remember being accosted, but it was the best she could do. She had to get out of the crowd.

"Until later!" said the young noble brightly. Her friends gathered around her, and they began to gossip about the handsome new head of the Apocrisarius.

Eilean crossed the flow with some difficulty and deduced from smells wafting from the front of the room that they were all going for supper together. Eilean's stomach did a little gurgle at the thought, but she focused on finding where to go.

Her gaze was drawn to another door across from her, and she felt a pull to go there. Thankfully, it opened to another corridor, which didn't have a press of people in it. She paused after shutting it, leaning back against the door with her hand to her breast, breathing fast.

The Medium led her to another door, this one opening to a staircase leading down, and as she descended, she noticed the walls were made of rougher stone, not polished marble. When she exited at the bottom, she realized she was at the servants' level. The fine decorations were gone, and there was rush matting instead of carpet or stone tiles. As she walked, she witnessed an army of servants wearing flaxen kirtles rushing back and forth, some carrying dishes, others flagons. They had urgent and anxious looks on their faces, and none of them spoke to Eilean. Their worried looks showed that they feared displeasing someone. A little while later, she heard a woman berating someone, then stepped around the corner and saw a middle-aged woman strike a young girl with a crop.

Eilean flinched at the sudden violence, and her stomach twisted with anger upon seeing the punishment and the girl's tears.

The woman noticed Eilean, and her brow wrinkled, and she quickly strode up to her. "My lady, what are you doing on this level?" she asked with growing concern. Eilean could sense from her thoughts that she was mortified to have been caught punishing someone.

Eilean gave her an arch look. "Be more patient. If you can."

The matronly woman bowed multiple times, and her eyes flashed with fear. Eilean could sense that this woman knew Kariss as well. Knew her and feared her.

"Yes, my lady," groveled the woman.

Eilean walked on and felt so lost, she wasn't sure where to go next. But as she passed another door, one with thick iron hinges, she felt prompted to go through it.

When she opened it, she saw rough stone steps leading down and smelled an ugly stench coming from below. She summoned her courage and descended. Partway down, she realized she was heading into a dungeon of sorts. Her throat thickened, and she longed to cover her nose and mouth. But she continued onward, determined to go where she needed to.

When she reached the door at the bottom, she opened it and found a room with a Leering in the center of it. It had been blasted by time, broken on many sides, and its grotesque face revealed an expression of anguish.

A guard stood before a row of several iron doors. His hand dropped to a dagger at his belt when he saw her, but then he lowered it.

"Back so soon, Kariss?" he grunted thickly.

Ask to see him.

Eilean felt magic ripple against her mind. "Open the door. Let me see him."

"He's been weeping, poor sod," said the guard dispassionately. "It won't take long to break him."

Eilean nodded to him, and the guard turned and withdrew a set of keys from his belt. He walked to one of the iron doors, which had a small window set at eye level and an empty spot for a tray at the base. There was a click as the guard twisted the key. He pulled on the door, and the sound of it squealing sent a shiver down Eilean's back as it opened.

The guard stood to the side so she could enter and then walked away.

She paused at the threshold, shocked by what she saw.

Hoel was kneeling against the far walls, chains fastened to his wrists. His head was hanging dejectedly. His cloak and weapons were gone.

When he lifted his chin, she saw another chain, this one a small threaded one, around his neck, showing the tip of a medallion beneath his open collar.

And his eyes, when they met hers at last, were glowing silver.

The other hunters of the Apocrisarius have fled Muirwood upon learning of the death of their captain. They did not believe his death was suicide. Rather, they blame me. We have only the sheriff's men to defend us now if the Naestors come.

And they will come. I've no doubt at all of that. If the pride of the maston order has blinded us to the machinations of the hetaera, we deserve the Blight that has come upon us.

—Sivart Gilifil, Aldermaston of Muirwood Abbey

CHAPTER
TWENTY-SEVEN

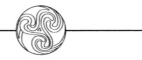

Too Many Enemies

When she saw the silver shining in Hoel's eyes, her heart clenched with pain. She felt the utter misery of his thoughts, the anguish he suffered because he had not listened to the Medium's warnings. Now he was in a cell. Now he would be transformed into an agent of the enemy against his will.

"You aren't Kariss," Hoel said, his voice thick with emotion.

Eilean realized she was still holding the illusion, and she released the magic, feeling herself growing weaker from having held it so long. When he recognized her, instead of looking relieved, he was horrified.

"No!" he blurted. "You have to go! She can *see* you. She can see you through my eyes! Run! They cannot take you too."

Instead of running from him, she ran to him and knelt opposite him, grasping him by the hands. His chains clinked. Glancing back, she saw the jailor wasn't in sight anymore.

"I'm getting you out of here, Hoel," she said quietly.

"You have to go!" he said, squeezing her hands. "I'm lost. There's no way to save me. I have a kystrel now. Run. She knows you're here. She's already on her way!"

"Then I'll stop her," Eilean said, feeling her heart throbbing with pain for him. She felt such pity for him, such tenderness. It swelled inside her like a flood and made her start crying. She covered her mouth to hold back the sobs.

"It's the kystrel," he said in anguish. "She's using it through me against you. Right now. Please, Eilean! Go!" He closed his eyes, shaking his head back and forth as if trying to fight a battle within himself.

"I'll break it." As Eilean reached to grab the necklace that tied the kystrel to him, Hoel grabbed her wrist and stopped her.

"You can't take it off me," he said. "It will *kill* you."

That's a lie.

She was grateful for the Medium's whisper. Hoel believed what he was saying was true. Or at least Kariss had convinced him it was true. Of course he was trying to stop her, given he believed ripping the kystrel off would kill her.

His grip was painful on her wrist.

"All right," she said and tried to pull away.

Hoel didn't let go. His eyes bored into her with a look of helplessness.

"Let go," she pleaded.

"She's . . . making me . . ." he grunted. His brow wrinkled with torment.

With her other hand, she grabbed at the chain to snap it from his neck. His reflexes were faster. He caught both of her hands and rose to his feet, wrenching against her arms to keep her down.

"No! No!" he groaned again, then let her go and pushed her so hard she fell on her back and rolled because of the awkwardness of her travel pack. He clutched his skull and let out a cry of anger.

Eilean stood, shrugging off the pack, and went up to him again. Still no sign of the guard. Her own emotions were churning. She realized how much she loved Hoel. She always had. She needed to rescue him. She was the only one who could save him. Yet, despite the power of her feelings, she knew they'd been twisted. Yes, she cared for him, but the violence of the emotions warring within her was unnatural.

"Stay back! She'll make me kill you. No!"

His emotions were being tormented by the kystrel as well.

"Hoel, listen to me," she said. "I can take the kystrel off you safely. She lied to you. Let me help."

"It's not just . . . the . . ." His teeth clenched, and the last words choked off. Groaning again, he shook his head.

She grabbed him by the front of his shirt with both hands and shook him. "Fight her! She cannot force you to obey her!" She wanted to kiss him. She wanted to smother his face with hers. The feelings were heady and intense, nearly uncontrollable in their savage compulsion.

"Can't . . . purge her . . ." he gasped, shutting his eyes. "Go! She'll make me!"

"She can't," Eilean said.

"They took my chaen!" he sobbed.

She placed her hands against his cheeks. "But they cannot take your oath," she whispered. "Heed me! Be still."

He grabbed her by the shoulders, and she could sense his swirling thoughts.

"You won't," she whispered. "You're stronger than her. You're Hoel Evnissyen. And I think I'm falling in love with you."

The fever was still there in his mind. But her words cut through it. Although he stood gripping her shoulders still, he did nothing further.

She sensed his thought.

Take off the ring. Please! I cannot speak of it.

She'd seen his hands dozens of times, and he'd never worn a ring before, so it took her no time at all to find this one, attached to the littlest finger of his hand. The band bore markings she recognized as the runes of Idumea. The writing was too small for her to understand the runes, but she could sense the relic's power.

"Close your eyes," she said to him.

He obeyed.

She kissed his forehead. Then she grabbed his wrist and twisted it so his hand was raised in front of her. *"Kozkah,"* she muttered, sending power and strength through her body so she could overpower Hoel.

His other arm wrapped around her throat, and his muscles bulged, cutting off her air. He was terribly strong, but she wrestled his hand with both of hers and pried the little finger up. The ring wouldn't budge. He was strangling her. In moments, she'd black out. But she held on to the word of power for strength.

She felt the Gift of Diligence thrum inside her, filling her with determination to save him. Through the ringing in her ears, she heard the guard outside address someone, but still she persisted.

Finally, she twisted the little ring off his smallest finger. With her magic, she was physically stronger than him at that moment.

Hoel released the chokehold and cried out in relief.

Eilean had doubled over to wrestle against Hoel's arm. As she straightened, she saw a man she didn't know enter the room. Closing her fist around the ring, she studied the new arrival. She recognized the hunter leathers, though, the gladius. He was an Apocrisarius, but from the dead look in his eyes, she knew he was a kishion.

Eilean rubbed her throat, coughing, trying to catch her breath. If she did not speak the words of power perfectly, they wouldn't work.

Kariss entered after the kishion with a young girl, no more than twelve years old, in a Dahomeyjan gown. There was a bit of food dabbed on the girl's mouth, as if she'd just been dragged from the meal upstairs. She looked frightened and confused, and her eyes kept going from the hunter to Eilean then to Hoel in bafflement.

A forewarning from the Medium struck her forcefully. They knew about the words of power. They knew that Eilean *knew* them. The dark druids who had attacked Muirwood had all been cut down by Mordaunt's words.

So they'd brought an innocent girl to act as a human shield.

Kariss had a hand on the girl's shoulder. In her other hand, she held a dagger.

"We meet again, my lady," said Kariss with a provoking smile. "You should have run when I warned you."

"I'm not running from you," Eilean said hoarsely. She tried to clear her throat.

"Excellent. I'm glad to hear it."

Glaring at Eilean, the kishion stepped to one side of the room. Kariss took the girl to the other side.

Eilean licked her lips. She and Hoel stood by the farthest wall from the door, in the middle of the room. The others were close, much too close. She heard Hoel's breathing behind her, but she didn't dare take her eyes off the other woman.

"Let's talk, shall we?" Kariss asked.

"I'm uninterested in what you have to say. I'm taking Hoel and the tome, and we're leaving."

"But the tome is no longer here," Kariss said.

Eilean tried to sense whether it was a lie or not. She felt nothing.

"I've already sent it back to my mistress."

Eilean wondered why the kishion hadn't rushed her yet. *"Gar-bool."* She tried to invoke a shield to keep them away, but her throat had garbled the word, and she didn't feel the power invoke. But did they know that?

"You are powerful," Kariss said. "But not as powerful as my lady."

"Lady Montargis?" Eilean challenged.

Kariss wrinkled her nose in disdain. "You know I didn't mean *her*. I'm speaking of someone much more powerful. A Wizr, like you are only *pretending* to be."

Eilean recognized the ploy, the subtle mockery intended to make her doubt herself. "And who is this lady? The Queen of the Unborn?"

"You assume I give credence to all the silly maston traditions of this world?" Kariss said. "Your superstitions are quite laughable to us. Are you beginning to understand now? I was hoping after being with *Myrddin* so long, you'd be more clever." Her eyes flashed with mischievous delight.

Except Eilean thought she did understand. She knew that Mordaunt used the name Myrddin in the other world. "You're not from this world, then. You're from the other. Is there a mirror gate here at Dochte Abbey?"

Kariss smiled with pleasure. "Good. Yes, to answer your question. There is. And you should also realize that if I do not cross it again within the proper time, it will be destroyed. If it is destroyed, you will not be able to get the tome. I've already sent it to my mistress, you see. She will be most pleased that her poisoner was successful where others were not."

Eilean looked at the young woman being held hostage. The girl had started to silently weep, undoubtedly sensing the danger she was in.

"I know that Myrddin wrote the tome in Glagolitic. Very few know that tongue. If my lady is to gain any benefit from it, she will need someone to translate it for her. Lady Montargis was one hope. The Aldermaston himself another. But it's probably better that he dies."

Hoel sucked in a breath.

Eilean sensed the other woman's thoughts. Aldermaston Kalbraeth's illness was no normal malady. Kariss had poisoned him, and she was gleeful that no one else knew. That she'd done it under the noses of the mastons, and their Gifts of Healing had all failed.

"So you intend to bring us to your mistress?" Eilean asked, glancing at the kishion again.

"Of course. The High Seer has named Hoel the new leader of the Apocrisarius. We've always wanted the kishion to be in charge of it, and now we have a chance of achieving that through him. And you will get to meet someone infinitely more skilled than you. Someone who will be grateful for the knowledge you can give her. I think we can work out something where everyone wins."

"You really think so?" Eilean asked.

"I can stop Hoel's father from dying. And the druid, Celyn's friend, who is in custody in Avinion." The words came as a slap. "Now, if you'll just let handsome Captain Hoel put a gag around your mouth, we can all be friends and end any . . . unpleasant events." She gestured behind the girl's back with her knife, aiming the tip at the edge of her throat.

Fear welled in the pit of Eilean's stomach. She'd faced a kishion before, and he'd nearly killed her. Now she was standing against Kariss, the kishion, *and* Hoel, who still had chains on his wrists and a kystrel around his neck. It was three against one, and the others' fighting skills exceeded hers.

"Who is the lady you serve?" Eilean asked, to gain time. "What kingdom does she hail from?"

Kariss's brow wrinkled at the question. "Hasn't Myrddin told you of her? The lady he loved, trusted, and who betrayed him?"

"I do not know her name."

Kariss laughed at that. "Even after all these years, he won't speak her name. How interesting."

Tell me, Eilean thought, pressing the suggestion into Kariss's mind.

The poisoner smiled. "Lady Essylt, High Queen of Brythonica."

"I'll give her your regards," Eilean said, inclining her head.

Kariss's brow wrinkled.

"Kozkah gheb-ool."

Talking had helped her clear her voice.

A boy was the only survivor. He fled in the night and followed the river to reach Muirwood. The Naestors had attacked before dawn and slaughtered the sheriff's men, who were guarding the village. They killed everyone—man, woman, child. All except the boy who fled to the abbey.

Dawn has come. And so have the murderers.

—Sivart Gilifil, Aldermaston of Muirwood Abbey

CHAPTER TWENTY-EIGHT

Unspoken Truths

T he words of power flung Kariss, the young woman, and the kishion away from Eilean, and all three collided against the stone wall of the cell. Kariss had been clutching her hostage, however, so the girl's weight slammed into the poisoner.

More of Eilean's strength drained from her, but she rushed to the girl and dragged her toward the door. A quick glance assured her the warden of the cells wasn't there.

"Anthisstemi," Eilean whispered, infusing the girl with strength. Her eyelids fluttered, and she came to, fear in her eyes.

Gripping the girl's shoulder, Eilean propelled her out the door. "Go! Run!"

The fear she already felt did the rest. With a scream, the girl took off to the other side of the corridor and ran away.

"Behind you!" Hoel shouted in warning.

Eilean was grabbed from behind and hauled back inside the cell. The kishion brought his arm up around her neck, but she managed to get both her arms up first so he couldn't constrict her throat. Kariss clearly wanted Eilean alive, so the kishion wouldn't kill her, but she was also no match for him in a fight.

At least Kariss still lay crumpled on the floor.

Anoichto, she said, gazing at the chains around Hoel's wrists.

They unlocked themselves and clattered onto the stone floor.

The kishion pried one of Eilean's arms behind her back and twisted it hard, making her cry out at the sudden pain in her shoulder.

Hoel charged them both and swung his fist into the kishion's face. There was a sickening smack of flesh against flesh, and the kishion rocked backward from the blow. Eilean stomped on his foot, and the suddenness with which he freed her nearly made her trip.

Her heart was in her throat as she watched Hoel and the kishion attack each other. She couldn't think of a spell that would work against one and not both of them, so she backed away, flinching as the kishion swiveled and kicked Hoel in the jaw. The two grappled, slamming first into the wall and then onto the floor, trying to overpower each other.

Eilean turned and saw Kariss had lifted herself onto her hands and knees. Urgency flooded her. If she didn't stop the poisoner, she'd use the kystrel to control Hoel. She kicked Kariss's knife, which had fallen from her hand after her collision with the wall.

Kariss sprang at her.

The sudden movement surprised Eilean, and both women went down. The look of rage on Kariss's face showed no more guile. Her hand squeezed Eilean's throat.

"No . . . more . . . words!" Kariss hissed.

Eilean grabbed Kariss's hair and yanked hard. A cry of pain came from the poisoner, and Eilean was able to knock away the hand that was choking her. She tried to rise, but Kariss made it up first and kicked her in the stomach, knocking the wind out of her. The need for air burned in her lungs. Panic and dizziness washed over her.

A feeling of dark power thrummed in the room. Eilean scrabbled backward, turning in fear as she watched Hoel's eyes begin to glow again.

She knew why, so she jumped at Kariss and pushed her back into the wall of the cell. She was determined to prevail. The two women beat at each other until Kariss landed another stunning blow, this time to Eilean's throat.

Eilean fell back, struggling to breathe. Before she could recover, the poisoner pushed her down, face nearly to the ground, her arm torqued behind her. Blinking with pain, she saw Hoel with the kishion in a headlock, squeezing hard to deprive the man of breath. His lip was cut and so was his eyebrow, but the kishion was faring worse. Blood dripped from the man's broken nose. Hoel stared at Eilean, his eyes flashing silver.

"Release him!" Kariss ordered. The dark vapor of feelings inside the room seemed to thicken at the command. A compulsion to obey came as a silent scream.

Eilean stared hard at Hoel. *Don't,* she thought, trying to bolster his strength with her own.

The pain in her arm intensified, and she groaned from it. Hoel looked tormented to see her suffering, but he didn't—couldn't—reach for her. Instead, he intensified his grip on the kishion's neck, suffering another blow from the flailing body of the suffocating man.

"Release him!" Kariss shrieked.

The jolt of magical compulsion was much stronger than the others Eilean had felt. Those had been milder, more insinuating.

Hoel's shoulders slumped in defeat. He was stricken with anguish, but he let go. The kishion flopped on his back, gagging and choking.

Eilean kept her gaze on Hoel. *It's not your fault,* she thought, and gave him an earnest look of understanding.

I failed you, he thought with despair.

Eilean coughed, trying to clear her throat, but Kariss torqued her arm farther, making her cry out in pain.

"No more," Kariss said angrily. "Hoel—gag her! Now!"

Eilean could barely think through the pain in her arm. She was almost on her knees, feeling weak and helpless. Her wrist had been twisted back, her arm locked straight. There was nothing she could do to unwind the position.

Hoel rose shakily to his feet, trembling. He removed his belt and wound it around his hands so he could use the leather to gag Eilean.

You should have run, he thought with despair.

She stared into his eyes. *Not without you!* She shook her head with determination.

There had to be a way out, but in the thrall of the blinding pain, she could not see it. Kariss was standing behind her, using her leverage to keep Eilean subdued. She had no idea how to get out of the situation.

But Hoel did.

He had trained in situations like this for years. And she saw, in his thoughts, what he would have done. He would have kicked Kariss's knee to throw the poisoner off balance.

Hoel reached Eilean with the belt and pressed it against her mouth.

Determined to fight, Eilean aimed a vicious kick at the inside of Kariss's knee, just like she'd seen in Hoel's mind. The poisoner gasped in surprise as her leg buckled. Eilean stood and twisted, and her injured arm came free. As she did so, Hoel brought his arms and the belt down around her chest and pulled her back against his body, lifting her off her feet.

Again she saw his thoughts, and again she followed them, kicking at Kariss's face as Hoel hoisted her up.

The kick knocked Kariss senseless, and she tumbled onto the floor.

The connection between her and the kystrel was again removed.

Hoel let her down just as the kishion lunged at them with a dagger.

Eilean didn't know who the blade was meant for, so she turned to the side, bringing her arm up to push Hoel away from harm.

She felt a jolt of pain down to her toes. A gasp came from her lips. The kishion had stabbed her in the back.

"No!" Hoel shrieked. Her vision blurred as her strength gave out. She collapsed onto the ground, unable to feel anything but the blade inside her body. Her muscles twitched and spasmed. Distantly, she heard the sound of fighting, the grunting and thrashing of two men determined to prevail.

Eilean tried to calm her breathing, but her air came in little pants. The pain in her back was awful. Her legs were numb.

Silence.

Then a body slumped to the ground next to her. The kishion's.

"Eilean," Hoel whispered, his voice heavy with dread.

He knelt by her, pulling her up. It made the pain worsen, and she stifled a sob. Craning her neck, she stared up at him, and he returned her gaze with a look of love and tenderness that stole her breath. There was no kystrel forcing his feelings now. She felt the connection binding them better than she felt her legs.

Hoel had cared for her for a long time. He'd painstakingly concealed it from everyone else, but it was raw and real, and she felt the softness of his heart, the wounds he'd been carrying silently since he'd gotten to know her. He would have done anything for her except forswear his oath of duty. Hunting her had been a torment to him. He'd secretly hoped he could win her over to his side. That he would win her affection.

"If I don't pull out the knife, you'll die," he whispered.

She reached up and stroked the side of his face. Weakness from her injuries and from using so many words of power was making her faint. The kishion next to her wasn't breathing, and judging by the angle of his neck, it was broken. Kariss lay still, unconscious.

"Wait," Eilean whispered. Her fingers traced Hoel's cheek, then his neck. She found the chain of the kystrel and tightened her fingers around it. She pulled. It didn't break. She clenched her fingers harder and pulled again. The chain finally snapped, and a sigh trickled out of Hoel's mouth.

He closed his eyes in relief. "It's gone," he whispered.

Her eyelids were getting heavier. "Do it," she pleaded. "Pull it out."

"I will see you safe," he said. He brushed his lips against her forehead. It struck her powerfully that she'd kissed him the same way at the Dryad tree, after saving him from the Fear Liath.

Then he slid the knife from her back. She stiffened with pain and gasped, wondering if she'd be able to walk or even stand again.

***

When Eilean revived, all was dark. It hurt to breathe, but it was the darkness that terrified her. The ground felt hard and cold. The smell—it was the same musty smell of the dungeon. She tried to push herself up, but her back screamed in agony, and she slumped forward. A cloak or blanket was underneath her, protecting her from the stone.

"I'm here," Hoel whispered. She felt his hand on her shoulder, pushing her back down.

"Where . . . ?"

"Shhh." He lowered himself until he lay against her. She smelled his sweat, smelled the leather of his bracers, and the warmth of him suffused her back.

His mouth came near her ear. "We're in another cell," he said very softly.

"Why?" she asked.

"Because it's the last place they'll search for us." She could sense the triumph in his thoughts. He was very good at being clever. "I've closed the wound on your back and added some padding. Just lie still."

Voices came from outside the closed iron door. One of them belonged to Kariss.

"They can't have gotten far! Find them! Are there guards hurrying to the mirror gate?"

"Yes, as you ordered. There's no sign of them." It was a man's voice. He sounded like the guard that Eilean had deceived earlier.

"I want them captured before nightfall," Kariss said angrily. "No one saw them in the corridors?"

"No one! The Aldermaston has people looking for them as well. None of the Leerings have detected them."

"She can become invisible at will," Kariss said with anger and approval. "The Leerings won't find them. Nor will they hold them. This is a wreck! Where could they have gone?"

"I don't know. What about the young girl you brought down here? We caught her wandering the tunnel."

"Send her back above. Tell her if she breathes a word of this, she'll be locked in the dungeon. She's weak-willed. She won't talk."

"Yes, I'm sure she won't. What to do with the kishion's body?"

"Burn it. I'll find her, Doran. I'll find her myself. That tome is useless to Lady Essylt without her."

The voices trailed off, and a door closed.

Sighing in relief, Hoel rubbed her shoulder. "How much pain are you in?"

"It only hurts when I breathe," Eilean said, but she was only half joking.

"Is that all?" he asked softly, his voice teasing. "So not much very much, then."

She butted him with her elbow. It felt strange lying with him in the dark, but in a pleasurable way. It was almost like they were cushing, a thought that made her smile and blush. She was grateful it was too dark for him to see it.

"It's going to take some time for you to heal," he said. "Unless you can teach me how you healed me back in the gorge."

"I didn't heal you," she said.

"That's strange, because I'm fairly sure I was bleeding to death."

"I meant I wasn't the one who did." She sighed. "I want to tell you things, Hoel. But I'm not sure where your loyalties lie."

He was silent. Then she felt his fingers stroke her cheek. "I'm loyal to the Medium. It's been prodding me for some time that I needed to take your side. I think I've been misinterpreting the visions I've had about you. I've been a fool."

"*Shaw*, you think so?"

He laughed softly. It was a delicious sound. "I'll admit it. I didn't want you to be right. But you were. You have been all along."

It felt very good to hear him say it. She nestled against him, drowsy again. Then she remembered the pack and sword she'd dropped in the other cell. It felt like a nudge from the Medium.

"Where is the pack I brought?"

"It's here with us. Do you need something?"

"Bring me the sword."

"Why do you need a sword? Was it Mordaunt's?"

"Yes. It's not from this world." She felt a little cold when he moved away from her, but he came back with the bundle, unwrapping it.

"There's a marking on the scabbard. What is it? It's too dark to see anything."

"It's a raven."

Hold the scabbard against you.

"Give it to me," she asked. She clutched the scabbard to her bosom while Hoel settled down behind her again, pressing his body to hers.

It will heal you both.

Now she understood. "Hold me," she whispered, nestling back against him again. A throb of pain came from her back, and she winced. He draped his arm over her, his hand resting on the scabbard, and kissed her hair. A strange blue light began to shine within the cell, coming from the scabbard.

"By Idumea," Hoel said. "It's glowing."

She turned her neck enough to study his face in the pale glow of the scabbard's light. "Like the eyes of a Leering," she said. "It has powers."

"I'll keep you safe," he promised.

Warmth glowed inside her heart. It wasn't the kystrel interfering with her feelings this time. Hers were real. And so were his.

"Good," she said. "Because we're about to go to another world."

Mordaunt came to me this morning. With his crooked staff clenched in his hands, he said he would stand with me against the Naestors. I know his words are powerful indeed, so I asked him if there was anything he could do or say to save us. He laughed and said that I was no longer being a pethet. *Then he reminded me of a passage from the ancient tomes. One that every first-year learner reads but only one in ten thousand ever puts to use.*

"We search the tomes, and we have many insights and even a share of the Gift of Foresight; and having this guidance, we obtain power by hope, and our faith becomes unshakable, so much so that we truly can command the very trees to obey us, or the mountains, or the waves of the sea."

Although he cannot stop the Naestors, he promised he would teach me how to do so with but a single word and the will to make it happen. "In the Bearden Muir there are many hills of different sizes at varying distances. Look for the right one, the one the Medium chooses, and then say this word. Atheq.

"And the mountain would be moved. It is a word from the Book of Creation."

—Sivart Gilifil, Aldermaston of Muirwood Abbey

CHAPTER TWENTY-NINE

To Be One

There was no way to tell whether dawn had come, for the dungeon was unvaryingly dark. The light from the scabbard had faded. Strangely, so had the pain in Eilean's back. She still clutched the scabbard, so she set it down next to her and then reached her hand back to where Hoel had bound her wound. She felt him start awake at the motion.

"I fell asleep," he whispered apologetically, rising and shifting away from her. She didn't want him to move away. In the quiet of the cell, they heard nothing else except their own breathing and the rustling of their clothes.

"It doesn't hurt," Eilean said, sitting up. She pressed tentatively against the spot where the kishion had thrust the dagger into her, expecting a jab of pain, or at least some soreness. Nothing.

"It couldn't have healed that quickly," Hoel said in a confused tone.

"I feel fine," Eilean said. She twisted at her waist, one way and then the other. Her legs felt normal as well. She was completely well rested. "We need a little light."

"There are no Leerings here, and I've nothing to burn. And the smell of smoke would—"

She pressed her fingers against his mouth to stop him. "You don't have to do everything, Hoel. *Le-ah-eer.*"

She said it in a whisper, with the intention of only summoning a very small light. A cold spark wriggled to life in the air between them, showing no tendrils of smoke, giving off no heat.

He stared at it with surprise, fascination, and a little wariness.

"Druid magic?" he asked her.

She shook her head. "No. It's the same magic that imbues our Leerings. It's the . . . origin. Primeval magic."

"Primeval?" he asked, eyebrow lifting. Was he impressed? She wasn't exactly sure, but she didn't sense any judgment from him.

As she studied his face, she noticed the dried blood on his lip and eyebrow, but the cuts were gone. She reached out a hand and gently touched his brow where the cut had been. He let her, his eyes gazing into hers.

Feeling her cheeks flush, she said, "You've been healed as well."

Just as the Medium had promised. The scabbard had healing properties.

With a knuckle, he rubbed the healed cut on his lip. The rasp of his whiskers sounded appealing. As did the thought of kissing him, an urge that filled her with surprising intensity. She looked down.

"The scabbard healed us both?" he asked.

"Yes. The magic did in hours what would normally take weeks or longer. I found the weapon with the tome, back at the chasm where you discovered me."

He tapped his lips and nodded thoughtfully. "I never thought of Mordaunt using a sword."

"He's been around for a long time. He knew the Harbinger person-ally." She gave him a meaningful look and then put her hand on his, which had dropped to his knee. "Did you know we were going to end up in this cell? Was it ever in a vision?"

"No," he confessed. "The visions aren't predictable. Nor do they always happen in order." He darted her a look. "Mostly they're about you."

"Me?"

He nodded. His thumb lifted and stroked the edge of her hand, sending a shiver down her arms. "There's something about you that summons them."

Her head tilted in confusion.

"When I met you at Tintern, I had a vision of you armed with a bow and a gladius, wearing hunter leathers. You weren't at Tintern, though. You were at another abbey." His eyes were serious. "It was Muirwood. There was . . . an . . . apple orchard. The kitchen. As I watched the abbey being built, I recognized what I'd seen in my vision. The vision was from years in the future, I think, for the trees weren't small. In the vision, you were walking with me, talking with me, and I was teaching you."

She swallowed, wondering what it meant. Confusion churned in her mind, but what he said sounded like truth, though not entirely.

"That's why you asked the Aldermaston to let me join the Apocrisarius," she said.

"I thought it was the Medium's will," he said with a perplexed sigh. "But nothing has turned out like what I saw."

"What about at Cruix? When you accused me of being a hetaera?"

His eyes widened with shame, and he looked away. "I'm sorry about that."

She squeezed his hand. "Just tell me what you saw."

"I don't know what it means."

She reached with her other hand and turned his face back to hers. "We'll figure it out *together*."

He sighed. "In that vision, it seemed to be winter. You were kneeling in the snow, your hair blowing in the wind. It was like I was standing behind you, looking at the Peliyey Mountains. They're distinctive, as you know. And I saw Cruix burning. It was in flames, from the lowest part of the abbey to the highest tower. The stone was burning by some sort of magic. As you knelt in the snow, weeping, you were rubbing your shoulder. And I knew, through the Medium, that there was a brand there." He fell quiet. "I truly believed you went to Cruix to destroy it. That you had chosen a path *against* what the Medium wanted for you. That you would ruin my father too."

Eilean nodded in sympathy. "Kariss was the one controlling things. Not me. And she's poisoned your father."

Hoel's look darkened with anger. "I want to save him if I can."

Her own heart hurt for him. "I don't think you're going to see him again. At least, that's what the Medium has communicated to me. I'm sorry."

His lips quivered from an onslaught of emotion within him. Anger wrestled with sorrow. Determination clashed with helplessness. "His fate is not in my hands."

She felt tears in her eyes, but she brushed them away. "He is a good man. And he raised a wonderful son. Not every prince-to-be would willingly give up their birthright. Yet you did."

Hoel smiled regretfully. "That life would have been easier; that much I know."

"But you allowed yourself to be the Medium's tool. You've come much farther because of it."

"Have I?" he said with a self-effacing smile as he looked around the cell.

She squeezed his hand again. "Yes. I know it. Have you had any other visions?"

JEFF WHEELER

"Several. And that's the problem. None of them have happened! In one you were swept away in an avalanche. In Hautland, I think. While I was waiting for you in Fenton, I kept going out and seeking you, afraid you'd die crossing the mountains. It was unbearable . . . thinking that you were buried in the snow."

He worried because he cared so much about her. It wasn't just his feeling of duty that had driven him. All this while, he'd cared for her, almost against his sense of right and wrong. But she understood that the Medium was trying to teach him something through his visions. What it was, she didn't know, but she had the notion that they would figure it out together.

"And these visions were all of me?"

He nodded with conviction. "Even though your garb was different, it looked like you. It *felt* like you."

"Clearly your visions aren't of the past or the present," Eilean said. "They must be of the future."

"Are they? Or are they different possibilities that *might* have happened? I remember reading a story in the tomes about a merchant who had visions from the Medium warning him to leave the city with his family. They left and inhabited a new land far across the sea. He had a vision of what would have happened *if he'd remained.* An alternate future where he and his family perished. I've wondered if my visions are like that. Might you have become a hunter? Did I do something *wrong* by asking the Aldermaston to let you join the order?" He bit his lip, clenching his other hand. "Or did I *drive* you to become a hetaera?"

Eilean could sense the anguish of his feelings. He was being honest with her, confessing his deepest worries and qualms.

"I don't know the answer, Hoel. And maybe you're right—maybe there were other possible outcomes for us. All I know is that when the Fear Liath ravaged you, I was given a choice. If I permitted you to be healed, you would continue to hunt me. If not, we would have been safer, obviously." She looked down, then back into his eyes. "I couldn't bear the thought of you dying because of me."

278

The little coil of a spark continued to hover in the air between them, bright enough that she could see how her words had stunned him . . . Twisting his wrist, he turned his hand over so that their palms were touching. Their fingers meshed together.

"Is that why you took that dagger for me?" he whispered.

She bit her lip and nodded.

He breathed in through his nose and let it whistle softly out his mouth. "Thank you, but don't do that again. I could have stopped it. I was going to." He closed his eyes. "Now I'm sounding ungrateful. We each have a part to play in this." He looked at her seriously. "Let me play mine. I'm not going to let anyone kill me, and by Cheshu, I'm not going to let anyone kill you either!"

She hadn't heard that expression in a while, and it made her smile. "Fair enough. But remember that you had a kystrel around your neck at the time. I wasn't sure what I could count on you for."

"And you freed me from it. And from that accursed ring."

"What did you do with it?"

"I left the kystrel and the ring there. I didn't dare touch it. It was worse than the kystrel."

"How so?"

"It robbed me of my free will," he said, "and forced me to obey the commands of my enemies. Even the thought of taking it off made me nauseous, but I knew, somehow, that it would lead me to murder people. The . . . the . . . lack of human feeling I felt while wearing it was a torture. It numbed every joyful feeling in my heart. I didn't care about anyone. Or anything. And that made the kystrel's influence even *more* powerful."

"That's awful," Eilean said in revulsion.

"Both were put on without my consent after they stripped the chaen from me. I'd never felt so much anguish in my life. I begged the Medium to deliver me from my fate."

"I knew you were in trouble," Eilean said. "The Medium sent me to you."

"Thank Idumea," he sighed. Then he reached out and hugged her to him, skirting around the tendril of magic which provided the light. His embrace was warm and tender, and although her own feelings were a jumbled mess, it felt wonderful to be united with him at last. She didn't imagine they'd always see things the same way, but their oars were no longer rowing at cross purposes.

After the embrace, she could see a little flush in his cheeks. Her own felt very hot.

"I need to tell you some things before we go. About Mordaunt and the other world he visited. From which he was exiled. Kariss brought his tome to that world and delivered it into the hands of the woman who betrayed him. If the language was too arcane for this world, I doubt she'll be able to translate it there. But if we are going to go there, we must first find the mirror gate."

"And what is that?" he asked.

"It's a translation from the old speech, so the wording is not exact, but a mirror gate is a bridge between the worlds. There are rules about traveling between them. You may have heard Kariss say that if she doesn't go back, there will be consequences. She said that, I think, because she was afraid I would kill her outright. And she threatened an innocent child to prevent me from stooping to it."

"That was very clever, by the way," Hoel said, brushing his thumb across her cheek. "Using the words to fling them back into the wall."

"Thank you. I'm sorry I had to use them against *you*."

"No apology needed. I deserved it. And I'm healed now. So what you are saying is we will have limits on how long we can be there."

"Yes. The time must be set in advance. It's part of the covenant. Failure to uphold it will cause the mirror gate to be destroyed. The only way to live permanently in that other world would be to trade places with another living person. A soul for a soul. But that must be done willingly by both sides. You cannot force another person to trade places with you. Intention matters. If not, the mirror gate is ruined, and a curse comes on those who broke it. A calamity will befall them both."

"So we must hasten the journey and not bring anyone back with us. But the tome isn't a person?"

"No. Artifacts can transfer between worlds."

His eyebrows arched, and he nodded in understanding.

"So I have a question for you, Captain Hoel. Where is the Cruciger orb? With it, we could find the tome easily. That is our first intention. The second . . . Mordaunt served a king of the other world, and he built a kingdom like Hyksos. A kingdom called Leoneyis. I should like to meet him and tell him what's happened to his friend. And possibly solicit his help to end the conflict with the High Seer and the Aldermastons. The high king's name is Andrew. His story is in the tome that was stolen. I believe he is still alive. He's a noble man, a benevolent ruler."

Hoel pursed his lips and studied her. "We are aligned on the need to take the tome back. Removing the High Seer . . . I'm not so sure."

"You've seen what she's done, Hoel. She won't relinquish power willingly. Your father had the right to call a—"

He held up his hand to forestall her. "I know all of it. I've seen the corruption in Avinion firsthand. Corruption caused by greed and power. And I agree that she *should* be replaced." It relieved Eilean to hear it. "I'm just not certain inviting another world to interfere is the best tactic." He pressed her hands between his. "But I promise you, Eilean, we will find a path that pleases us both. I won't act against you. My loyalty is to the Medium. And if the time has come for the Dagenais family to fall, I will help that happen. I think I will see the future more clearly if we are unified in our purposes."

Eilean agreed wholeheartedly and hugged him again. Their cheeks touched, and she savored the simple contact. It felt so good to have him on her side.

"Now, about the Cruciger orb," he said. "That's the hard part. I don't have it. Kariss took it when she took my chaen."

My hand trembles as I write this. We are saved. The Medium has saved us. I take no credit or honor for it. The Naestors left their longboats by the river, and a crew of over fifty came to slay us. I stood before the abbey, trying to calm my raging emotions. Staring across the horizon, I saw a short, crouch-backed hill in the distance. Invoking the word of power Mordaunt taught me, I lifted my arms to the sky, and the hill lifted into the air. The Naestors began to flee.

And then the shadow of the hill came down on them. It was over. The danger was gone. Mordaunt approved of my choice. And he approved when I deflected all recognition and praise for the deed. I asked him if the druids had a name for that hill. He said no, that all bulging hills are called tors in their order.

And so that is what we named it. The Tor.

—Sivart Gilifil, Aldermaston of Muirwood Abbey

CHAPTER THIRTY

Mirror Gate

They walked side by side down the inner corridor beneath Dochte Abbey. A spell of illusion had transformed Eilean and Hoel, so no one stopped them or asked who they were. Eilean was surprised to find her connection to the Medium was strong enough to hold the spell, as long as she and Hoel were together. It reminded Eilean of Mordaunt's story about High King Andrew's wicked father, who'd transformed himself into the husband of the woman he'd lusted after.

"That door, on the left," Hoel said in a low voice. They'd paused at the kitchen earlier and claimed some food to eat and take on their journey. Now they were headed for a room controlled by the Apocrisarius stationed at Dochte.

When they reached it, the handle was locked. Hoel looked both ways down the corridor and, finding no witnesses, nodded to Eilean.

"Ephatha," she whispered, and the locking mechanism rolled on its own. Hoel gripped the handle with one hand and the gladius he'd

stripped from the dead kishion in the other. The sword and scabbard she'd been carrying were strapped to his back, providing him with another weapon. He listened at the door and then twisted the handle and pushed it open.

Eilean breathed out in relief. No one was inside. From the light streaming in through the curtains, it was midmorning of the next day. Most of the learners were probably at their studies.

Hoel quickly did a search of the room, waved her in, and then barred the door behind them. While he disappeared into an inner room, Eilean walked the outer area, examining the shelves lined with neatly stacked tomes and scrolls stored in canisters with brass fittings on the ends.

After a moment, she joined Hoel in the other room, which proved to be a cloakroom full of weapons. He'd acquired a bow and a quiver of arrows and was now feverishly searching the desk, pushing aside papers, opening drawers.

"I hope it's here," Eilean said. She noticed some small chests stacked in one of the corners next to a cloak rack, so she went to it, knelt, and opened the first.

The Cruciger orb was in the top one, sitting atop a thin-coiled chaen with the markings of the maston order on it.

"I found both," she declared excitedly. She gingerly lifted the orb out of the chest, the metal feeling cool against her skin. It was about the size of an apple, with stays and an interconnected web of spindles supporting the inner part of the orb.

Hoel came to her side, touching her shoulder, and heaved a sigh of relief.

"I am so . . . thank you. Thank you, Eilean." He went straight for the chaen, pulling it out of the chest.

"I need to put this on," he said. "I've felt so vulnerable without it."

Immediately, he began stripping off his cloak and then his shirt. Her cheeks flamed with embarrassment, and she set the orb on the table

284

and turned away, though not before she caught a glimpse of his chest and arms, carved with muscles and scars. The sight of his half-clothed body overwhelmed her. Although she'd seen plenty of men this way during harvest days at Tintern, none had looked like *him.*

Kneeling back down by the chests, she pulled the top one off and looked in the next, wondering if Kariss had lied about the tome's location. The second one was filled with an assortment of vials and stoppered bottles that exuded an air of danger. Setting that chest aside, she opened the bottom one and found it full of pouches of coins. One of them held coins that bore the same raven marking as Mordaunt's sword.

"We might need this," she said, looking back as Hoel finished dressing. Part of her wanted to see his scars again. To ask him about them. But the time wasn't right for such talk, and she shoved the thought away.

"Bring it," he said. He lifted the orb, staring into it, and she could easily hear the thought in his mind. *Where is the tome we seek?*

The orb began to whir softly, like the sound a kitten made when it was content. The spindles moved faster than she could track with her eyes, and writing appeared on the lower half of the orb.

"What does it say?" she asked.

"See for yourself." He showed her the orb.

The writing on the lower half was in Pry-rian. It said: *You will find the tome in Brythonica.*

"The spindles are pointing the way," he said. "They provide a direction to follow. Or instructions when simple directions are impossible."

"It is wondrous," she said in awe. She felt the gentle thrum of the Medium's power. "This is a curious piece of work. Who made it?"

"No one knows. It appeared long ago. Only the High Seer can authorize its use. It's how I knew you were in Hautland."

"You'll need another pouch to carry it," she suggested.

He looked in the chest she had left open and chose one of the money pouches, emptying the coins from it. The orb fit inside.

"Do you know what a mirror gate looks like? Will we recognize it when we find it?" he asked her.

She shook her head. "It's a rock formation, a natural bridge carved by water. So that means it'll be on the lower part of the island."

"We best get going before Kariss returns." He stacked the chests again, rearranging them so that they weren't out of place. Then he went back to the desk and began quickly reading some of the letters on the top.

"The High Seer is in Paeiz with the emperor," he said. "At least she has some protection. I wish there were a way I could warn her about Kariss."

"Hoel," Eilean said. "We have to do this. She might already *know* about Kariss."

Hoel shook his head. "I don't think so. And now we know that she's in league with the kishion." His brow furrowed. "It doesn't bode well that we've run into another one. I'll admit it's hard for me to walk away from trouble . . . and from my oaths. But your path is where I must go. I know that now."

She took his hand and squeezed it. "Together."

***

Once they left the abbey, which was at the top of the hill on the island, they walked down the narrowed cobblestone streets descending from the peak. Shops of every kind lined the streets, and locals urged them both to see their wares, as if they believed Hoel and Eilean were nobles from the abbey with coin to spend. But the two kept walking, intent on their mission.

As they went lower, the narrow streets blocked their view of the abbey they'd left. The buildings were so close together it would have been possible to jump from one roof to the next. Iron signs had been fastened to the walls, announcing the different shops, inns, and services offered. The streets all wound in circles before reaching major forks, which led sharply down to the next lower level of the hill. The buildings were surprisingly tall, four or five levels high, with stone first floors and upper floors of wood and plaster. Unlike the colorful buildings of Isen, these were all either pale gray or butter-colored.

They stopped for a drink at a Leering fountain at the lower level and asked one of the locals loitering there about the coming tide.

"The fishermen will be returning before noon when the tide comes. You want some fresh fish? I know a fishmonger who could get you a good price on his catch, eh?"

"No, thank you," Eilean said. Then she switched to Pry-rian and said to Hoel. "They are all about money here, aren't they?"

"That's common in Dahomey," he answered, then nodded to the fellow, who looked confused at their change of language.

"Midday is not far off," he said as they walked away. "The orb said we'd need a boat to reach the mirror gate." They had checked the orb for further directions as they'd made their way to the wharf.

"Probably a small one," she said. "Maybe we should have asked about the fisherman."

"We're going to," he said. "But not from that person. It would have left a trail for others to follow." It was her turn to give him an impressed look. It made him smile. "I've been to Dochte; I know where the fishermen gather. We'll pay someone to take us where we need to go."

"But our guide won't be able to come with us. Not unless we explain the covenants that control the mirror gates."

"I wasn't intending to let him come with us." He gave her a smirk, and she saw the thought in his mind of tossing someone overboard.

"That's not very kind, Hoel."

He shrugged. "He'll be paid for his swim. And the loss of the boat. I don't fancy arriving in your other world without any kind of boat. Won't help us much if we find ourselves in the middle of a sea."

"You may be right. But let's not ruin the poor fellow."

They finally reached the lowest level of Dochte. From this vantage point, she could now see the abbey at the top of the island in all its glory. It was truly an impressive sight, so much grander and larger than Cruix, Tintern, or Muirwood. It crowned the top of the island and had a collection of walls, turrets, and a single spire that rose like a spike to pierce the sky.

She'd watched in fascination at Muirwood being built. But an abbey the size of Dochte was an even more impressive feat. She could only imagine the train of floating stones that must have crossed from the mainland in order to construct such a grand building on an island.

"You should see Avinion," Hoel told her. "It's even grander."

"And meanwhile, so many suffer in poverty," she said. "It's not bad to build beautiful things. But must there be so many wretcheds too?" A series of clouds could be seen on the horizon, she noticed, indicating the coming of a possible sea storm.

His look softened to one of compassion. "There should not," he agreed. "I don't know why so many are abandoned. Why *you* were."

She'd never known her parents. Or why she had been abandoned at Tintern. It dawned on her that the orb could supposedly find anything. Gnawing her lip, she asked, "Could I use the orb to find out who they are?" she asked.

"You could. Are you certain you wish to know?"

"You answered that quickly," she said, thunderstruck. "Have you already asked it?"

He looked at her seriously and then nodded.

"Truly?" she asked in disbelief.

"I was curious," he said. "And I was sent to hunt you. I wondered why you were so strong in the Medium. So naturally I wondered about your parents."

She grasped the front of her gown by her heart, as if preparing for a blow. "So you know?"

"I do."

She wasn't ready to hear it. Not yet. "Don't tell me. I need . . . time."

"All right," he said softly. "When you are ready." He gestured for them to keep walking. "Let's find a fisherman."

The tide was coming in by the time they reached the wharf. Ships could be seen approaching as well, large holks and smaller cogs. Hoel was fluent in Dahomeyjan and didn't need magical help to speak it like a local. After asking around, they found a fisherman just returned who hadn't fared well at sea. He agreed to take them for a ride on his rowboat if they would wait for him to get a drink of ale first.

Hoel agreed and paid the man an upfront fee. The dock was busy with the fishing trade and exclamations of joy as well as complaint. The boat was a small thing, peaked at both ends, with a single set of oars. Hoel watched the crowd, exchanging occasional good-natured banter with the locals.

Eilean saw them first. A small group of guards coming toward them, led by another Apocrisarius armed with a bow. The fisherman was talking to the guards animatedly, a greedy look on his face.

"Hoel," she called.

He turned, followed her gaze, then nodded. "Thought that might happen. He was too eager to help. Get in the boat."

Eilean promptly obeyed and then unslung her pack as she settled down. It rocked so fiercely she feared it would capsize, but the movement quickly stabilized. Hoel came over and slashed the rope with a dagger before leaping down into the boat, which immediately began to lurch away from the pier. He thrust the oars at her.

"Start paddling."

One glance revealed the Apocrisarius on shore had lifted his bow to aim. Heart thumping, she dipped the oars in the water and mimicked the motions she'd seen often enough. Hoel had brought up his own bow, but she feared it would be too late, and—

Cries of alarm had already begun from the dock, and people were yelling and pointing at them. The shriek of a seagull sounded, and a large white bird swooped down and pecked at the Apocrisarius with the bow. What was even more unusual, the seagull had a tail like a mouse and floppy ears. The púca! The hunter waved the nuisance away, but it had given them a few precious moments.

Bracing one boot against a seat, Hoel leaned against another as he pulled the string back and aimed.

A quick glance at the shore. The Apocrisarius was preparing to take another shot, but Hoel loosed his arrow first.

Eilean watched in disbelief as his arrow struck the other man's bow and shattered it. The recoil from the string flapped around, and the other hunter stared after them in shock.

A small smile played on Hoel's lips as he set down his own bow. "You'll send us right back to the dock that way. Let me have them."

She was grateful to hand the oars over. The boat glided against the rippling waves, and soon the wharf faded from sight. The seagull swooped toward them and let out another cry, though it sounded more like a snicker.

Thank you, she thought to it, grinning in spite of herself.

"They'll be getting another one to follow us," he said over his shoulder as he heaved against the oars. She saw the muscles on his forearms knot like ropes beneath his skin. The boat cut through the water like a knife, continuing to gain speed.

"Where are we going?" she asked.

"Pull out the orb. It's at my waist."

Leaning forward, she stumbled a bit and had to steady herself against his shoulder. But she managed to untie the knot cinching the pouch and withdrew the orb.

Holding it in her palm, she gave it the thought. *Bring us to the mirror gate.*

Nothing happened.

"You're not authorized to use it," he said. "Here." He stopped rowing a moment and held out his hand. She layered his palm beneath hers and repeated the thought. Immediately it began to whir and spin. The narrow spindles pointed the way.

He was right. It didn't take long for another boat to pursue them, this one a skiff with a sail that began to gain on them quickly. Hoel rowed until the sweat was streaming down his face, which was tightened into a grimace of determination. There was still no sign of a natural arch.

"Can you . . . set their sail . . . on fire?" he asked while exerting himself.

Eilean turned back to look at the skiff. "No, but I can set the wind against them." She thought a moment and then held out her hand, her palm extending toward the skiff. *"Keraunos."*

The wind immediately began to change direction—whereas it had been blowing from the north, pushing them away from the isle, it now began to blow against them. In moments, the waters began to heave. The skiff's sail had been rendered useless, and the sailors struggled against the turning of the wind.

"Impressive," Hoel said, out of breath. "We're about to pass the north tower. See it on the left?"

She did. There were stone walls built around the lower portion of the island, but they terminated at a round tower. There were no buildings beyond that point, only a densely wooded area and rocky crags. It was too steep and rugged for anyone to use such a path to climb up to the abbey high on the top of the hill.

"So the town of Dochte is only on the southern side?"

"Yes. Just that side. These waves are impossible! I'm glad you summoned the wind, but we've made our own job harder."

"I could stop it," she said.

"Not until we're out of their sight."

Eilean felt her hair flying wildly. Excitement mixed with the sea breeze. "You're tired. Let me have a turn."

"I can manage it."

"I know you can, Hoel. But I can do hard work too. It won't hurt your pride to rest for a while."

He turned his head, looked at her, and then lowered the handles against the oarlocks and scooted over a seat. She settled in where he'd sat and, gritting her teeth, pulled on the oars as she'd watched him do. Although she wasn't as efficient at it, she was strong and used to hard work, especially during the flax harvest at Tintern.

Hoel wiped the sweat from his brow and watched her row with admiration. "You're getting it."

"I know I am," she huffed, her breath already struggling.

"There's an arch, over there," he said, pointing. "I think it is the one."

She turned to look at it and saw the seagull heading toward it. "You're right."

"Are you willing to go to another world?" she asked him.

"I am. How long should we take?"

"A week might not be long enough. What about two?"

"I agree. We'll need to find Brythonica, which the orb can do, retrieve the tome, and then return."

"I want to meet High King Andrew," she said. "And tell him what's happening."

"There might not be time. We could come back?"

"It will be easier to accomplish both goals with the Cruciger orb. Can we agree on this?"

"Meet him, yes," he said, his tone immovable. "Solicit his help to overthrow the High Seer? I'm not ready for that."

"Very well. We'll just meet him, then."

"How do we make the agreement?" he asked.

"There's a Leering . . . at the top of the arch," she said, panting. She'd tired much more quickly than he had. Sweat was trickling down her ribs, her back, and her cheeks.

"Did you know . . . about our friend? Stright?" she asked.

"That he was captured? Yes. I had some hunters watching in the woods for him. I warned them about his ability with fire." He put his hand on hers, the gesture tentative. "They'll keep him in the dungeon for quite a while, hoping he'll be useful. There's still time."

Her heart hurt for Celyn. Had her friend made it back to Hautland already? Her mind summoned up Aldermaston Utheros, Prince Derik, and the others she'd met along her journey. She never would have imagined that it would bring her here, in a boat with Hoel. At least, not without her being trussed up first.

The strenuous rowing was making it harder to breathe.

"I've rested," he said, breaking into her thoughts. "Let me finish."

"I can do it," she panted.

He smirked. "That or you'll crash us into the rocks."

"*Pethet,*" she told him, putting down the oars and returning to her previous seat.

"Is that a compliment?"

"Does it *sound* like one?"

He laughed and started rowing again.

As they approached the stone arch, which was about twelve spans higher than their heads, she watched as the waves crashed in and through it with surprising violence. Rocks poked out from the sea as it sloughed off, revealing the danger Hoel had just warned her of.

She sensed the Medium's power throbbing in the air as Hoel said, "I see the Leering."

Eilean gazed up at the ancient carving. The face was so worn by time and storms that it was hardly more than a gnarled beard and two eyes.

"Are you sure about this?" she asked him.

His look was confident and steady. "I'll protect you, Eilean."

She was so grateful they were together, finally, that they were on the same side. That he was the man she had thought he might be. Flashes of his own feelings filtered through to her. He wanted to kiss her, but he was unsure whether he should—not because he thought her beneath him, but because he respected her. Because he wanted to make no mistakes with her. So she led the way and leaned forward. Their minds touched before their lips did, and she could sense he'd wanted it as much as she did. It was a hesitant kiss. An acknowledgment of shared feelings. A *promise*.

And it was sweeter than any of the moments she'd shared with Aisic.

As she drew back after their lips had brushed together, a shy smile forming on her mouth, she saw a contentment in his eyes she couldn't recall ever seeing there.

Reaching up, he caressed her cheek and then tucked her hair behind her ear. He nodded. "It's time."

In her mind, she invoked the Leering's power by using the words she'd learned in the tome of creation, *"Mar-ah shaw-ar."* Then she repeated the terms of the covenant in her mind. One fortnight.

Would it be long enough? What if something stopped them from returning? The arch could collapse, and their way home would be destroyed.

Maybe Hoel could see the reluctance on her face, for he gave her a determined look and nodded again.

The eyes of the Leering flashed in acceptance as they neared the mouth of the portal.

"What do we do?" he asked.

"We go through."

Hoel shifted his shoulders and began to row steadily, bringing their boat to the mouth of the arch.

As soon as they passed beneath its shadow, it felt as if they'd plunged off a waterfall.

CHAPTER
THIRTY-ONE

Epilogue

By the time they'd climbed to the top of the Tor, the Aldermaston found himself wishing he, too, had brought a staff to ease the journey. He was huffing for breath, with a stitch at his side. His companion, Maderos of the Twelve, didn't look winded at all.

The view from the summit was well worth the climb. From the rounded top, the Aldermaston could see the expanse of the Bearden Muir surrounding the wetlands. The starlings were swarming to the east. Pockets of mist and fog followed the streams and brooks, which fed into the larger rivers that wove through the sedge grasses. Remembering how the land had looked before Muirwood Abbey was built, he recognized that the Tor's present position would have been in the middle of the lake that had once dominated the area. His heart swelled when he looked at the majestic abbey, the first in the kingdom of Moros. A quickening feeling in his chest made him catch his breath. Standing where he was, he felt that he was on holy ground.

"Aye, but it is," said Maderos to him with his distinctive accent. "The Medium brought this bit of earth to save the abbey. You *should* feel grateful to be standing on it."

"Not only do I thank the Medium, but I thank my teacher." He looked up at him. "You saw something in me worth saving."

"Pfah, none of us are entirely good or ill. I hoped you'd come around. You did the hard part."

The Aldermaston sighed. It could have ended much worse. He was indeed grateful that the abbey had been spared, although his heart ached for the loss of the villagers who'd been destroyed by the Naestors, including the sheriff's men who had fought to save lives. One of them, Aisic, had once been a wretched at Tintern. He grieved for a life cut off too soon. But in the world they lived in, such tragedies could happen without warning.

"This is sad country, lonely country," said Maderos. "Far from the machinations of King Aengus's court."

"Will you be returning to him, then?" asked the Aldermaston, dreading the response. He'd destroyed the Leering that had bound the prisoner to the grounds.

"No. I served him as best I could. Just as I have done for you, Aldermaston Gilifil."

"You will depart soon?"

"Did you think I would stay at Muirwood forever?"

"No." A pang of sadness filled his heart. "I hoped you'd stay a little longer, though."

Maderos gripped his crooked staff, the one he'd taken from the dark druid who'd come to abduct him all those months ago. Resting his other arm atop it, he gazed down at the valley, his nose pinched in thought.

"I go where the Medium sends me. Maybe I will go and preach among the Naestors next? They are a violent and heartsick people. In that land of darkness, they fear the light. They fear the maston order."

"Their coming has been a punishment."

"You could say that. But it also served as a reminder. When ill winds blow, remember they came from somewhere. Before you can change a person's heart or mind, you must first see how they live. What ails them. What pleases them. I came to Moros to do the same. That is why I joined the druids. As my friend Ovidius said, 'You can learn from anyone, even your enemy.'"

"He spoke the truth," the Aldermaston said. "I thought of you as an enemy at first. Now I see things more clearly."

Maderos chuckled. "Good. But how good are your eyes truly? Do you see those two mastons walking this way?"

The Aldermaston frowned. He did not. "Where?"

Maderos extended his arm and pointed. "There, from the north."

"They must be coming from Tintern," the Aldermaston said.

"Let us see what news they bring," said Maderos.

At least the climb down would be easier than the way up. The Aldermaston's legs were still trembling from exertion.

"There is wisdom in climbing mountains," Maderos said thoughtfully. "For they teach us how truly small we are."

Taking in the view one last time, the Aldermaston gazed down at the abbey, his gaze dipping to the kitchen where Ardys and Loren worked. They were still grieving the loss of Eilean and Celyn, still hurt that they'd abandoned the abbey and the Aldermaston. He had told them that the two young people had departed according to the Medium's will and would be welcomed back with open arms if they ever returned. From this height, he could barely see the small orchard of apple trees. The cider that had been produced so far had turned out to be quite popular. When he had first come to Muirwood, he'd seen it as a stepping-stone to greater things. Part of the pavement on the road to ruling Avinion. He harbored no such ambitions or delusions now.

"Let us go down," Maderos said, giving him a wry smile.

They walked side by side down the more gradual slope of the crouch-backed hill. The two mastons coming their way had spotted them. They reached the base of the hill first and were waiting for the Aldermaston and Maderos to arrive. Both men wore packs around their shoulders and looked as if they'd been walking for days. There were smudges under their eyes and days of growth on their chins from not shaving. One was markedly older than the other.

"Where do you hail from, my friends?" the Aldermaston asked warily.

The younger man turned to his companion, deferring to him to begin.

"I am Sizel Mosk, and this is my companion, Dominic Shavelae. We hail from Cruix Abbey," he said. "We serve Aldermaston Kalbraeth."

"My countryman," said the Aldermaston.

Sizel nodded. "He's counting on that, Aldermaston. He summons a conclave of the Aldermastons at Cruix Abbey to judge the High Seer, Tatyana Dagenais."

"We came by Apse Veil to Tintern first," said Dominic, the younger man. "I see the abbey at Muirwood is complete. But is there no functioning Apse Veil?"

"There is not," said the Aldermaston. "We are being shunned by the High Seer at the moment. She has not activated the Leerings that control it."

"That is unfortunate," Sizel observed. "It would have made our return to Cruix safer."

"The Naestors have been invading the northern kingdoms. Truly, they are a scourge on us all."

"Have any Naestors come this far?" questioned Sizel.

The Aldermaston turned to Maderos and smiled. "Indeed, but the Medium preserved us."

"That's a relief. At Tintern, we learned that they sacked Krucis and Holyrood Abbey. Many fled to Tintern because it is in the mountains."

The Aldermaston was stunned. "*Both* abbeys have fallen?"

"Aye. Krucis fell first. The king and his sons went to Holyrood to defend it. They were slaughtered, their bodies were desecrated in a heathen way as a warning against those who would defy the Naestors."

The Aldermaston's stomach fell. He stared at both of them, aghast, and Maderos frowned at the news.

"The royal family of Pry-Ree is dead," said Dominic. "The Aldermaston at Tintern said that the people are clamoring for Aldermaston Kalbraeth to renounce his role and return to claim his right to the throne—"

"We told them," interrupted Sizel, "that he is very sick. Gifts of Healing have not helped him. So now the people of Pry-Ree are asking for his son, Hoel Evnissyen. He was at Cruix recently with the High Seer. They came to take a tome from that noblewoman. The one the High Seer has been after."

"What noblewoman?" demanded the Aldermaston.

The two exchanged a look. Dominic said, "The one who came to Cruix with the tome. Lady Gwenllian."

"Who?" he asked.

Maderos put his hand on the Aldermaston's shoulder. "They're speaking of Eilean."

So Eilean had made it all the way to Cruix Abbey? And Captain Hoel of the Apocrisarius was in line for the throne of Pry-Ree?

"This is strange news indeed," muttered the Aldermaston. "I cannot leave Muirwood to attend the conclave. We have been attacked once, and the Naestors may come for us again. All the abbeys are at risk. How did the Aldermaston of Tintern Abbey answer?"

"He said he would come to the conclave," replied Dominic. "He was already preparing to cross the Apse Veil when we left him."

"You *must* come," implored Sizel. "The High Seer has overstepped her authority. She refused to acknowledge Aldermaston Kalbraeth's right to call a conclave. She was going to arrest him for suggesting it!"

"But Lady Gwenllian stopped her," broke in the younger man.

The Aldermaston held up his hand to silence them both. Turning to Maderos, he said, "I cannot leave Muirwood for a long journey. Is there another way to get to Cruix quickly? Even returning through Tintern to cross through their Apse Veil would take too long. Would *you* consider representing me?"

Maderos had an inscrutable look on his face. There was no way of knowing what he thought of the situation.

"I cannot go," he said. "But there is no reason you should not."

"But the abbey," the Aldermaston implored.

"The High Seer is not the only one who can activate the Leerings controlling the Apse Veil. I have the same authority to do so. Given me by the Harbinger herself."

Both of the mastons looked at Maderos in confusion.

"Who are you?" asked Dominic.

The Aldermaston felt hope stir in his breast. "His name cannot be spoken, for the High Seer has locked its utterance under a binding sigil. But he is one of the original Twelve. The tome the High Seer seeks belongs to him."

The two mastons both dropped to one knee before him.

Maderos sighed. "Up, lads. That's enough fluff. Let's go to the abbey. Then all three of you can cross to Cruix and speak to Aldermaston Kalbraeth directly. Enough! Stand! I am a fellow servant."

Both of the younger mastons rose in reverence. "You're the druid," said the first. "The one being kept prisoner at Muirwood."

Maderos arched his eyebrow. "I'm no prisoner now. Hasten to the abbey. Tell them we are coming."

The two mastons hurried away, racing one another to be the first to reach the abbey.

The Aldermaston began walking swiftly alongside Maderos, who set a pace that was difficult to match.

"Do you think there's a chance for a conclave to overthrow the High Seer?" the Aldermaston asked.

Maderos didn't break his stride. "No. The pride runs too deep. Too many have been swayed or empowered by the wealth of her family. No, I see where this is going. The Harbinger warned of it."

"Truly? What did she say?"

Maderos kept walking. "She said it would cause a schism. One that would bring the maston order to its knees."

AUTHOR'S NOTE

A love of history has been with me for as long as I can remember. While I was in high school, I deliberated between wanting to be a history teacher or an English teacher. I chose history. Most of my story ideas come from episodes in the past. You might recognize some of them in this book.

When I wrote the Legends of Muirwood trilogy, the maston order was already in decline. Their peak influence was over, and the hetaera had begun to influence things behind the scenes. I wanted to delve more into that era, the tipping point in time. I found an unattributed quote that said "the door of history turns on small hinges."

For inspiration on such "small hinges" moments, I went back to my college days and refreshed myself on the era of Martin Luther and the Reformation. I've actually visited Wartburg Castle where he was hidden following his excommunication and saw the little dwelling space he lived in during those years. The story about the storm frightening him is real, as well as legends of him having verbal encounters with spiritual creatures. I also leveraged research into the Great Schism of 1378 when there were two rival popes, one of which ruled from the French city of Avignon. Even though these time periods were centuries apart, I borrowed elements from both, including the organization of the Apocrisarius. I changed the spelling slightly because I thought it sounded better phonetically another way.

The original title of the book was *The Fugitive*, because that is what Eilean is throughout the novel. I wasn't totally happy with the title because it was the same as a Harrison Ford movie and old TV show, so I worked with Adrienne, my editor, to try to come up with a better one. We traded several ideas, but kept going back to the drawing board. Finally, I brought the short list to my wife, Gina, and asked for her input. She looked at the list, then at me, and suggested *The Hunted*. It was the clear winner. We all loved her idea. Thanks, sweetie!

It has been interesting writing this series during a global pandemic and with so much political and cultural turmoil in the world. We've been losing, as a society, the ability to see another's point of view. To respect divergent opinions. To even admit when we're wrong. In many ways, this series isn't just Eilean's story. It's Hoel's story too. It's about how someone can become so fixed in their mindset and traditions that they reject the inner whispers of truth that guide and steer us to be more compassionate, understanding, and willing to listen.

I love collecting quotes that contain nuggets of wisdom. This is a modern one that I heard from a friend and found the original quoted in an interview with Rabbi Jonathan Sacks (who passed away in 2020). Rabbi Sacks was invited to meet with a vocal atheist. He was asked if he was going to try to convert the man. "No, I'm going to do something much better than that. I'm going to listen to him."

Listening to someone, truly listening, is the greatest way we can show our love.

ACKNOWLEDGMENTS

No story is ever the lone creation of a singular person, and I wanted to express my gratitude for the team that continues to help make my books even better. Whether it's coming up with the perfect title for the book (which is truly a group effort), the dazzling cover art, the heart-felt narration, crafting the wording of the descriptions on the back cover as well as what appears online and in ads, 47North has been an amazing team to work with over the last decade. Individuals have come and gone during that time, but the team has only gotten stronger. Thank you all!

I would also like to offer encouragement to other budding authors out there. I enjoy each opportunity to try to add to the creative spark in the world. I recently visited my sister-in-law's class of fifth graders and shared my publishing story and answered their questions. To me, those more intimate settings are the best, when you can look into the eyes of eager kids and inspire a love of reading or of wanting to create worlds of their own. I used to be one of those kids. And I'm grateful for the many teachers and mentors who added fuel to the flames (Mrs. Reidy, Mr. Darren, Mr. Spring, Mr. Galliart, Mr. Hannah, Mr. Brooks, Ms. Penman—just to name a few).

Thank you for inspiring me.

ABOUT THE AUTHOR

Jeff Wheeler is the *Wall Street Journal* bestselling author of the First Argentines series (*Knight's Ransom*, *Warrior's Ransom*, *Lady's Ransom*, and *Fate's Ransom*); the Grave Kingdom series; the Harbinger and Kingfountain series; the Legends and Covenant of Muirwood trilogies; the Whispers from Mirrowen trilogy; and the Landmoor novels. Jeff is a husband, father of five, and devout member of his church. He lives in the Rocky Mountains. Learn more about Jeff's publishing journey in *Your First Million Words*, and visit his many worlds at www.jeff-wheeler.com.

Printed in Great Britain
by Amazon

86034470R00181